Finding Molly Parsons

Alyson Root

J&M Books

Published by J&M Books

Lytchett House, 13 Freeland Park, Wareham Road, Poole, Dorset, BH16 6FA

Print ISBN: 978-1-917785-00-6

Ebook ISBN: 978-1-917785-16-7

Developmental Edit & Cover Design by:

Tara Sullivan, The Write Gal Co.

www.thewritegal.com

Line & Copy Edit by:

Linda Slate

Proofread by:

Morgan Bonito

For everyone who found their chosen family

1

Faith

The relentless ticking from the clock on Faith's wall sent her nerves through the roof. Normally indifferent to its presence, tonight, the clock became an unwelcome reminder of the daunting task ahead.

Faith had planned her escape for months. She was meticulous, acutely aware any lapse in detail could spell utter disaster. With each passing minute, her heart quickened its pace, mirroring the march of time itself.

So far, everything was going to plan. That was the one good thing about her parents; they were painfully predictable. But that wasn't the reason Faith craved freedom. No, her reason for all the plotting and lying was for her future life and the right to live it as she saw fit.

If Alan and Maureen Parsons ever found out who Faith truly was while she lived under their roof, Faith would... Well, she dreaded to think what would happen.

There was no point dwelling on the 'what ifs' now. Faith was thirty seconds away from irrevocably changing her life.

Straining her ears, Faith listened for any sign her mother or father were awake. It would be the first time in history either parent stirred before 6 a.m. but Faith couldn't take any chances. This was too important. The house remained silent, only the gentle creak of the wooden rafters pierced the stillness.

Stepping lightly, Faith gathered her backpack. With gentle steps, she made her way over to her window. It had taken an hour to jimmy the lock open, earlier that evening, all while trying to stay as quiet as a mouse. If her dad heard anything out of the ordinary, he was guaranteed to burst through her door.

She gently lifted the window, thankful it didn't snag or squeak. Taking one last look over her shoulder, Faith slipped her pack through the narrow opening before climbing out as quickly as possible.

As much as she hated this house, she was grateful it was a single-story bungalow. Having to scale down a wall didn't hold any appeal and there was no way she would have been able to do it without disturbing her parents.

As soon as her feet touched the ground, she eased the window closed and swiftly took off. Skirting the edges of the yard, Faith avoided the gravel. Now all she had to do was make it to the back of the garage. After a quick look behind her, Faith set off, praying the security light she'd relieved of its bulb had gone unnoticed by her father.

With no blazing light to illuminate her escape, Faith smiled. Luck was on her side tonight. Maybe it was divine intervention?

A glance at her wristwatch reminded Faith she had to hurry if she was to succeed with the next part of her plan.

At the back of the family garage sat Faith's trusty bicycle. Her father had refused to let Faith get her driver's license, insisting she only cycled. Faith knew the reason was to prevent her from leaving. Alan Parsons wasn't a stupid man.

Faith wondered how he would feel when he realized that by enforcing the 'no driving' rule, he'd given her the perfect way to escape. Bicycles were silent, unlike cars.

Wheeling the bike to the road, Faith placed one foot on the pedal and used the other to push off. Summoning all the energy she could, Faith peddled. There was no time to admire the moonlit streets or the twinkle of the stars. Faith had to remain focused on her goal: getting to the bus station within the next five minutes.

With labored breaths and sweat on her brow, Faith made it with one minute to spare. Rushing over to the ticket desk, she gave her name and collected her pass. Leaving her pre-purchased ticket at the station had been the right choice. Faith never knew when her mother would overturn her room, looking for contraband.

The bus rumbled to life just as she threw herself onboard. The driver drew up his eyebrows as she puffed and panted. Only when she waved the ticket in his face did he turn away.

Inhaling deeply, Faith made her way to the middle of the bus, choosing a window seat. There wasn't time for her to get comfy, though. Her ticket might have read "Destination: Dallas," but that was *not* where Faith planned to leave the bus.

When her parents found her missing from her room, they would come for her. Faith had no doubt in her mind. The first place they would look would be the bus station. Once they found out her ticket information—and they would—Alan and Maureen would be hot on her tail.

So, to keep them in the dark, Faith would change buses prior to Dallas. With all the bobbing and weaving she planned, it was going to take her days to reach Seattle;

her final destination. The stops and changes were a must, though.

Closing her eyes, Faith mentally ran through the rest of her plan. It wasn't complicated but it would stop her parents from getting law enforcement involved. That was the reason she'd waited until she turned eighteen. God knows she'd wanted to escape for years, but without the law on her side, it would have been foolish and deadly to have left before her last birthday.

Now, though, she was a legal adult. She'd even managed to sneak her birth certificate out of her father's office. With her documents safely stowed away in her backpack, Faith finally allowed herself a reprieve from the anxiety she'd suffered with for months.

Maybe a bit of sleep would help? No, don't fall asleep. Stay vigilant.

The bus was nowhere near full as she cast her gaze over the other passengers. There were a handful of people, most of them snoring. She saw a girl who looked to be about her own age, sitting in the back of the coach, eyes closed, bopping her head and silently mouthing the words to her music. Faith saw the AirPods and naturally became curious.

What is she listening to? Stop it, Faith. Stay focused. No distractions.

Admonishing herself for her wandering eye, Faith turned her head back to the window, and the possibilities that lay ahead.

The bus had barely stopped before Faith was up and out of her seat, heading for the door. Thankfully, the bus had made good time, leaving Faith with ample opportunity to buy her next ticket—with cash, of course.

The sleepy bus station only had one ticket operator, who clearly detested his job. Faith was a naturally shy person who avoided confrontations at all costs, so when she heard the ticket clerk arguing with a customer, she wanted to hide away. Raised voices were a trigger. In Faith's experience, they were usually followed by a swift backhand.

When the irate customer finally purchased her ticket, Faith stepped up to the window. "One-way to St. Louis, please."

The ticket agent sighed and bashed his keyboard dramatically. Faith wasn't sure why he behaved that way, and frankly, she didn't care. As long as he gave her the ticket, he could do as he pleased.

Faith smiled sweetly as she waited. Finally, he shoved the printed paper through the little slot. Faith thanked him and left. With an hour to wait, Faith prepared the next stage of her plan.

Alan and Maureen would go straight to the Sheriff's Office and tell them Faith was missing. To make sure that didn't happen, Faith entrusted her best friend, Alice, to deliver a letter to the sheriff at first light. The letter stated Faith had left town of her own free will. Hopefully, that would be enough to stop *law enforcement* looking for her. It wouldn't deter her parents.

Pulling out the burner phone she'd picked up in town yesterday, Faith sent a message letting Alice know she was okay and to make sure her letter got delivered. As soon as she got a reply, Faith turned off the phone and dumped it.

Waiting was the hardest part. If she wasn't moving in some way or other, Faith felt vulnerable. To stave off the inevitable anxiety that came with stillness, Faith paced the station. After a few restless minutes, a rumbling stomach gave her the perfect excuse to find somewhere to eat. A diner was a better option than driving herself insane, walking in circles.

The smell of coffee and grease slapped her across the face as soon as she opened the door. Normally, that smell would be nauseating, but Faith was too hungry to care. In fact, her mouth was salivating. Taking a seat at the counter, Faith scanned the board.

"Hey, honey, what can I get you?" The woman behind the bar was short and stout. She had an infectious smile and her golden curls bounced as she moved. Faith didn't know many people who could sport a genuine smile like that, first thing in the morning.

"Coffee and pancakes, please."

"Coming right up."

Faith let out a little giggle. This would be the first time she tried coffee. Caffeine probably wasn't the best thing in her current state as she was already wired, but screw it. This is why she'd left; so she could make her own decisions and try new things. Her reasons for leaving ran a lot deeper than coffee, but it was still a valid example.

Faith's wristwatch beeped. She'd set it to go off at six. Like clockwork, Alan and Maureen would climb out of bed at 6 a.m. sharp. Her mother usually rapped on Faith's door at two minutes past.

Faith's eyes were glued to the digital display. As the numbers changed to 6:02, Faith clenched her fists. They would now know.

"Here ya go, honey. Coffee and pancakes. There's extra syrup just over there. Call if you need anything."

Unfurling her hands, Faith placed them on the counter, closed her eyes, and counted to ten. She was okay. She was safe. For now, anyway.

Not wanting her first experience of tasting coffee to be marred by all the things that could go wrong with the upcoming travels, Faith shook out her body and smiled. The coffee looked like mud, which Faith was sure meant it wouldn't be great. Yup, the first swallow almost made her cough up a lung.

"Eat your pancake. It will help," a soft voice said from beside her.

The unfamiliar voice poured from a familiar mouth—it was the girl with the AirPods from the back of the bus.

"Thanks, wow, yeah, that's something," Faith spluttered. The woman laughed, which made Faith smile.

"Do you mind if I sit here?"

"No, go ahead." Faith shuffled in her seat.

"I'm Nathalie," the woman said, holding out her hand. Faith gripped it lightly and shook.

"Faith."

"Are the pancakes any good?"

Faith cut a small bite and popped it in her mouth. Warm butter spread across her tongue, causing a delighted moan to leave her mouth.

"So good," Faith mumbled.

"Hey, can I have the same as her, please?" Nathalie asked the same smiling server.

"Sure thing, honey."

"So, where are you off to?" Nathalie asked, turning her attention back to Faith.

Faith's defenses rose instantly. It was silly, because Faith knew there was no way Nathalie had any knowledge of her plans, or reasons for leaving Kentucky. That didn't stop her body from visibly reacting. Nathalie must have seen Faith stiffen, because she quickly changed the subject.

"Ugh, I hate traveling by bus. My back goes into spasm. I'm only nineteen. That shouldn't happen, right?"

"Definitely not," Faith laughed, thankful for Nathalie's understanding.

Nathalie smiled as the server placed her food and coffee down. "Well, these pancakes should help."

The women fell silent as they ate. Faith wished she had better social skills. Maybe then she would know how to traverse these kinds of interactions. Unfortunately, socializing was not important, according to her father. As long as she could be polite when spoken to, that was all that mattered. If it weren't for Alice, Faith would have been completely alone and friendless.

Faith didn't even have the respite of school. Maureen Parsons had homeschooled her. Well, she'd taught her daughter the basics, never straying into anything remotely liberal. As long as Faith could read, do basic math, and recite the Bible by heart, that was a job well done in Maureen's eyes.

"I...I saw you listening to music on the bus," Faith stuttered. Was her face red?

"Oh yeah. God, I couldn't do without music. What sort of stuff are you into? I love everything. Honestly, my playlist is a mixed bag."

Great, another uncomfortable question. Faith didn't know any music, unless it was for the church. Her parents didn't even have a radio.

"Oh, I like everything, too. I don't really have a preference."

"That's cool. I like a woman who is open-minded."

Something stirred in Faith's stomach: butterflies; the real reason she'd run from the only place she'd ever known: her attraction to women. And, boy, was she finding herself attracted to Nathalie. She was tall, fit, and had gorgeous blue eyes. Yep, very attracted.

Instead of replying, Faith smiled shyly and finished her food. As much as she'd like to pursue this flirtatious chat with a gorgeous woman, Faith had to keep on task. With her pancakes eaten and her coffee drunk, Faith stepped off her stool.

"Um... it was nice to meet you Nathalie. Safe travels."

"Wait. Before you rush off, let's see if we can turn your cup of mud into something palatable." Faith watched Nathalie signal to the server. "Hi. Can we have these coffees to go?"

"Sure thing."

Faith played awkwardly with the strap of her bag. There were literally no words in her head. Nathalie was so calm and collected...and hot. The woman behind the counter interrupted Faith's internal meltdown, placing her to-go cup on the bar.

"Here," Nathalie began, sliding over the cream and sugar. "Pour in a good glug of cream and add a couple of spoons of sugar. It makes all the difference."

Faith watched Nathalie scoop in three large spoons of sugar and a dash of cream. Curious, Faith added both condiments, gave it a stir, and took a tentative sip.

"Oh wow, that's so much better!"

"Yup! I couldn't let you go without knowing the joys of a good—okay—semi-decent, cup of coffee."

Popping the lid onto her cup, Faith cradled it to her body. "Um, thanks, Nathalie."

Would it be weird if she kept the empty container forever? Probably, but at least she'd have something that reminded her of this wonderful woman.

"I really have to go." And with that, she hurried out of the diner and towards the bus station.

Faith stood in line, waiting for the driver to allow the passengers to board. Once again, she wouldn't complete the journey to her ticketed destination and would hop off before getting there.

Choosing the back seat this time, Faith settled down. This leg of the journey would take longer than the first. Knowing she should catch up on some much-needed sleep, Faith set the alarm on her watch.

Resting her head against the back of her seat, Faith allowed herself to indulge in the memory that was Nathalie's lovely face. She wondered what Nathalie's story was, where she'd come from, and where she was going. The comment about liking open-minded women played at the forefront of Faith's mind. Did it mean Nathalie liked women?

A smile trickled across her face as she pondered Nathalie. Could she dare to believe, that one day she could have a Nathalie of her own? A woman who was beautiful and interesting?

The thoughts left her a little breathless. Thank God her parents couldn't read her mind.

Faith was twelve when she first realized boys held about as much appeal as contracting scabies. The girls, in their Sunday best, were the ones who stole her attention. Faith quickly learned her feelings were not to be divulged to anyone within the church community. It took one innocent question about girls liking girls, and Faith had found out how angry her father could get. Safe to say, Faith never brought up the subject again.

Any fantasies she had of living her truth had been firmly put to one side until she was sure she could be safe—far away from her parents. The knowledge that Alan and Maureen would know she'd left, was niggling. Faith replayed her every move, making sure she'd covered her tracks well enough.

Flashes of Nathalie smiling at her helped quell her fears. No matter what, Faith would be free. A sliver of regret settled in her stomach. If she'd just had the confidence, she could have asked Nathalie for her email or something. Would Nathalie have thought she was nuts?

Chuckling at her internal monologue, Faith calmed her mind. Falling into slumber, thinking of Nathalie, was a much better option than worrying about her parents.

Faith jolted awake as her watch beeped repeatedly. The dream she was ripped from was an unfamiliar experience; something that made her clench her thighs together. The dream had been so vivid, she wouldn't have been surprised to learn she'd been writhing around on her seat.

"Wowzer," she muttered to herself as she straightened her clothes. Clearing her throat, she took a long pull of the water she'd packed in her bag. Craning to see out the window, she noticed the bus was approaching the station where she planned to get off.

Giving herself a little pep talk, Faith steeled herself for the next changeover. She had plenty more to come, and even though swapping buses was already tedious, she knew it had to be done.

"Eyes on the prize" was her mantra. She could rest when she got to Seattle. In Seattle, she could be herself with the one person who knew what it was like to be gay and also a part of the Parsons family.

Faith just hoped she had the right address. She also hoped her Aunt Molly would welcome her. It had taken months of stealthy trips to the library to find out about her aunt. There was no trace of her existence in the family home. Faith's parents had only ever uttered the woman's name once. That one time caused so much anger, Faith feared her mother would be beaten within an inch of her life.

Alan Parsons was not a man to cross. Obviously, Maureen had been ordered to never speak of Molly, Alan's sister, ever. Faith wasn't sure what caused her mother to disobey, but one thing was for sure: After the whooping Alan gave her, Maureen never spoke the name again.

Faith's natural curiosity won out, and after a few weeks, she'd begun the search for her elusive aunt. The library—which she could only visit for half an hour, once a week—yielded a treasure trove of information.

Molly Parsons was two years younger than Alan. She'd been a pillar of the community and the church until her seventeenth birthday. Then, Molly had simply disappeared.

The mystery of Molly, plagued Faith. A gut feeling told her she needed to find out about her aunt. That gut feeling had led her to do some perilous things, such as rifling through her father's office and closet.

The danger was worth it, though, because Faith found what she was looking for. It was the moment, finding Molly Parsons became Faith's number one priority. However, as she sat draining the last drops of Nathalie-inspired coffee, Faith's head was far from focused on finding her aunt. Nathalie's eyes swam in her mind. Gosh, she was simply lovely.

Yes, she was definitely keeping the cup.

2

Carmen

Carmen stood by the kitchen counter, rubbing her eyes, and scratching her ass. God, she hated mornings, especially after a late night looking after Mateo. That man could party like he was still twenty-one.

"Coffee, that's all I fucking asked for. Coffee! Did I get coffee? Of course not," she grumbled to herself.

Why she'd believed Mateo last night, when he'd promised breakfast and coffee in bed, was anyone's guess. That man was flakier than pastry.

"You always fall for it, Carmen. Always. *'Come on Carm, just stay out a little longer. I swear I'll treat you like a queen in the morning, with coffee and breakfast.'* Yeah, right."

"*Chica*, are you talking to yourself again? It's not right, we need to get you a woman," Mateo called from the living room.

Carmen ground her teeth. Not only did her best friend fail to deliver on his promises, he also woke up fresh as a daisy, unlike Carmen, who felt like death warmed over. The universe was a cruel mistress. Mateo had been the one to sink tequila shot after tequila shot.

"He's your best friend, you can't kill him," she continued to grumble.

"Oh shit, Carm, you look like trash."

Carmen stopped scratching her ass and turned around. Mateo stood, in all his five-foot-nine glory, wearing a pink silk robe. His hair was still immaculate and set above the complexion of a fresh-faced youth. Right then, Carmen kind of hated him.

"Stop scowling at me. That's why you're getting lines. I'll give you a facial later."

"Oh, just like you were going to bring me coffee and breakfast this morning?"

"Is that why you're being such a delight? *Chica*, I tried to wake you for breakfast earlier and you slapped me upside the head, mumbling something about pandas."

Huh. Pandas?

"Whatever," she griped, sounding like a sullen teenager. Turning back to the coffee machine, Carmen poured herself an extra-large cup. Bringing the black gold close to her nose, she inhaled deeply.

Oh yeah, that's the stuff.

"Anyway, it's not breakfast time anymore. Hell, it's past lunch."

Carmen peered up at the clock above the kitchen door. Well shit, Mateo was right.

"Pizza?" she asked, still unable to get over Mateo's breakfast betrayal.

"Sure, *hermana*, I'll call it in. Maybe after you've inhaled that coffee, you can take a shower." Mateo wrinkled his nose.

Carmen nodded and shuffled into the living room. She'd shower later. It's not like she had to go anywhere. Plus, her boxer briefs and tank top were comfy.

As the caffeine worked its magic, Carmen felt half human again. They had to stop partying so hard. Carmen was pretty sure her liver was ninety percent pickled by now. But when Mateo asked for something, Carmen knew she wouldn't refuse.

That man had been through enough shit to last a lifetime. He deserved to get whatever he wanted, and if that was for Carmen to bust a move—and a gut—dancing and drinking in some skanky-ass gay club, then that's what would happen. She just wished he didn't need that every Friday and Saturday night.

Mateo sashayed into the living room and gracefully lowered himself to the sofa. "I got you a veggie supreme with a side of mozzarella sticks."

"*Gracias, hermano.*"

They sat in silence for a few minutes. Carmen knew it couldn't last; Mateo detested silence. Sure enough, he shattered the peace.

"*Chica*, did you see that fine man get all up in my space last night?" Mateo was fanning his face with the pizza takeout menu. "Damn, I could have had some fun with him."

"Why didn't you? He was up for it."

"Now, Carmen, you know that's not my style. I like the chase, but I'm not a one-night kind of guy."

"Did you get his number?"

"No. Luis pitched a fit about that drag queen ripping the tiara off his head. I had to deal with that. When I got back to the dance floor, Mr. Fine was dancing with someone else."

"There's always next time," Carmen laughed. There was always a next time.

A knock on the door interrupted the conversation.

"I'll get it," Mateo sang. Carmen rolled her eyes.

One hundred bucks, Daniel is the delivery guy.

Daniel was Mateo's not-so-secret crush. Whenever they ordered pizza, they went to Vinnie's. Not only because it was the best pie in Seattle, but because Mateo enjoyed looking at Daniel.

"Hey, *chica*, there's a white girl at the door for you."

Carmen scrunched her eyebrows. Who the hell had turned up? Becky, maybe?

No, she's out of town.

Donna, possibly? They were the only white girls who would come knocking, but it was far too early in the day for either of them, regardless of whether they were actually in town.

Hauling herself off the sofa, Carmen studied her attire. Rainbow boxer briefs and a scraggy tank top did not scream sexy.

"Eh, it is what it is," she mumbled.

Mateo passed her in the hallway with a judgmental look on his face. "Damn, Carmen, she's young, even for you!"

What the hell did that mean? Carmen didn't sleep with young women. Twenty-five was the lowest she'd ever go, and that was stretching it. Ten years her junior was the limit.

Carmen arrived at the partially closed door. As soon as she opened it, she understood Mateo's concern. The girl in front of her barely looked eighteen. She was gonna kick Mateo's ass for thinking this girl was Carmen's booty call.

"You're not Molly," the girl barked, her eyes wide, and face pale.

"And you're not an extra-large veggie supreme with a side order of mozzarella sticks. Looks like we both lost out, huh?"

"Damn," the girl growled. "Damn, damn, damn."

Carmen had no idea what was happening, but she knew she wanted to extricate herself from whatever it was.

"Sorry for disappointing. Um...bye."

"No wait, please," the girl begged. "Do you know Molly Parsons? This was her last address."

"Sorry, kid, no idea who that is."

"How long have you lived here?"

Carmen could see the desperation on the young girl's face. "Six months. The property was already vacant by the time I moved in."

The girl nodded, her eyes vacant. "Was there any mail or anything left behind? Anything with a forwarding address?"

"Nope, nothing. Sorry, look, I gotta go. Take care." Carmen gave a weak smile as she shut the door.

A weight sat in her stomach. A second knock made her jump. Daniel stood in the doorway, pizza box in hand. Over his shoulder, Carmen could see the young girl sitting slumped over on the sidewalk, her head in her hands.

"Hey, Carmen, I got your delivery," Daniel said, setting her food down on the hallway table. He'd delivered enough to their address, they were almost friends. Of course, at the sound of Daniel's voice, Mateo appeared.

"Hey, D," Mateo cooed.

Carmen rolled her eyes. Their flirtatious banter was nauseating. Carmen's racing mind muted their conversation. Watching the girl on the street was tugging at her chest. There was something familiar about the situation; something desperate.

Brushing past Daniel, Carmen approached the girl. "Hey."

"Oh, sorry, I'll move. I just needed a second," the girl croaked. Carmen could see the tears streaking down her face.

"I was gonna ask if you wanted some pizza." Carmen hooked her thumb over her shoulder and gave the kindest smile she could. Whatever was going on in this girl's life, Carmen knew she needed help.

"Oh, no, you don't have to do that, but thank you."

"Come on. No offense, but you look like you could do with a good meal."

Carmen regarded the girl. She was a waif of a human: thin, almost gaunt, with pale skin. Her hair was long, almost down to her ass. Her clothes...well, they would look good on the set of *Little House on the Prairie* if she were being honest. This kid was not from around here, that was for sure.

"I'm Carmen."

"Faith."

"Okay, then. Let's get some food." Carmen held out her hand. She could see Faith weighing up her options. After all, Carmen *was* a stranger.

A few moments passed before Faith grabbed Carmen's hand and let herself be pulled to her feet. Turning on her heel, Carmen gestured for Faith to follow. Daniel and Mateo were still flirting, so she paid them no mind, though Mateo shot her a confused look when he saw Faith.

"Just stick your backpack near the door," Carmen said as she took the pizza box into the living room. "I hope you like veggies," she added. Faith's reaction was strange. The girl was looking at the takeout box as though she'd never seen one before.

"I love vegetables. I don't know if I like them on pizza."

"What's your favorite topping?" Carmen was happy to make small talk. She could see Faith relaxing a bit.

"I don't know. I've never had one before."

Is she being serious?

The red tinge on the girl's cheeks told Carmen that yes, in fact, she was telling the truth. That raised a bunch of questions, but Carmen knew better than to pepper the girl.

"That's okay. We all have to start somewhere. And how good is it that your very first pizza is going to be from the world's best pizza place?"

"I'll take your word for it," Faith replied, smiling.

Mateo flounced in, looking from Faith to Carmen. "I didn't know we were expecting a guest." He smiled, offering his hand to Faith.

"Mateo, this is Faith."

"A pleasure."

"Did you finally ask Daniel on a date?" Carmen asked, hoping to take the focus away from the young woman who looked like a deer in headlights.

Mateo tutted, "Girl, I'm not gonna do that. We flirt; that's it."

"That's stupid," Carmen mumbled.

"You're stupid," Mateo shot back, causing Faith to giggle.

"Ignore him." Carmen smirked. "He's just moody because he's bloated."

Mateo gasped, bringing his hand to his chest. "How dare you!"

Carmen smiled when she saw Faith laugh. There was a time to find out what Faith's deal was, but now wasn't it. Carmen knew better than anyone that sometimes a person just needed company; someone to make them feel safe, without adding pressure.

"You know you bloat after a night out. Stop lying to yourself."

"I might be bloated, but I'm still better looking than you."

"In your dreams, *hermano*."

"Are you brother and sister?" Faith asked, her voice quiet.

"In every way but blood, honey. We took the same surname." Mateo smiled.

"That's nice," Faith replied.

"What about you? Any siblings?" Mateo was less patient than Carmen. He wanted the gossip.

"No, just me."

Carmen looked at Mateo when Faith dipped her head and took a small nibble of the pizza Carmen had put on a plate for her.

Carmen shook her head before Mateo could even open his mouth. Faith needed some time, and Carmen was happy to give that to her.

"How's the pizza?" Carmen asked through a mouth full of mozzarella sticks.

"Wow, it's awesome. I think I could eat this every day."

"Amen, sister," Mateo chimed.

"Do you...do you think there's a way I can track down my aunt?" Faith was nibbling on her lip now, instead of the pizza. Carmen wanted to scoop the girl up and give her a big hug.

"I'm sure there are ways. Um...do you have more information?"

"Not much, just that she was supposed to be living here. Apparently, she moved to Seattle three years ago. I tried searching for her on the internet at the library. But there is nothing."

"And you don't have her phone number?"

"Nope, just this address."

Carmen nodded and then looked at Mateo for support. What should she do? The girl clearly needed help.

"Do you have anyone else in Seattle you could ask?" she inquired.

"Nope. I...I had to leave home, you see."

Carmen sat patiently, waiting for Faith to open up. Mateo, remarkably, did the same, even though he looked ten seconds away from firing a thousand questions Faith's way.

"Um...my parents...they're...well, they aren't wonderful people."

Mateo moved to sit next to Faith, his hand rested gently on her forearm. "You can talk to us, sweetie. You're safe."

"My dad is an angry man. He has a certain way of thinking. He believes things that meant I couldn't stay at home."

"Did he hurt you?" Carmen asked.

"Nothing too bad. The thing is...well, I'm gay, and if he or my mom ever found out...it would be really bad."

"So you ran away?" Mateo asked, his voice full of understanding.

"No, I left. I'm eighteen. I waited until I legally turned into an adult."

Carmen had to give Faith her due. The kid had thought it through.

"I had a letter sent to the sheriff's department letting them know I left of my own free will. My parents will come after me, and I didn't want the police involved."

Mateo smiled. "Smart."

"I left in the middle of the night." Tears formed in Faith's eyes. The stress of her journey must have been getting to her. "I found out about my aunt a few months ago. She left for the same reason I did. I thought, if I could just find her, I would be okay," Faith sobbed.

Carmen scrubbed her face with her hands, regretting it immediately when she felt pizza sauce smear across her face.

"Let it all out," Mateo cooed softly as he hugged Faith closely.

"We'll help you," Carmen announced. She and Mateo knew exactly what it was like to be scared and vulnerable. They'd grown up in the system together. By the time they were fifteen, they'd run away and started a life of their own;

away from foster parents who used them as their personal punching bags and servants.

"What?" Faith spluttered.

"We'll help you find your aunt. Right Mateo?"

"Damn right, honey. We got you."

"You don't even know me," Faith replied, her eyes wide. "Why would you do that?"

"Because everyone needs a little help now and then. Plus, you're family." Carmen could see the confusion on Faith's face. "I'm a lesbian and Mateo is gay. See? Family!"

Mateo chuckled when Faith gasped and smiled. "I've never met anyone else like me."

"I'm sure you have; you just didn't know it. We gotta get your gaydar working, *chica*," Mateo clucked.

"All in good time," Carmen laughed. "First, let's get you settled in. We have a third bedroom. It's only small, though. You're welcome to it."

"I...I haven't got any money," Faith whispered. Carmen's heart was breaking for this girl.

"Unnecessary. If you could help with a few chores, that will be enough."

"Of course—you name it."

"And," Mateo added, "I get to play dress up!"

Carmen huffed out a breath. She should have known Mateo would want to use Faith as a mannequin. Kudos to the man, he had impeccable taste, and Faith could definitely do with a change of wardrobe. But Carmen wasn't sure Faith was ready for the full Mateo Ruiz experience yet.

"Dress up?"

"Honey, I'm gonna make your entrance onto the scene..."

"The scene?" Faith looked more confused than ever.

"Gay scene. A place of wonder," Mateo said with as much dramatic flair as possible.

"Mateo, maybe we should get her settled in first, before..."

"Nonsense. We want Faith to look awesome when she meets her aunt again."

There was no point in arguing with him. In a flash, Mateo pulled Faith up and dragged her to his room. Carmen closed the pizza box and followed. Faith was already sitting on his bed, laughing, as Mateo held up different women's garments to his torso, showcasing them with a twirl.

"What's your style, Faith? Dresses? Pants? Shirts?" Mateo called from inside his closet.

Carmen sat next to Faith on the bed and gave her a smile. "He loves fashion. He especially loves a chance to dress someone. That being said, if this is too much, just say. He won't be offended."

"It's...it's a little overwhelming. I've worn the same style of dress since I was tiny. I was never allowed to pick clothes."

"Has anything Mateo showed you looked appealing?"

"The jeans were nice. And the T-shirts. Although, I'm not sure I'd want them that sparkly all the time."

Carmen chuckled. Mateo loved anything that sparkled. "He does have some that won't blind you in the sunlight."

"Who got blinded?" Mateo asked, exiting his closet with an armful of clothes.

"I was just explaining that not all of your T-shirts are glittery."

"Oh no, girl, I have every style you could think of."

"Um...why do you have women's clothes?" Faith asked.

"I own a women's boutique."

"Do you work there too, Carmen?"

"God no. I'm a graphic designer."

Mateo snorted. "I'd go out of business if Carmen worked with me. She has no interest in fashion...as you can see."

"These are my sleep clothes, you ass."

"Uh-huh." Mateo smirked.

"I like comfort, nothing wrong with that."

"Comfort is fine. You living in sweatpants is not," Mateo punctuated with a perfectly arched eyebrow. Carmen muttered under her breath.

"You really don't have to give me clothes, Mateo." Faith said once she'd stopped giggling at Carmen and Mateo's bickering.

"Let me, please. That dress," he said, waving his hand at Faith, "is hurting my soul. You are a baby gay that needs some guidance. Let me be your fairy queer mother."

"*Por Dios*," Carmen laughed.

"Okay." Faith smiled.

"Excellent. Now, I think we know what needs to happen immediately, right Carmen?"

This is what Carmen had been afraid of. "I'll get the disco ball," she sighed.

"And the red carpet!" Mateo shouted at her retreating body.

"Disco ball?" Faith parroted.

"Oh yes. It's fashion show time," Mateo squealed.

Outside Mateo's room, Carmen rolled out the red carpet. She'd love to say that this wasn't a frequent thing she did, but that would be a lie. Mateo loved himself a fashion show.

Carmen shivered when she recalled the swimwear show Mateo and his friends put on last summer in their old house. No lesbian should ever be subjected to that many men in Speedos.

Laughter filtered out into the hall. Carmen hoped they could help Faith find her aunt. Now they just had to figure out where the hell to begin their search.

3

Faith

Faith excused herself to the bathroom so she could get a little space. Today had not gone to plan.

At all!

Not only was her Aunt Molly still a mystery yet to be unraveled, but now Faith found herself in the company of two people she didn't know, but had still taken her in and were offering to help her. For all her months of planning, Faith hadn't accounted for any of this.

It could be worse. The plan could have gone completely wrong.

The sound of Mateo laughing pulled a smile from her lips. Sitting on the edge of the bath, Faith gripped her knees and let out a breath; the first full breath she'd exhaled since running from Kentucky.

The constant worry Faith had dealt with for the past few months was still there, but becoming a little easier to keep at bay. Now and then, a shiver of anxiety would ripple through her body when her mind turned to thoughts of her father discovering Faith had escaped his control.

In a few days, she would think about contacting Alice again, just to check in. Faith was sure her parents would have gone straight to Alice, after the sheriff, of course. Hopefully, Alice and her parents hadn't suffered at Faith's expense.

Another laugh, this time from Carmen, roused Faith from her thoughts. Why were these people being so accommodating? Could she trust they had good intentions?

Faith had no answers, but she had her gut feeling, which had always steered her right. Now, her gut was telling her she was safe. Even if her safety and accommodation were temporary, at least Faith had a little time to collect herself and figure out her next move. Finding her aunt seemed an impossible task. After all, the one lead Faith had was a dead end.

"It will be okay," she whispered under her breath.

"Hey, are you okay in there?" Carmen's soft voice asked, slightly muffled through the bathroom door.

"Yeah, I'll just be a second."

"Take your time. Mateo is entertaining himself now," Carmen laughed, which made Faith chuckle.

It had been a couple of hours at most, since Faith met Carmen and Mateo, but without sounding like a cliché, it really felt like they'd known each other for a lot longer. Both Carmen and Mateo gave off older sibling vibes. And Faith could do with a bit of that in her life right now.

Straightening her dress, Faith stepped out of the bathroom. Mateo was catwalking like a pro while Carmen stood at the end of the hall taking photos.

"There you are, *chica*. Come on, it's time to get this show on the road. I've laid out a couple of outfits for you to model."

Faith's face glowed with embarrassment.

"Hey, you don't have to do anything you're not comfortable with," Carmen reassured. It wasn't that she was uncomfortable, as such. How could she explain how she was feeling? Maybe overwhelmed was a better word than uncomfortable.

Mateo was so full of life and his enthusiasm was infectious, but how would he react when he learned Faith really had no experience with clothes or modeling? Even letting go and just having fun was a foreign concept.

"No...I'm...I'm   not   uncomfortable,"   Faith stuttered.

Mateo walked over to the small music pod blasting out Madonna's *Vogue*. After pressing pause, he tapped the couch, beckoning Faith to sit down.

"Sorry, honey, I tend to get carried away. Come on, let's chat."

Faith sat down, flattening out the skirt section of her dress. Carmen watched her and gave an understanding smile. Carmen knew Faith was nervous and probably struggling with all the feelings bubbling under the surface.

"I..." Faith began, "I...don't know how to do all this."

"What, *chica*?" Mateo asked.

"I don't know... This..." Faith pointed to the red carpet.

"Oh, Faith, no one does. Mateo is just crazy and thinks everyone knows how to strut down a cheap-ass carpet, pretending to be a model," Carmen laughed.

Faith smiled. How did she explain the life she had led until now?

"I told you my parents aren't very nice people."

Carmen and Mateo nodded silently.

"My dad is the kind of man who believes a woman's place is to serve her husband. A daughter's place is to remain silent and do as she's told until married off."

Shuffling in her seat, Faith readied herself. "My father believes all women are sinners. He believes anyone different from him and his beliefs are sinners. Homosexuals, especially. So you can imagine what would happen if he found out about me."

Faith didn't need Carmen or Mateo to answer. They knew exactly what she was inferring.

"From a young age, I learned not to cross him. The few times I did, I was struck, usually across the face. My mother suffered worse if she stepped out of line."

A few deep breaths helped stave off the panic forming in Faith's chest, as she remembered all the times she'd witnessed her father's rage.

"I was homeschooled. My father didn't want me socializing with other children, including the kids from our church. Except one, that is. Alice. She's my best friend—probably my only friend. My father and her father grew up together, so he tolerated my friendship with Alice. She was the one who helped me escape."

That sliver of anxiety was making its presence known again. Screwing her eyes shut, Faith willed her body to calm down.

"I could go to the library once a week for half an hour, unsupervised. That's how I learned about things outside of my very limited world."

Carmen's hand on her shoulder grounded Faith, allowing her to continue.

"My dad planned to marry me off to one of the pastor's sons after I turned eighteen. I already knew I was different. Even from a young age, I had no interest in boys. Foolishly, I asked my dad about homosexuals once. Let's just say the experience was harrowing. That's when I knew I had to leave as soon as I was old enough."

It had taken every ounce of Faith's patience to stay put until she was a legal adult.

"Although I could learn some things at the library, it wasn't much. I have no understanding of the world. Today was the first time I'd tried pizza, rode on a bus, and met two other people like me. I don't know the clothes I might like or how social media works. I'm an eighteen-year-old with no life experience."

"That's alright, Faith. You'll pick it up with time." Carmen spoke so softly it made Faith's chest tighten. "How did you learn about your aunt?"

"By accident. The first time was when I walked in on my parents arguing and my mother let the name slip.

I've never seen my father get so mad. He nearly beat her to death. The second time was when Alice's parents were whispering. They didn't know I was listening. Obviously, Alice's father knew Molly, having grown up with my dad."

"Couldn't you have asked him about her?"

"No. Alice's parents were great to me. They're the reason I could afford my bus tickets. Mr. Carter may have grown up with my dad, but he doesn't share his beliefs. I wonder why my father is still friends with him. Normally, he shuns anyone with opposing views to his own."

"Probably because they share a past," Mateo remarked.

"Possibly. Anyway, Mr. and Mrs. Carter knew how my father treated me and mom, but they couldn't really help. Not without us suffering more. They did, however, set money aside for me, like they did for Alice. On my sixteenth birthday, they tried to give it to me. I tried to refuse, but they insisted. Alice said she would keep the money in her room. There was no way I could take it home. Asking Mr. Carter about Molly would have put him in a terrible position. I couldn't do that, not after everything they did for me."

"They could've gotten you out of there," Carmen shot. Faith could see anger simmering in her eyes.

"No, *hermana*, they couldn't. You know situations like that are impossible," Mateo chided softly.

Carmen huffed, clearly not happy. Faith smiled at her.

"Mateo's right. There would have been hell to pay for them, and for us, if they'd tried to intervene. They gave me a way out in the end. For that I'm grateful."

"I suppose," Carmen mumbled.

"When I started to plan my escape, I thought about this Molly woman. Although I'd heard her name, I didn't know who she was, or why my father hated her so much. On one of my library visits, I did some digging. I found out she was my dad's sister. I say that in the past tense, because as far as my father is concerned, Molly Parsons is dead to him. There were a couple of local news articles about her, up until she was seventeen, and then it was like she vanished."

"She ran away too?"

"No, my father cast her out. A local woman, Mrs. Baker, saw me researching Molly. Mrs. Baker has lived in Loretto all her life. I think she's around eighty now. Anyway, she came into the library and saw me looking at the news clippings. She sat next to me. It was the first time I'd ever spoken to her. My father forbade me or my mother from talking to her. Now I know why. Mrs. Baker told me about Molly."

Faith cast her mind back to the conversation with Mrs. Baker. She was so grateful the woman had shared Molly's story with her.

"According to her, my father caught Molly with a girl from church. By that time, he was nineteen and Molly was seventeen. Both their parents, my grandparents, had passed away, leaving Dad to raise Molly."

"So he caught her and threw her out?"

"Not right away. Mrs. Baker said he tried to get her to repent. If I know my father, he would have tried to beat the gay out of her."

"Bastard," Carmen hissed.

"When it became clear Molly wouldn't do as my father wanted, he banished her. Told Molly to never return, otherwise there would be severe consequences."

"Fuck, what century does he live in?" Carmen barked.

"Carmen," Mateo warned.

"And that was the last anyone heard from her," Faith concluded.

"We'll find her, Faith, I swear it."

"Carmen, you can't promise her that. Molly could be anywhere," Mateo scolded.

Tensions were running high and Faith felt awful she'd created such a heated atmosphere. Carmen and Mateo didn't need her baggage upsetting their lives. Faith was the one who decided to look for her long-lost aunt.

"Thank you, both of you, for welcoming me into your home. I think it best I go, though. You guys don't—"

"Faith, let us help."

"But you're getting upset with each other." Faith looked between Mateo and Carmen, their bodies tense.

Carmen looked at Mateo and softened. "Hey, we're not fighting."

Mateo took Carmen's hand and winked before turning his attention back to Faith.

"No, *chica*, we're not fighting; we're just passionate. Carmen is right. We want to help find Molly."

"Why?" Faith couldn't understand why they wanted to get involved. This was more than two people wanting to do a good deed.

"I was abandoned at a fire station as a baby," Carmen began. Faith's eyes widened with shock. "Mateo was left in a dumpster."

"Oh my god," Faith gasped.

"Yeah, not the greatest introduction to life," Mateo chuckled.

"We ended up in foster care together. There were times we would get sent to different foster families, but we always ended up coming back together."

Carmen gripped Mateo's hand. Faith could see the unshakable bond between them. Mateo's comment about being brother and sister in every way but blood made sense now.

"We didn't go through what you did, Faith, but we understand some of the hardship. Neither of us would have survived without the other," Carmen said, smiling at Mateo.

"We want to help you because you need someone in your corner. We can be those people until you find your aunt. We learned quickly that family isn't just the people you are born to. Family can be the people you choose to surround yourself with. Mateo is my brother. I chose him and he chose me. Now, I know we don't know each other well yet, but we're here, and we would like to be your chosen family, even if it's temporary."

Faith sat silently. Carmen and Mateo waited patiently for her to respond. The problem was, Faith was sure the moment she uttered any words, the floodgates would open.

For so long, Faith had craved the support and love her parents should have given her. Now, in this unfamiliar house, with these two strangers, Faith finally experienced what it was like to be truly seen, supported, and, dare she say it, loved.

As soon as Mateo squeezed her hand, Faith sobbed.

The sky had dulled considerably by the time Faith calmed down. Carmen and Mateo stayed by her side the entire time. Faith cried for her parents' inability to love her. She cried tears of relief that finally, after so long hiding and being scared, she was finally free to be who she wanted to be. And last but not least, she cried for her Aunt Molly. Faith knew how fortunate she was to stumble across Carmen and Mateo. God knows if Molly ever found people like them to take her in when she found herself alone at seventeen.

Wiping her nose on one of the tissues Mateo had continually supplied, Faith sat up. "Sorry about that." Her voice was hoarse after so much crying.

"You needed to let it out, honey," Mateo replied.

"You've had a lot to carry around with you," Carmen added.

"I didn't mean to disrupt your lives so much," Faith hiccupped.

"No disruption, *chica*. Anyway, it stopped me from having to watch Carmen eat Cheez Whiz out of a can and scratch her ass again, so really, you did me a favor."

Faith burst out laughing when Mateo received a pillow to the face from Carmen.

"Asshole," Carmen chuckled. "Hey, how about we get you settled into your room? You can grab a shower and we'll order some food?"

"Oh, Mateo, you didn't get to do your fashion show!"

"Relax, girl, there is plenty of time for that. Let's chill tonight, yeah?"

Faith nodded. A hot shower and a chance to relax was just what she needed.

Following Carmen to a door at the far end of the corridor, Faith surveyed her new room. It was twice the size of the one in her parents' house. The walls were painted a burned orange. There were dozens of pictures hung on the walls.

"Will this do?" Carmen asked.

"It's...wow...I love it," Faith breathed. The color was warm and inviting. The bed looked so soft; Faith couldn't wait to dive under the covers.

"There's a TV and radio/CD player. Feel free to watch and listen to whatever you like. Mateo sleeps like the dead, and I wear earplugs because he also sounds like a rhino when he gets his motor going." Carmen grinned.

"Carmen, I…"

"It's all good, kid. We want you to feel comfortable. If you need anything, just ask."

"Maybe we could talk more tomorrow?" Faith yawned. The day had thoroughly caught up to her.

"Absolutely. Breakfast at eight, if you want fresh pancakes, otherwise it's coffee and cereal," Carmen said with a smile. Before leaving, Carmen turned back to Faith. "It gets better. I promise."

"Thank you," Faith replied in a whisper. She was far too close to sobbing again.

When the door closed, Faith fell face-first onto the bed. There were still lots of things to talk about and decide, but right now, Faith let herself bask in the warmth that spread throughout her body. She never made it to the shower.

The sound of music and laughter jolted Faith from sleep. Looking around the room, it took her a moment to remember where she was. Her heart thudded in her chest.

It's okay, I'm safe.

Mateo's deep voice boomed through the house as he sang along to the music. Carmen begging Mateo to stop wailing, relieved Faith of the residual tension coursing through her veins.

"I'm safe," she said one last time to herself.

Faith stood in the doorway to the kitchen watching Mateo and Carmen kidding around. Mateo twirled Carmen and then dipped her. They laughed before turning back to the stove.

"Morning," Faith greeted the pair.

Carmen turned around with a spatula in her hand. "Hey kiddo, how'd you sleep?"

"So good." Faith smiled.

"Pancakes, *chica*, and lots of them. Sit down," Mateo said, waving at the long breakfast bar that was already adorned with fruit and cereal.

"Coffee?" Carmen asked, pouring three big mugs. Faith hoped it would taste better than the sludge from the diner.

Nathalie.

The thought was in Faith's mind before she could stop it; Nathalie's pretty face smiling at her.

"Hey, are you alright?"

Faith jumped slightly. When did Carmen sit next to her?

"What...yeah, sorry, sort of zoned out for a second."

"Oh, no, *chica*, I've seen that look before." Mateo grinned, his eyebrows wiggling. "That's the look of love."

"Faith, you've been holding out on us," Carmen teased, knocking Faith's shoulder.

"No," Faith shot, her face getting hotter.

"Uh-huh," Mateo chuckled, shoving a pancake in his mouth.

Faith nibbled on her bottom lip. She was so used to shutting anything down that might cause her trouble with her parents, the idea of sitting with people and talking about her crush was mind-boggling.

"I..." Faith cleared her throat. "I met a girl in a diner when I was on my way here. Her name was Nathalie."

"And was this Nathalie a cutie?" Carmen asked.

Faith wiped her face with a napkin, even though she hadn't eaten anything yet. Could she wipe away a blush?

"Um...yeah, she was nice."

"Did you get her number?" Mateo pushed.

"No, of course not, we just talked for like five minutes. She was just being nice. I don't even know if she likes girls."

Mateo and Carmen must have sensed her rising panic.

"Alright, honey, settle down. Sorry for teasing."

Mateo didn't look sorry; he still had a stupid grin on his face. Faith rolled her eyes and started on her pancakes. She desperately tried to hide her grin.

Is this what having siblings is like?

4

Carmen

Carmen listened to Mateo regale Faith with one of his clients' mishap stories. Faith was crying with laughter as Mateo performed his tale with dramatic flair. Smiling, Carmen polished off her pancakes and coffee.

Sleep hadn't come easily last night. As soon as Carmen was alone in her room, panic set in. Welcoming Faith into her home was the right thing to do, but something was telling Carmen their lives were about to get complicated.

Never mind the fact that finding this Molly woman was going to be a massive undertaking and might not turn out the way Faith hoped. There was also Faith's family to consider.

Because of the way Faith described her father, Carmen knew they would have to deal with some kind of fallout. Yes, Faith was an adult, but Carmen had met men like him. He wouldn't give up control that easily.

If Faith's parents showed up, Carmen had to take into consideration how that would affect Mateo. It had been a long time since either of them had dealt with people like that. They tended to stay far away from assholes nowadays.

Carmen and Mateo's childhoods had been tough. They'd both been through a lot, and they'd both tried their hardest to put those memories in the past, where they belonged.

A shot of pain reminded Carmen not everyone in her and Mateo's life had been bad. Camila Ruiz was the one, and only, person in their younger lives who'd given a damn.

The older woman worked at the group home. It was Camila who taught Carmen and Mateo Spanish. When Camila passed away from a heart attack, it felt as real as losing their own mother. That's why Carmen and Mateo adopted the surname Ruiz. It was the only time they'd felt seen, and in some way, loved...wanted.

After Camila, the two Ruiz kids only knew pain and suffering, especially Mateo. The worry that a run-in with Faith's father might trigger Mateo, played heavily on her conscience.

Carmen suffered busted lips and bruises at the hands of her so-called caregivers. Mateo had suffered so much more. How was Carmen supposed to keep him safe and help Faith, at the same time?

Those had been the thoughts rolling around Carmen's head for most of the night. By the time the sun was peeking over the horizon, Carmen was almost bouncing off the walls. Music hadn't helped. TV just irritated her more. So Carmen did the one thing she hated: exercise.

Plugging in headphones and running at the ass crack of dawn was not her idea of a good time, but nothing else was working. Carmen didn't want Mateo or Faith to see how unsettled she felt.

A three-mile jog had done the trick. By the time she got home, the sun was up. Mateo and Faith were still in bed, which gave Carmen the chance to shower and put on a clean boxer brief and tank combo. Just because she'd showered didn't mean she had to get dressed, right?

Maybe Mateo was on to something? Maybe Carmen had become a little too comfortable working from home.

"Hey, Carm, how about a movie marathon today? We can introduce Faith to a few essential movies and TV series."

"Is this the beginning of her *lesducation*?" Carmen chuckled. Mateo had a twinkle in his eye. That man was over the moon to be Faith's guide into Queerdom.

"Absolutely. Plus, it's Sunday. You know Sundays are sacred."

"Oh, are you religious?" Faith asked.

Carmen snorted. "If by religious you mean with face masks and manicures, then yes, Mateo is devout."

"At least I'll look good when I get to those pearly gates," Mateo tutted.

"I've never had a manicure," Faith remarked, studying her fingernails.

"Well, that's about to change, *chica*. I'm going to *Pretty Woman* the shit out of you!"

Carmen laughed again. Poor Faith. She had no idea what she was signing up for. At least Carmen wouldn't have to suffer another Sunday of being attacked with wax strips and tweezers.

"Don't think you're off the hook, *hermana*. Those eyebrows are close to becoming a single unit."

Faith giggled behind her hand, and Carmen scowled at Mateo. "My eyebrows are fine."

"No, honey, they are not. Plus, you need your undercut shaved."

Carmen grazed her fingers along the back of her neck. Okay, she needed a little maintenance performed on her hair, but that didn't mean she was going to let him go all *Miss Congeniality* on the rest of her body.

"Faith, why don't you grab the robe on the back of your door while I get my kit. Meet us in the living room."

Faith nodded and scampered off; her mood was much lighter than the day before. Carmen sighed audibly.

"Okay, what's wrong?" Mateo asked.

"Nothing, I just didn't sleep much."

"Give it up Carmen. What's wrong?"

Carmen shot a look towards the door. The last thing she wanted was Faith to hear her worries.

"I'm worried. I don't know where to look for Faith's aunt and—"

"You're worried about dear old dad showing up," Mateo finished, slipping onto the stool next to Carmen.

"Yeah," Carmen sighed.

"Are you worried for Faith or for me?"

Carmen should have known Mateo would see straight through her. They shared a bond tighter than blood relations. Their survival as kids had depended on trusting each other.

"Both?"

Mateo gave Carmen an understanding smile. "You know, I'm like six months older than you right? Yet here you are, acting all big-sisterly on me."

The tut he gave for effect helped break the tension.

"Carm, I know this is going to be tough for us both. First, we've never had to look out for anyone but each other. I mean, what do kids eat these days? Is she potty trained? Gosh, so many things to think about."

Carmen knocked his shoulder playfully.

"But at the end of the day, Faith is a young woman who needs our help. And I think we are uniquely qualified to offer her that. Yes, sure, if her parents show up, it could trigger me and possibly, you. Don't forget, I'm not the only one that went through shit, but that's why you forced us both into therapy. I can handle myself and I trust you to do the same."

"Things have just been so good for us; I'm worried about breaking our luck."

"*Hermana*, it's not luck. We've worked hard to get where we are. Nothing will change that. Faith needs us to be the role models *we* so desperately needed growing up. She also needs adults who understand her and can help guide her through what I'm sure is a really exhausting time. Not only is she fresh out of the closet, but the way she was brought up means she has so many other things to learn and experience."

"I hear you," Carmen replied thoughtfully.

Taking on Faith was a massive decision. Yesterday, Carmen's heart had overruled her brain. In the cold light of day, though, was it the right decision to involve themselves in Faith's business?

"No, you don't. I can hear your cogs grinding from here. We're not teenagers who need to keep the world at bay anymore, Carmen. That girl needs our help and I intend to give it, with or without you!"

Carmen gritted her teeth as Mateo stormed out of the room. Damn it. She shouldn't have opened her mouth. It was rare Mateo and Carmen disagreed, but when they did, Carmen usually found herself in the wrong.

Out of the two of them, she was the one who struggled to let go of the past. Even at thirty-seven, Carmen let her past dictate her present and future. Most of the arguments between Carmen and Mateo were about her inability to let herself fully live. Mateo hated Carmen working from home because he thought it gave her an excuse to shut out the world. He wasn't wrong.

"Fuck," Carmen hissed.

She could hear Mateo laughing with Faith in the living room. How Carmen wished she could be like him. It would be great to go through life not expecting the worst in people. Instead, Carmen was in a constant state of awareness and suspicion.

"Carmen, get your ass in here. My tweezers are itching to pluck your unibrow."

Rubbing her face vigorously, Carmen prepared herself. Mateo would play nice in front of Faith, but the second they were alone, he would be pissed at her all over again.

"I didn't know my skin could feel so soft," Faith whispered.

Carmen, Faith, and Mateo, all sat in a row with their heads leaning back on the sofa. Mateo had given them each a facial.

"Honey, this is essential maintenance," Mateo replied.

"I feel tingly," Faith giggled.

"That's because your face can breathe now that all the dead skin is gone."

Carmen gagged. "Ew, gross, let's not talk about dead skin, please."

"We wouldn't have to if you exfoliated once in a while, Carm."

"I exfoliate."

"You two are hilarious," Faith cackled.

Carmen smiled. It was nice to see Faith relaxing. It was also good for Carmen to have spent some time with her and Mateo. Just being around those two helped quell Carmen's worries.

Mateo was right. There was a reason Carmen felt the need to offer Faith their home. Stripping away all the uncertainty left Carmen clearheaded. Faith was a good kid from the little Carmen knew of her. Everyone deserved support, and that's what Carmen would give. Now she just had to channel that thought to Mateo, so he didn't rip her a new asshole as soon as Faith left the room.

"Right, now that we are silky smooth, I suppose I should tackle your hair, Carmen. No self-respecting lesbian is going to jump into bed with you looking like that."

"Wow, you're just full of compliments today, Mateo. So good for my self-esteem."

"Just telling it like it is, *hermana*. Now into the bathroom you go."

Carmen hauled herself up from the couch and trudged to the bathroom. Stripping off her tank top, Carmen surveyed herself in the mirror. Her undercut was overgrown. Her skin was also pale.

"Jesus," she mumbled as she prodded the skin on her face, "you're getting old."

"No, you're just not getting enough sunlight," Mateo stated.

He directed Carmen to sit on the stool that was reserved for haircuts. Carmen had argued until she was blue in the face, when Mateo first told her he planned to set up a hair station in the shared bathroom.

The idea of Mateo using their space to play hairdresser had irked Carmen, until she actually allowed Mateo to give her a full treatment. Now their bathroom resembled a salon and Carmen loved it.

"Listen, before you jump all over me about earlier, I know I was wrong. I was just panicking a bit."

"Alright," Mateo replied, leaning Carmen's head back against the sink to wash her hair.

"That's it? Just, 'alright'?"

"Yes, that's it. I know you needed your freak out, but I also knew you would come to the right decision."

"Are you...are you sure you will be okay if her dad turns up?"

"Yes, I'm sure. My time fearing asshole men is well and truly over. Faith needs us to be strong for her. She's a good kid."

"You get on well with her."

"You will, too. Just let yourself, Carmen. For once, don't overthink—just connect. I can't be your only constant, *chica*. I *will* be, you know that, but I shouldn't be the only one."

"I don't understand how you're so chill about everything."

"How else should I be? Yeah, we had a shitty start in life, but Carmen, look at us. We fought and worked, and we survived. Hell, we did more than that. I have a successful business I love, and you are stupid intelligent, with not one, but two, companies. There will be people who hurt us—that's life—but none of them will break us."

"I'm so proud of you, Mateo," Carmen choked. It was unlike her to get sappy, but for whatever reason, Faith's situation was bringing a lot of emotions to the surface.

"I'm proud of myself too," he laughed. "I love you, Carmen. You are my person and I'm damn proud to call you *Hermana*. But please, stop letting old shit dictate your life. At some point I'm going to meet a hunky man, move out, and have a pack of kids. I want to know you are settled and happy, before that."

"A pack of kids?" Carmen laughed. "God help us all if there's a bunch of mini-Mateos running around the place."

"Imagine how perfect their skin will be," Mateo mused. Carmen chuckled. Mateo's kids would have the most flawless skin in the United States.

The pair fell silent as Mateo washed and rinsed Carmen's hair. Hauling her long locks into a messy bun on top of her head, Carmen rolled her neck, dispelling the tightness that always formed after bending over the sink.

"Do you want an inch trimmed off?" Mateo asked, flicking Carmen's wet bun.

"Sure, why not."

Silence fell again. Carmen wondered what Faith was doing. There was no sound coming from the living room.

"Where's Faith?"

"Relaxing on the sofa."

"Didn't she want the TV on or anything?"

"I don't think it even occurred to her. I pointed out your books, just in case she got bored."

Carmen whipped around to face Mateo, her eyes bugging. Carmen's books were not exactly PG.

"Mateo, she can't read them."

Mateo barked out a deep laugh. "Of course she can. It's about time the girl—"

"No, Mateo. Jesus, she'll have a heart attack."

"Relax. She'll put it down if it's too much. Stop panicking."

Carmen squirmed on the stool. Faith was a grown woman—sort of. Of course she could read whatever she wanted. That didn't make Carmen feel any better; not when she felt it was her responsibility to help ease Faith into the sapphic world.

Was it her responsibility? Did Faith even want her help? Maybe it was best to leave anything like that up to Faith's aunt. But what if they couldn't find Molly?

"Will you stop moving?" Mateo snapped.

"Wait one minute," Carmen replied, grabbing a towel, then launching herself out the bathroom door. Nope, she couldn't sit back. She needed to warn Faith.

Rounding the corner to the living room, Carmen looked crazed, with her hair pulled up haphazardly and a towel wrapped precariously around her chest.

Faith was just about to flip the page on one of Carmen's sauciest books.

"Wait!" Carmen practically screamed, causing Faith to launch the book halfway across the room.

"Oh my Lord, you scared the bejesus out of me," Faith panted, clutching her chest.

"Sorry, I just...I just wanted to warn you?"

"Warn me?" Faith's eyes went wide with fear.

Oh, for God's sake Carmen, don't go blurting out something like that!

"No, no, don't panic. You're fine—we're fine. Mateo told me you might read my books," she said, quickly pointing to the novel on the floor.

"I'm sorry. Didn't you want me to? I should have asked."

"No, it's not that. Um...the books are sapphic stories."

"Okay."

"And...um...well, they're a little spicy."

"Spicy?" Faith furrowed her eyebrows.

Oh, Christ.

"Yeah, the sex scenes in them are quite explicit."

Faith's face turned a deep shade of red, as did Carmen's.

"I just didn't want you to feel uncomfortable." She tacked on in a voice far less confident than it should be.

"She feels uncomfortable now, *chica*," Mateo hollered from the bathroom.

"Shit, sorry—"

"No, it's okay. Thank you for warning me...um...but I'd still like to read one, if that's alright?"

"Yeah, sure, go for it." Carmen gave an awkward thumbs up. Hating herself a little, she turned on her heel and headed back to the bathroom.

"Well, that was entertaining," Mateo chuckled.

"Shut up."

"Now that you've successfully embarrassed yourself, and Faith, can I continue with your hair?"

"Wow, I love your hair," Faith gasped when Carmen stepped into the kitchen.

"Thanks, me too." Carmen smiled. "I was thinking," Carmen added, "I have a friend in the Seattle Police Department. Maybe I could ask her how we should begin our search for your aunt."

"Really? That would be great."

"I was also thinking we could ask the neighbors. Maybe Molly got friendly with them and may have told them where she was going."

"Of course. Why didn't I think of that?"

"Because you've had a super stressful few days," Carmen laughed. "Don't beat yourself up about it."

"Who's beating whom up?" Mateo asked. Carmen threw her head back in laughter when she saw what Mateo was wearing.

"No one needs to see you in spandex, Mateo!" Carmen howled.

"I have a fitness video to finish," he huffed.

"And that requires you to dress like Richard Simmons?"

"Don't knock Ricky, Carmen."

"Don't assault my eyes with spandex, Mateo."

"Carmen was saying she has a friend on the police force who might give us a clue where our search for Aunt Molly should begin."

"Ah, would that be the delectable Detective March, by any chance, *hermana*?"

Carmen rolled her eyes. Rachel March had been, at one time, a friend with benefits. Although the "friend" part of that title was questionable. The "benefits" part certainly outweighed any friendship time they shared.

"Yes, I'm going to call Rachel. We need a starting point. I'm also going to talk to the neighbors." Carmen bypassed Mateo's attempt at teasing her about Rachel.

"Maybe you could go for a drink? Make an evening out of it?"

"That's unnecessary. I'll just call her."

Carmen scooted past Faith and headed to her room. Hopefully, Rachel would be happy to hear from her. It's not like they parted on bad terms. Carmen hadn't wanted Rachel to get the idea she wanted more from their arrangement, so she'd cut off communication a few months ago. They still sent the odd text now and then, but the benefits had been put on a permanent hold.

Tapping the little green icon on her phone, Carmen only had to wait three rings before Rachel's sultry voice invaded her ear.

"Well, well, well. If it isn't Carmen Ruiz."

"Rachel, hey, how are you?"

"Intrigued. I thought our little bedroom adventures were over after you all but ghosted me."

Carmen bit her lip and made a fist with her free hand. She should have known Rachel would be pissed.

"Sorry—"

"Oh stop, I'm teasing. We both knew what it was. Is everything alright? You're not in trouble, are you?"

"No, but I have a few questions, if you have five minutes?"

"For you, kitten, I have ten."

Carmen chuckled. Maybe they *could* find their way back to their bedroom adventures, just one more time.

5

Faith

Even though the last twenty-four hours had been an emotional whirlwind, Faith was feeling pretty good. Whether it was because Mateo and Carmen made her feel safe, or simply because she could stop running long enough to take a break from the usual feelings of anxiety, she wasn't sure. Whatever the reason, Faith was happy to go along for the ride.

The simple acts of sitting with her new friends, eating pancakes this morning, and having a facial and manicure, were so far from her norm, Faith reveled in it all. It was a hard pill to swallow sometimes, when she thought about how much of the world she didn't know.

What eighteen-year-old didn't know about current affairs? Or which TV show was popular? Running from her previous life in Kentucky didn't just mean Faith could finally live as an out-and-proud queer woman. It meant she had bought some time to learn about the world and her place in it.

There were so many things about herself Faith had yet to discover. Her style, for instance. Hanging around Carmen and Mateo had shown her just how dowdy she looked and felt.

Mateo was tall, trim, and immaculate. His clothes were wild, and often feminine, but Faith adored everything Mateo wore—probably because the man had so much confidence in himself, it was almost infectious.

Carmen was a little different. For Faith, Carmen was more of a role model. Sure, Carmen was the first lesbian Faith had met—that she knew of, anyway—but that meant nothing. Faith could have met a thousand lesbians and would still hold Carmen up on a pedestal. There weren't many people in the world who would selflessly help a complete stranger, but Carmen Ruiz had.

If Faith was going to walk the rainbow road, she wanted to have someone like Carmen guiding her. Like Mateo, Carmen seemed confident in herself. Yes, she walked around in boxer briefs and an old tank top most of the time, but she was still herself—maybe even more so than Mateo.

"Hey, I just wanted to apologize again, for freaking you out earlier," Carmen said awkwardly, as the two of them sat in the kitchen drinking coffee.

She'd returned from her room after talking to her police friend. Faith wanted to know what they'd discussed, but didn't want to push.

When Carmen had come running into the living room earlier, Faith had thought the worst, especially when Carmen said she'd just wanted to warn Faith.

That word had instantly made Faith feel sick, until Carmen explained she meant the warning had been for the book Faith was about to read. Then the panic had turned to embarrassment, for them both.

Faith knew the basics about sex. Her mother had given her a God-fearing version of sex education. Only when Faith had a conversation with Alice, did she actually learn the important, and relevant, aspects of sex.

Sex with a woman, though? Nope, nothing. Maybe Carmen's books could help her in that department, not that she was anywhere close to actually sleeping with a woman.

"It's fine, honestly," Faith replied, hoping to make Carmen feel better.

"I'm going out. Back in an hour," Mateo called from the hallway.

"Where are you going?" Carmen hollered.

"Just out. I won't be long."

"Bring tacos."

Faith chuckled again. The dynamic between Carmen and Mateo was fascinating. They were best friends, but fought like brother and sister.

"I really do like your hair," Faith commented. With a freshly shaved undercut, Carmen looked great.

"It's a good style for me. Look," Carmen began, freeing her hair from its bond, "I can wear it down for meetings and I look all professional and strait-laced," she grinned, dramatically flipping her curly locks over her shoulder.

"But in an instant, I can wear it up in a ponytail or top knot, and I become stylish as hell." Carmen then whipped her hair into a messy bun. "Two styles in one."

Faith had been thinking long and hard about who she was since stepping into Carmen and Mateo's world. "I wish I had a style."

"You may not know what your style is yet, but you do have it. Tell me, what do you want to change?"

"Um...maybe have some length taken off my hair? I was never allowed to cut it."

"That's easily done. What else?"

"My clothes. This," Faith pointed to her dress, "is not my style. I know that much. I hate it."

"Again, easy to fix. Mateo is itching to make you over," Carmen laughed. "Letting him give you a facial and pedicure was just the tip of the iceberg."

"I really enjoyed it. I think it's the first time...in forever, that I feel like me. Just a girl enjoying life."

"As it should be, Faith. You're still young, and there is plenty of time for you to figure everything out. I'm here for you, in whatever capacity you need, okay?"

"I have so much to learn."

"Yeah, but how exciting is that?"

Carmen's enthusiasm stunned Faith for a second. She was so used to being cautious and looking at her upbringing as a negative, Faith forgot she was on a journey.

"We all learn and grow. Most of us don't even recognize when that happens. But, for you, Faith...you are coming into your new world with your eyes wide open. You are old enough to understand the significance of your new life, but young enough to learn freely, and without the cynicism we often gain in adulthood. Your life sucked before; I get that. Hell, I lived that, but now? Wow, Faith, now you get to explore and learn about love, and everything that makes time on this rock worth living."

"You should be a motivational speaker or something," Faith gasped.

Carmen was so enthusiastic and upbeat, Faith found herself nodding along as Carmen's words poured out and engulfed her.

"Ha, I don't know about that. I do know a little about re-inventing yourself and learning who you are."

"Can I ask you something?"

"I'm an open book, Faith."

"When did you...you know...*know*?"

"That I liked girls?"

"Yeah."

"When I was around fourteen, I think. It was the year before Mateo and I hightailed it out of the system. Mateo had just got back to the group home after his most recent foster dad beat the crap out of him. Anyway, he arrived with another kid—a girl called Brogan. Well, after I made sure Mateo was okay, I sort of fixated on Brogan. At first, I thought it was because she was a little shy. You know, like I just wanted to help her out. But then, after I had a dream about her—one where she kissed me—I knew my feelings were something more.”

“Did you ever tell her?”

“Hell no,” Carmen laughed. “The one thing I learned in the system was to keep your shit to yourself. I didn’t trust anyone but Mateo. It was funny really because we didn’t even come out to each other.”

“What do you mean?” Coming out had been Faith’s worst nightmare for a long time.

“Well, there was no deep discussion. We just sort of knew already. Mateo had boyfriends, and I had…friends that were girls.”

Faith laughed at Carmen’s unique description of her relationship with women.

“Have you had a serious girlfriend before?”

“Nope, and I know why. I’m not ignorant of the fact that my childhood has shaped how I interact with people. It’s just something I struggle with. It drives Mateo nuts.”

“I hope I have a girlfriend one day.” Faith longed to have someone to love her completely, without conditions and expectations.

“I have no doubt you’ll get what you want, Faith. But...”

“But?”

"But don't be in a rush, okay? Take your time exploring this side of yourself. Learn to love yourself, entirely, including the parts of yourself that connect you to your parents. Once you do that... I think you will make some girl really fucking happy."

Tears sprung from Faith's eyes. No one had ever spoken to her the way Carmen just had.

"Why is Faith crying, Carmen?" Mateo barked, causing both Faith and Carmen to jump.

"Jesus, *hermano*, give us a little warning next time. I almost peed my boxers."

"Why is she crying?"

"I'm crying because I can't believe how lucky I got when I turned up here yesterday. I already feel seen and heard. More than any time in my life. I hardly know you, but I feel like I *do* know you."

Mateo wrapped his arms around Faith. "What the hell did you say to her?" Mateo chuckled as Faith sobbed.

Those sobs turned into mirth when Faith saw the "deer in headlights" expression on Carmen's face. Pulling back from Mateo, Faith reached for Carmen. Together, the trio hugged each other tightly.

Forget love at first sight. For Faith, this was *family* at first sight.

"Are we all adequately cried out yet?" Mateo asked a few minutes later. Faith giggled.

"I'm good now," she replied, wiping her face.

"Yeah, all good," Carmen added, clearing her throat.

"God. Lesbians!" Mateo huffed. "Now, I didn't get to do a full fashion show yesterday," Mateo began, pulling Faith into the living room. "So we are having one now."

Faith looked at the bags piled on the sofa. "What's all that?"

"I went to the store and picked up a few items for you. Now, I don't know if you'll like everything, but I'm feeling confident."

Faith looked from the mountain of bags to Mateo and then Carmen, who was smiling affectionately.

"Mateo, this is..."

"If you say anything along the lines of 'it's too much' or you 'can't accept it', I'm going to throw a massive fit. And trust me, you don't want that."

"You really don't," Carmen laughed.

"Okay, I won't say anything, but thank you."

"Great, let's get started."

"Yes, yes, yes, I'm a genius," Mateo crowed loudly.

Faith stood in the living room, dressed in lightly distressed overalls rolled up above her ankles, a black short-sleeved T-shirt, and new Converse All-Stars.

"What do you think?" Carmen asked.

"I love it. I feel comfortable, but stylish, without having to put a ton of effort into it."

"See? Genius!" Mateo cried, thrusting his fist in the air. Faith laughed, and Carmen rolled her eyes.

"What about the other stuff you tried on?" Carmen pawed through the ridiculous amount of clothes piled on the sofa.

"I liked all the jeans. I think I prefer the darker ones."

"Yes, you looked great in those black skinnies," Mateo remarked, holding up the aforementioned jeans.

"Yeah, I agree. What about the shirts and T-shirts?"

"Love them all. Thanks for dialing back the glitter," Faith grinned. It hadn't escaped her notice that Mateo had chosen darker colors.

"It was difficult to do, but for you, Faith, I rose to the challenge."

"Um…" Faith fumbled. She wanted to ask Mateo to cut her hair. Nothing drastic, but something new. "Would you…um…would you cut my hair?"

Mateo jumped up from the sofa and began running his hands through Faith's long locks.

"What are you thinking? You have gorgeous hair, *chica*. Has it ever been cut?"

"Not really. My mom trimmed the ends once a year, but that's it."

Faith loved her hair, but she hated the fact she'd never been given the choice of what to do with it.

"It's such a rich blonde—almost like honey," Mateo muttered, more to himself than anyone else in the room.

"It comes from my father's side."

"Are you wanting a trim? Or something a little more drastic?"

Faith twisted her hands together. "Um…I'd like it to be shoulder length and um…"

"An undercut at the neck?" Mateo supplied.

Faith's face went red. She wanted her neck shaved, but she didn't want Carmen to think she was being lame by copying the style.

"I think that would look awesome," Carmen interjected.

"Really?" Faith didn't mean to sound so timid, but she couldn't help the nerves. Apart from Alice, she'd never really had anyone to look up to. The last thing she wanted was to irritate Carmen.

"Hell, yeah. I think it's gonna really suit your face. And your new style. Get in that bathroom and let that old queen do his thing."

"Who the fuck are you calling *old*?" Mateo shot.

"Notice he's offended by the age thing, but not by being called a queen," Carmen laughed.

"I am a queen, and don't you forget it," Mateo tutted. "Now, get in the bathroom, *chica*, I have work to do."

Faith skipped into the bathroom and internally squealed with excitement. Mateo guided her to a chair and then leaned her head back. The water was warm, and the head massage Mateo was performing, felt heavenly.

"Wow, I could fall asleep," Faith muttered, her eyes closing.

"You do you, honey," Mateo chuckled.

"Are you a hairdresser by trade?"

"Not professionally, no. I learned early. There weren't a lot of things I enjoyed growing up. One thing I loved, was playing with Carmen's hair. It's so thick. She would always let me fiddle about with it when we got placed in the group home together. It was a way for me to de-stress."

"I'm sorry you went through that, Mateo."

"Me, too."

"How are you so open and relaxed about it?"

Honestly, it staggered Faith how either Carmen or Mateo could talk so openly about their childhoods.

"Therapy," he laughed. "When we were older and making money for ourselves, Carmen forced me to see a therapist. That girl worked her ass off to make sure we could both get weekly sessions. I don't know what I would have done without her."

Faith mulled over all the information Mateo was freely giving her. As much as she hated hearing what they'd gone through, their life story also reassured her. If Carmen and Mateo could go through all that, and come out the other side, so could Faith.

"You're both amazing."

"Yeah, we are," Mateo stated. "Okay, you're all washed and rinsed. Sit up and we'll get to work."

Faith sat up. Mateo wheeled her over to the mirror opposite the sink. After a quick towel-dry, Mateo gathered Faith's hair and brought up his scissors.

"Ready?"

Faith looked him in the eye through the mirror. She'd never been more ready. With a quick nod, Faith watched Mateo snip the first tendrils of hair. As the pieces drifted to the floor, Faith took a deep breath and smiled.

"Hey, I'm going to go get the tacos Mateo didn't bring back," Carmen called.

"We need hot sauce," Mateo bellowed back.

"Mateo, we have five bottles in the cupboard. Stop buying, or asking me to buy, hot sauce."

Faith's shoulders vibrated as she tried in vain to conceal her laughter. The door banging closed ended the hot sauce argument. Mateo reached over and pressed a button on the wall. A cacophony of noise boomed through the house.

"I need to dance as I cut," he shouted over the music.

"I'll say it again: I'm a genius!"

Faith studied her new look. Her blonde hair fell in layers, just past her shoulders. The texture made her look a little older, which she liked. Paired with her new clothes, Faith was almost unrecognizable, even to herself.

Carmen whistled. "Nice job, Mateo." After dumping the taco bag on the kitchen sink, she turned Faith in a circle. "You look great, kiddo."

"I feel great."

"Well, I hope this adds to your good mood." Carmen reached inside her rucksack and produced a new iPhone. "It's not the newest model, but it should get you by."

"No, no way," Faith protested. iPhones, no matter how old, were still expensive. Faith knew that because Alice was given one for her birthday a couple of years ago.

"Look, you need a phone, and honestly, I know how to use an iPhone, so I shouldn't have a problem helping you set it up."

"Carmen, this is too much."

"No, it's a necessity," Mateo interrupted before Faith could continue.

"You can have our numbers. We can set up the find-a-phone thingy. You can study up on all the things you've missed out on. You need it, and I'm not taking it back." Carmen turned back to the tacos and began dividing the contents between them.

Faith's mind instantly went to Alice. She desperately wanted to call her friend. Deciding that arguing with either of the Ruizes was foolish, Faith vowed there and then, she would somehow find a way to pay back their kindness.

After inhaling three tacos, which were the best thing she'd ever eaten, Faith settled on her bed and began setting up her phone. Before calling Alice, Faith thought it prudent to send a message asking Alice to save her number under a different name. Alice responded immediately, informing Faith she'd done as asked.

The call connected after one ring.

"Hey Spencer, it's good to hear from you," Alice all but shouted down the phone.

Faith chuckled to herself. "Am I Spencer from camp?"

"Yeah, I saved you under Spencer's name. My parents won't think anything of it. How are you? Where are you?" Alice whispered.

Faith could hear the worry in her friend's voice. "I made it to Seattle. My aunt wasn't at the address I had—"

"Are you safe? Do you have somewhere to stay?"

"I'm good, Alice, I promise. The people who live at the address took me in."

"You're staying with complete strangers! Fai—Spencer, what the hell?"

"Alice, calm down. They are lovely. Both gay, and both with a tough childhood like mine. I'm lucky to have found them."

"Are you sure?"

"Positive. Really, Alice, they are wonderful. Carmen and Mateo have already done so much for me. They've agreed to help me look for Molly."

"Any idea where she is?"

"None, but Carmen has a police friend she talked to and we'll quiz the neighbors."

"Faith, your dad…"

So much for the Spencer charade.

A sharp stabbing pain hit Faith in the gut. She knew they would need to talk about her father, but she was hoping for a little more time before that came up.

"What's happening?"

"He did what you said he would. Went straight to the sheriff. After that didn't go the way he wanted, he came here, just like you predicted. Thankfully, Dad calmed him down and convinced him we don't know where you are."

"Well, that's good."

"Yeah, but my dad told me this morning your parents have packed up the car and are on the move. He's coming after you, Faith."

Even though the news wasn't a surprise, it still sent a wave of dread to Faith's stomach.

That ticking clock was counting down again.

6

Carmen

Monday mornings weren't usually a big deal in the Ruiz household. Mateo left for the boutique around 8:30 a.m. and Carmen would set up her laptop in the kitchen at 9:00 a.m.

Few people would think Carmen owned two successful graphic design companies; not with the way she operated. Most of the time, she left the running of both companies up to her VPs. They were a solid and reliable bunch of people who enjoyed the professional freedom Carmen gave.

Before her success, Carmen's motivation had always been Mateo, and providing a life they both deserved. When she became financially stable, Carmen took a step back from the stress of running two businesses, much preferring the design side of things than the management. Carmen was the owner on paper only, if she were being honest, which suited her fine.

Carmen's goal wasn't ever to have wealth for wealth's sake. As long as she had money for Mateo's retirement, she was satisfied. Everything she earned went into savings. The house they lived in was rented. The car she drove was pre-owned, and she never spent recklessly. Carmen knew how things could change in an instant and she would never find herself compromised financially—not for the sake of a fancy car or house.

With Faith in their lives, Carmen had to think a little differently. Faith needed help financially, at least until they could track down her aunt. That begged a few questions. Did Faith have a bank account? What about medical insurance? Carmen guessed she had neither.

Now the weekend was over, and Faith was a little more settled, they needed to discuss the next steps and how Carmen could help Faith begin her new life. Clothes and a makeover were all good fun, but there was a serious side to starting over; a side that Faith probably didn't know how to navigate.

After shooting off a few emails to her VPs, Carmen worked on creating a spreadsheet for Faith; one that would help her check off important tasks that needed to be done ASAP, as well as planning for her future.

Satisfied with her work so far, Carmen thought back to the conversation she'd had with Rachel yesterday. There wasn't much Rachel could offer, apart from advice, which was to talk to the neighbors, which Carmen already planned to do.

Molly wasn't a missing person; therefore, Rachel couldn't get involved. The detective said she'd poke around a little, but Carmen felt uneasy about that. Rachel getting into trouble with her boss wasn't what she wanted.

Pouring herself another cup of coffee, Carmen heard Faith's bedroom door open. It was almost 10:30 a.m., and later than expected. Faith shuffled into the room wearing unicorn sleep trousers—courtesy of Mateo—and a faded black T-shirt. Faith's newly shortened hair stuck out in different directions.

"Hey," the young woman yawned.

"Morning. Sleep well?"

"Like a baby. That bed has magical powers, I swear."

Carmen chuckled. It was more likely Faith's body needed rest after such a turbulent time.

"Want some?" she asked, holding up the coffee pot.

"Mmm, please."

Setting about preparing another mug of coffee and turning on the stove, ready to make some scrambled eggs,

Carmen realized how regular the whole setup seemed. It felt like Faith had been in the house for months, rather than hours.

"Here, get that down. I'll make you some breakfast."

"Thank you," Faith mumbled, her eyes almost closing again. The kitchen fell into a comfortable silence as Carmen made eggs and Faith sipped on her coffee. Only when Faith finished demolishing her breakfast, did the girl seem to fully wake up.

"Do you have a lot of work today?"

Carmen scanned her laptop, noting a couple of new emails, but nothing that couldn't wait.

"Some—nothing crazy. I wanted to talk to you, if that's cool."

Faith sat up straight, a flicker of fear washing across her face, causing Carmen to feel bad. It seemed Faith didn't feel completely safe just yet.

"Do you have a bank account?" she asked.

The question took Faith a second to answer. It was probably not the conversation Faith thought they were going to have.

"Um, no."

"I'll go out on a limb and say you don't have any savings, then."

"No, nothing." Faith began fiddling with the handle of her coffee cup.

"Hey, relax. I'm not asking because I want you to pay us," Carmen chuckled, hoping to relieve some of Faith's tension. "I've just been thinking about where we go from here. You need a bank account and you need spending money."

"I can get a job," Faith blurted.

This wasn't going the way Carmen hoped. Instead of reassuring Faith, she was making the girl panic.

An idea struck her. Faith wouldn't accept money for nothing. That was clear.

"I have a job for you."

Faith narrowed her eyes. "What job?"

"I need a personal assistant."

"Did you just make that up?" Faith asked, continuing to regard Carmen with suspicion.

"Yes, and no. I only thought of it now, but actually, I could have used some help a while ago. It's basic: answering certain emails, organizing my schedule...that sort of thing."

"Carmen, I don't know how to do any of that."

"You can learn and it would be good experience for you. Plus, you can earn some money."

"I can't take your money, Carmen." The flush in Faith's cheeks rose with the tone of her voice.

"Shit, I'm not doing a very good job of this at all," Carmen chuckled. "Faith, you wouldn't be taking money from me. You would earn it, legitimately. You can go into the office and shadow an experienced PA. When you feel ready, you can then take up the role of *my* PA."

"Carmen—"

"Faith, you've made the choice to start out on your own. Getting a job and earning money needs to be your priority."

"What about finding Molly?"

"Absolutely. That's one thing that should be at the top of your list, but neither of us know how long that will take. And when you find her, you will still need money and a job. Why not take advantage of the time you have now to get a head start? There are other things to consider as well. You need an I.D. Do you have a driver's license or a passport?"

"No, neither. I have my birth certificate, though."

"Okay good. Let me help you organize the basics. Please, Faith, it makes me uncomfortable knowing you have nothing set up."

Carmen sat waiting for Faith to decide. She could understand Faith's reticence about accepting help. Faith was proud and wanted to make her own way without others interfering. She'd clearly had enough of that at home, and now she needed some control over her life.

After a few more minutes of silent contemplation, Faith inhaled deeply. "Thank you, Carmen. I would really appreciate your help."

"Excellent. Let's get started."

Carmen was exhausted. Who knew setting up someone's life would be so draining? Thank God for Mateo, who strolled in at 5:30 p.m., armed to the teeth with food and beer—and soda for Faith.

"You are my hero," Carmen gushed. Hours on the phone, trying to help Faith, had seriously depleted her batteries.

"How was your day? You look terrible."

"Mateo. We need to work on this. You telling me I look like crap every five minutes, is not cool."

"Carmen, you need to get out of the house once in a while. You're turning white. It's summer in Seattle and you have zero tan."

"It's my fault," Faith interjected. "Carmen has been helping me sort out a few things and that took nearly all day."

"How about we take dinner outside?" Carmen suggested. Mateo was right, she needed some vitamin D.

With the outside table set up, the three of them ate, drank, and chatted about their day. Everything seemed fine until she noticed Faith squirming in her seat.

"Hey, what's going on with you?"

"I called Alice last night," Faith began. Carmen set her beer down on the table. "She told me my parents left the house looking for me."

"Okay, but you expected that, right?" Mateo asked softly.

"Yeah, I did. But now it's happening and I'm scared. Guys, if he finds me, I don't know what he'll do."

"How would he know where you are, though? Even if he traced you to Seattle, how would he get this address?"

Faith pinched the bridge of her nose. "The same way I did."

"Faith?"

"I found a letter in his office. Molly wrote to him several times over the years, updating him of her whereabouts. Clearly, she's a better person than him, because he was awful to her, yet she still wanted to keep in touch with her brother."

"So, he has the address?"

"I think we should assume he does."

"But he doesn't know for sure you were heading this way?" Carmen asked, needing clarification.

"No."

"We should prepare for the worst," Mateo added.

Carmen hated this.

"What do you want to do?" she asked calmly, even though her insides were clenching.

Faith had to take the lead. If it were up to Carmen, well...what she had in mind wouldn't help anyone, but it might make her feel better. There seemed to be no justice in this world for assholes like Faith's father.

"I don't know. I thought I would already be with Aunt Molly and she'd know what to do. You two shouldn't be in the middle of this."

"We're in it with you. You might not have Molly, but you have us. I'm going to call Rachel back and ask her for advice. If he turns up, we will deal with it. You're safe here, Faith. We *will* keep you safe."

"What she said, *chica*," Mateo added. Faith pulled them both in for a hug.

"Let's finish our evening and get some rest. We still have a life to lead, and unfortunately, that means work." Carmen sighed good-naturedly.

With the day drawing to a close, Carmen made a call to Rachel. There wasn't much that could be done until Faith's father turned up, but at least Rachel was aware of the situation.

The next morning, Carmen found Faith subdued. Determined to turn the girl's mood around, she suggested they go knock on a few doors and inquire about Faith's aunt.

"Where are you going?" Mateo asked, just as Carmen and Faith were about to leave the house. It was still early and Mateo hadn't left for work yet.

"To knock on some doors. We told you that."

"You're going to introduce yourself to our neighbors dressed like *that*?" Mateo screeched.

Carmen looked herself up and down. Not seeing an issue, she looked back at Mateo, who had his face screwed up in disgust.

"What's the problem?"

"Carmen, you cannot speak to these people in your lounge pants."

"Lounge pants, really?" Carmen laughed. "The rest of the world calls them sweat pants, Mateo."

"That word is offensive to me now. I'm banishing it from the house. In fact, I'm banishing the offending item too."

"Mateo, you can't banish my sweatpants."

"Oh yes, I can."

"Mateo, come on," Carmen whined.

Mateo scooped Carmen by the elbow and dragged her towards her bedroom. "This is for your own good."

"Alright, alright. I can dress myself, thanks."

"That is *highly* debatable. All I'm asking, is for you to put on some jeans and maybe a fresh t-shirt."

Grumbling the entire time, Carmen sifted through her closet. An unease crept its way over her shoulders as she skimmed through the rail of clothing composed of power suits, jeans, slacks, and dresses. Carmen certainly wasn't in need of a new wardrobe.

Mateo's concerned look played over and over in her mind. At first, Carmen thought he was just busting her ass because that's what he did, especially where fashion was concerned, but now, a different thought invaded her mind: Carmen had let herself slip.

Boxer briefs and sweatpants had replaced skinny jeans. Baggy tank tops had replaced slim-fit T-shirts. Mateo was right. Carmen *was* hiding herself. But why? And when was the last time she could honestly say she'd made an effort with herself?

Selecting a pair of tight-fitting black jeans and a white short-sleeved T-shirt, Carmen changed. Just the act of putting on something more fitting made her feel different; made her feel...more.

"Now that's more like it, *hermana*," Mateo gushed when she exited her bedroom. A slight blush settled on her cheeks.

"Let's go, Faith," Carmen mumbled, ushering the girl out the front door. Heat from the sun licked Carmen's skin. Taking a moment to bask, she turned her face to the sky and soaked in the warmth.

"Which neighbor do you want to try first?" Faith asked, hands on hips, looking from one neighbor's house to the next.

Carmen mimicked Faith's stance. Unfortunately, in the six months Carmen and Mateo had lived in the rental, neither of them had introduced themselves to the neighbors. They'd meant to, obviously, but life took over. Mateo was busy with the boutique, and Carmen didn't want to interact with anyone if she didn't have to.

Shaking her head in annoyance with herself, Carmen gestured to the house on her left. They had to start somewhere, and that neighbor had a car in the driveway.

"Let's start there."

Faith nodded and set off towards the neighbor's house, keen to get their search for Molly underway. The well-kept residence was two-stories, unlike Carmen and Mateo's bungalow. Carmen peeked back towards her home and noted it could use a bit of sprucing up. The landlord wouldn't mind if she added a fresh coat of paint.

Faith was already on the front porch before Carmen had stepped a foot into the yard. Knocking loudly, Faith rocked on her heels, looking back over her shoulder at Carmen. A nervous energy buzzed around them. Carmen was equally impatient; not because she wanted the girl gone, but because she wanted Faith to have one more person in her corner.

A loud banging noise echoed from inside the house, followed by a string of curse words. Carmen and Faith looked at each other, both sets of eyebrows reaching for the sky. Whoever was behind the door, had a mouth like a sailor.

"One minute—just gotta reattach my fucking leg," a woman's voice shouted.

"Did she just say..."

"Yup."

The door finally opened, revealing a woman Carmen would put close to seventy, leaning on a cane.

"If you're here to sell Jesus, don't bother. That fucker gave up on me years ago."

Carmen and Faith were stunned into silence. Whoever this woman was, she was intimidating, which was a little ridiculous. At a maximum of five feet in height, dressed in a neon-pink tracksuit, with short, permed hair, the woman looked like she should be power walking in Florida, not living in the suburbs of Seattle.

"Did you want something, or are you just gonna stand there all day, looking like a pair of stunned fish?"

Clearing her throat, Carmen willed herself to speak. "Sorry, yes, hello. I'm Carmen Ruiz. I live next door to you."

"Ah yeah, with that gay fella, right?"

"Um...yeah."

"That man can strut in a pair of heels. I might invite him over for some lessons," the woman said to herself. "Although, he needs to lay off the manscaping. He's smoother than a Ken doll."

Faith guffawed, quickly hiding her mouth behind her hand. Carmen found it hard not to giggle.

"Anyway, you were saying, dear?"

"Right." Carmen inhaled, trying to calm herself down. "So, I'm Carmen and this is Faith."

"Hello, dears, I'm Enid Butcher. I know it's a fucking terrible name, but what can ya do? Well, maybe not marry a man with a surname like Butcher, I suppose. Well, that's beside the point. What are your last names?"

The rate at which Enid spoke was making Carmen's head spin.

"I'm Carmen Ruiz and this is Faith Parsons."

"Parsons, you say?" The flicker of recognition in Enid's eyes was unmistakable. Faith noticed too, her body instinctively moving forward, her hand reaching out to touch Enid's arm.

"Do you know the name?"

"I know a *Molly* Parsons," Enid supplied. "Huh. Actually, you look just like her, although your hair is a little more honey-colored, whereas she is on the brown side of blonde, if you know what I mean."

"Oh my God, you know Molly. That's excellent!" Faith cried. Her excitement was palpable.

"Of course I know her. She was my neighbor for a couple of years. Such a shame she moved away. That woman was a godsend to me. After Ernie died, I didn't have anyone to open my cans. Molly always came over for a coffee and a can opening session."

"Do you know where she moved to?" Carmen asked.

Enid scratched her chin. "Vermont, I think. Hang on, I'm sure I have an address somewhere. Molly left it with me in case I needed her. I'm not sure what she thought she could do from the other side of the country, but the offer was nice."

Enid pushed off the door and hobbled back inside her house. Carmen and Faith shot a quick look of triumph at each other.

"Are you coming in or what?" Enid called.

"I can't wait to rib Mateo," Carmen whispered to Faith as they went inside. Faith snickered.

"Wow," Faith breathed as she took in Enid's house.

"Do you feel she would rather be somewhere tropical?" Carmen asked. Enid's house was adorned with bright colors, plastic flamingos, and pineapple pictures. It was an interesting choice of decor, that was for sure.

"Ernie made me move to Seattle, when *I* wanted to move to Hawaii," Enid shouted from another room.

Jesus, did the woman have bionic hearing?

"The old bastard made me live in a rainy state, so I made him live in a tropical nightmare," Enid chuckled.

Carmen laughed, thinking how she would have done the same to Mateo.

"Did you not think of moving after Ernie passed?" Carmen asked, not sure if that was an inappropriate thing to ask a stranger.

"I thought about it. I still do, to be honest, but I'm used to this place now."

"I like it!" Faith beamed.

"Here we go," Enid said, handing Faith a piece of paper. "That's the address she gave me."

Faith clutched the paper to her chest as tears welled up in her eyes. "Thank you."

"She didn't mention a daughter."

Clearly, Enid was out to get some gossip.

"I'm Molly's niece."

"She didn't mention a niece, either."

"I doubt she knows I exist," Faith sighed.

7

Faith

Finally, Faith was getting some answers. After everything in her plan had gone wrong when she'd arrived in Seattle, it was a relief to know Molly wasn't just a myth; she was real, and there was someone who knew her, and by all accounts, liked her a lot.

"Molly moved in about two years ago. I wondered at first, how she could afford to rent that house. It's a three-bedroom, and let's be honest, the prices around here are fucking atrocious," Enid barked from the kitchen, where she was fetching the three of them some iced tea.

Hearing such language spill out of a lovely old woman was a little surprising. It wasn't like Faith had been around a lot of curse words. Even her father refrained from cursing, mostly.

"Did you know her well?"

"Oh, yes," Enid said, shuffling into the tropical monstrosity that was her living room. "Molly came over the day she moved in."

Faith noticed the disapproving look Enid shot at Carmen. Carmen noticed too and ducked her head, causing Faith to chuckle.

"She came over with a batch of muffins. Introduced herself, and spent an hour chatting with me. Well, after that, Molly would visit me several times a week."

"Did she tell you what she did for a living?" Faith was eager to learn as much as possible about her elusive aunt.

"Something to do with young people, I think. She didn't talk much about work. Whenever she came over, we chatted about all sorts of things. She told me a little about her home life."

"Molly is my dad's sister. He's..."

"Difficult," Enid answered. Faith nodded. She didn't have the energy to explain all the terrible things that her father had done and said.

"Well, Molly turned out to be a wonderful woman. A right looker, too." Enid shot Carmen another look. Carmen scrunched up her eyes in confusion.

"She's a lesbian, you know," Enid commented, clearly aiming it at Carmen again. Faith wanted to laugh. Enid was relentless, and Carmen looked petrified.

"Oh, right..."

"I bet she'd be right up your alley," Enid continued.

"Um..."

"Heart of gold. Gorgeous long hair. A figure to die for."

Carmen looked pleadingly from Enid to Faith. Faith didn't know what to do to curtail Enid's clear enthusiasm at the prospect of Carmen and Molly.

"Are you single dear?"

"Y-yes." Carmen shuffled in her seat.

"You should ask Molly out when you find her. You'd make a striking couple."

Carmen shot iced tea through her nose and then began coughing.

"I don't...we..." Carmen spluttered.

"No need to choke, dear. It's not that outrageous. I just think you could do with a nice girl. Heaven knows you haven't brought a good one back to the house in a while."

Faith had to pinch her nose to stop a snort from coming out. Carmen looked at Enid, agog. As far as Faith knew, this was Carmen and Enid's first interaction, although, by the look of things, Enid had been keeping an eagle eye on the Ruiz household.

"You need to tell that fella you live with to ask Daniel out. What are they waiting for? I've never seen anyone eat as much pizza as you two."

"You...what..." Carmen shook her head. Faith silently laughed. Poor Carmen.

"Oh, don't look so surprised, Miss Ruiz. I'm an old woman with jack shit to do. Your comings and goings are my entertainment. Well, not as much as Ted across the street, that is. You should see him try to walk in his wife's stilettos. Why the woman thinks it's sexy is beyond me. It's not like Ted is built to be on stilts. The man weighs as much as a bus and has the balance of a potato standing on its end."

Faith couldn't stop herself after that. Her laughter ricocheted through the house. Enid sipped her tea as if nothing had happened. Carmen looked shell-shocked before bursting out in tears of laughter. Both Carmen and Faith held their bellies. It took them a good five minutes to calm themselves down.

"So, will you go to Vermont?" Enid asked.

Faith nodded. "That's the plan. I traveled to Seattle thinking Molly would be here, but...you know how that turned out. Carmen and Mateo were kind enough to take me in and help me out."

"I'm glad there are still some kind souls left in the world. Is there anything I can do to help, dear?"

"If you think of anything else about Molly, I'd love to hear it."

"I'll see if I can find some pictures for you. I'm sure I have a couple. How about I fetch you over when I have them?"

Faith beamed in delight. Would she finally get to see what her aunt looked like? "Oh Enid, that would be wonderful, thank you."

"My pleasure, Faith. You're a chip off the old block. I can see that."

Faith felt a chill run through her. She naturally thought of her parents when she heard comments like that, but after a moment's contemplation, Faith calmed. Enid thought she was like Molly, not her parents. Finally, she had someone worth measuring up to in her family. That meant more than Faith could articulate.

After another glass of iced tea, Faith and Carmen said their goodbyes with a promise to visit again soon.

"Enid's lovely," Faith mused as they walked back to the house.

"She has a potty mouth," Carmen laughed.

"I think it suits her, though. Do you know what I mean?"

"Yeah, you're right. Now, how are you feeling about the information she gave you?"

"Honestly, relieved. I just hope she's still there."

Carmen let them in through the front door. The sound of salsa music boomed through the house. Faith strained to see what Carmen was staring at. Oh, boy. In the living room was a very pink and glittery Mateo, dancing his heart out to the music, while vacuuming the floor.

"Why?" Carmen shouted. Mateo looked up and smiled. His eyes were just as glittery as his body.

Shutting off the vacuum, Mateo danced his way over to them. "What did you say, *chica*?"

"I asked, 'why,'" Carmen replied.

"Why what?" Mateo looked confused.

"Why are you vacuuming dressed as a unicorn on steroids? And where in the hell did you get that tutu?"

"Oh, it's fabulous, isn't it? Luis gave it to me. Anyway, I'm wearing it because it's my dress rehearsal. I need to see how I move in the outfit. Don't want chafing."

Faith stood silently, watching the two converse. She'd never tire of their back-and-forth.

"What the hell are you rehearsing *for*?"

"I think you look spectacular," Faith interjected. He really did look magical.

"Don't encourage him," Carmen mumbled.

"Thank you, Faith. At least *someone* around here appreciates my style. And, Carmen, I knew you would forget. I can't believe it."

"What did I forget?"

"It's Pride on Saturday. This is my outfit."

Faith's ears perked up. She'd heard about Pride events. They were supposed to be spectacular. Her heart raced. Would Mateo and Carmen let her go with them?

"I have the cutest outfit for you, Faith," Mateo said, answering her question without her needing to ask it.

"Mateo, do you think that's a good idea?" Carmen asked. Faith's heart immediately sank. Carmen didn't want her to go with them. Faith couldn't blame her. Who wanted a kid hanging around when they were sure to be with their friends?

"It's okay. I can stay here."

"Absolutely not. Faith, this is Pride—an essential rite of passage for any baby gay."

"But you don't think it's a good idea?" Faith asked Carmen.

Carmen smiled at Faith and then looked at Mateo. "I fully understand Faith attending Pride would be a great experience. But Mateo, I don't think taking her with you and your friends is a good idea."

Faith slumped her shoulders. "It's fine, really. You guys have fun."

"I've already called Luis and told him I won't be with them," Mateo huffed. "Do you really think I would subject Faith to those crazy bitches?"

"Well, alrighty then," Carmen laughed, her posture instantly relaxing. Faith wondered why the idea of her being around Mateo's friends would be a problem.

Mateo pulled Faith by the hand and twirled her. "My friends are intense. They party hard and I...no, *we,* want you to really enjoy your first Pride. We will follow the parade and then..." Mateo paused for dramatic effect, which worked, because Faith was on tenterhooks, "we will go to our friend's place. Rita is a doll. She throws amazing parties at Pride. There will be a bunch of people, of all ages, so hopefully, you can meet someone your own age. I can't imagine how awful it is for you to be stuck with us old folks."

Faith laughed. "I can't wait. Really, thank you. Oh my gosh, I'm so excited."

"I knew you would be. Oh girl, we are gonna have a blast."

"Okay, before you kidnap Faith to play dress up, we need to tell you what we found out."

In all the excitement, Faith had totally forgotten Enid had given her Molly's location. A pang of guilt buzzed through her stomach.

"Yeah, Enid knew Molly."

"Who the hell is Enid?"

"Enid is our neighbor...and she knows things," Carmen laughed. Mateo gave her a puzzled look.

"She also has the mouth of a sailor," Faith added. "Oh, and one leg, I think."

It was a complete guess that Enid had a prosthetic leg, but from her comment, and the way she limped, Faith would bet she was right.

"What do you mean, 'she knows things'?'" Mateo asked in a hushed voice, his eyes comically darting around the room.

"That woman is the neighborhood Nosy Nelly."

"Oh, I have to meet her," Mateo chuckled. Faith shared a look with Carmen, because she knew damn well what Carmen was about to say.

"Enid also mentioned...you're as smooth as a Ken doll, and to tell you to stop all the manscaping."

A beat of silence settled in the space between them before Faith giggled, Carmen slapped Mateo on the shoulder with a shit-eating grin, and Mateo stood aghast.

"Smooth as a Ken doll? Well, shit." Mateo huffed. "Did she happen to notice you have enough hair on your body for the both of us?"

His quick comment earned him a jab in the ribs by Carmen. Faith giggled before running to the bathroom. Those two were gonna make her pee her pants.

Pride morning arrived, swept in with a shimmering sea of sequins and glitter. Amazingly, Mateo had somehow become even gayer. His limits, for all things shiny and queer, were endless.

After the conversation with Enid, the three of them decided to drive to Vermont the Monday after Pride. Faith was happy with that plan. Carmen and Mateo needed the rest of the week to organize themselves so they could travel without worrying about work.

"Faith, get your cute behind in the bathroom. I need to start your makeup."

Faith had been looking forward to Pride all week. Mateo's enthusiasm was infectious. He treated the whole thing so seriously, as if it were an integral part of Faith's *lesducation*, as Carmen liked to refer to it.

Not only had they done multiple fashion shows that week, but Mateo had also given Faith homework. Every day, she had to watch something queer. It hadn't taken her long to exhaust Netflix's LGBTQIA2s+ content. Carmen had put the Deezer app on her phone so she could listen to the list of songs Mateo had instructed her to get familiar with. By Friday night, Faith was feeling gay as hell.

Wrapping her fluffy robe around her body, Faith sat diligently in the salon chair. Mateo laid out a myriad of tools to help him complete his work. "Let the magic begin," he announced, turning up the music.

What felt like hours passed as Mateo painted Faith's face. They agreed to a rainbow flag on one cheek and the lesbian flag on the other. Glittery eyeshadow and blush followed. Her hair was given a slight curl and—of course—sprayed with even more glitter.

"Okay, you're done. You only need to get dressed and you'll be good to go."

Jumping out of the chair, Faith hugged Mateo tightly. Carmen received the same treatment seconds later, after Faith left the bathroom.

Pulling on her short black overalls and rainbow tank top, Faith almost toppled over with excitement, literally, as she hopped around trying to put on her Converse.

"Calm down," she muttered to herself.

Picking up her phone, she snapped a selfie and sent it to Alice. Faith knew her friend would be shocked at the transformation. Seconds later, she received a reply. It mainly consisted of OMG, a flame emoji, and Pride flags.

"Faith, let's go," Carmen bellowed. "Mateo, you do not need any more fucking glitter."

Faith grinned, slipped her phone inside her front pouch, and headed to the front door.

"Wow," she breathed when she saw Carmen. "You look awesome."

Carmen had old black Doc Martens, ripped, skin-tight black short-shorts, and a camo tank top. Her hair was up in a topknot and her eyes were smokey. Faith saw Carmen as an older sister, but that didn't mean she was blind. This Carmen, was very attractive.

"She's hot, right?" Mateo said, sliding up next to Faith, leaning his arm on her shoulder.

"Yeah, she is," Faith answered honestly.

"Now do you understand why I badger you? Your body is killer and there are going to be so many thirsty lesbians wanting to get all up in it."

"Gross. Don't speak about thirsty lesbians. I agreed to this," Carmen said, waving at her attire, "to shut you up. My ears were bleeding with all of your whining. That does not mean anyone will be 'getting all up in this.' We're going to have fun as a family, end of discussion."

"She's gonna get so much attention," Mateo whispered, and Faith had to agree.

Faith's jaw hit the floor when they arrived. Her eyes couldn't process what she was seeing. Thousands of people lining the streets and waving flags. Couples and families standing together, holding hands and kissing. Joy and excitement rippled through the air, and Faith wanted to soak up every last drop.

"You okay?" Carmen shouted over the music and whistles.

"I'm fantastic," Faith shouted back.

They wound their way through throngs of Pride goers, eventually finding a place to stop. As the parade passed them by, Faith couldn't stop the tears from falling. Never in her wildest dreams did she think she would get to feel like this.

The atmosphere around them was alive. The crowd was electric and Faith felt every bolt of joy and pride, zip through her body. This was why she'd risked everything—for this feeling.

Suddenly, a hand grabbed her arm and Faith felt herself being pulled forward. Looking behind her in a panic, she saw Mateo and Carmen following her. Carmen gave her a wink, which settled her racing pulse.

The crowd parted, and Faith found herself in the middle of the parade. A six-foot Amazon of a drag queen held her hand, encouraging her to join in with the other dancing parade participants.

Mateo didn't hesitate. He twirled Faith, and then Carmen. To Faith's surprise, Carmen got right in the middle of it all, moving to the music with the rest of the crowd. As Mateo predicted, it took less than a minute for Carmen to be surrounded by... What did Mateo say? *Thirsty lesbians*?

Faith hadn't really understood what he'd meant, but now, seeing the scene play out in front of her own eyes, Faith understood. Each of the women circling Carmen looked like they wanted to inhale her.

They danced all the way through, until they reached the end of the parade route. Faith was completely high on adrenaline.

"That was so... wow, oh wow." She gushed.

"It's not over yet," Carmen called, her voice hoarse from singing and shouting.

"Let's get to Rita's before all the good booze is gone." Mateo hooked Carmen and Faith by the elbows, pulling them out of the crowd.

Rita's house was enormous, with two gigantic Pride flags posted on either side of the wooden door. Music was already blaring, and the house looked filled to capacity.

"She's gone all out this year," Carmen commented.

"Her niece is here this year, so I think she wanted to make it special. Faith, did you put on a bikini like I said to do?"

"Sure did."

"Excellent. Let's find Rita, then grab a drink." Mateo strutted off before either Carmen or Faith could answer.

"Hey," Carmen said, turning to face Faith. "I'm not your mom or anything, but you are still underage. Have a drink if you want, but be reasonable."

"I'm not interested in alcohol. Don't worry, I just want to have some fun."

It wasn't a lie. Out of all the things she'd missed out on, alcohol wasn't something she was overly excited about.

They made their way through the mansion until Carmen pointed to Mateo and an older woman with luscious red hair.

"Carmen, my God, you look stunning."

"Thanks, Rita, you too. May I introduce you to Faith?" Carmen gently squeezed Faith in a side hug, which was comforting. There were so many stimulating things swirling around them. Carmen's touch was grounding.

"It's a pleasure to meet you. Thank you for having me." Faith said, holding out a hand.

"Oh, my, aren't you just the most adorable thing ever?" Rita replied, ignoring the hand and stepping forward to give Faith two air kisses. "Feel free to swim. There's a hot tub, too. Drinks are in the kitchen and the dance floor is wherever you want it to be. Oh, hang on, there's my niece."

Rita waved to someone over Faith's shoulder.

"That's her cousin's daughter, but they're more like aunt and niece," Carmen whispered. Faith turned to greet the newcomer and almost gasped out loud.

Standing there, in a forest green bikini with a rainbow wraparound, was Nathalie.

The Nathalie from the bus station.

Faith's Nathalie.

8

Carmen

So that was Nathalie; the girl who clearly got under Faith's skin. Carmen grinned as the two young women stared at each other with wide eyes. Both were a little shy, and more than a little surprised at their reunion.

"Hey, why don't you two go and catch up? You don't want to be hanging around us oldies," Carmen said, nudging Faith. She could see that Faith was embarrassed and needed an excuse to duck away.

"Um...are you sure?" Faith asked, only momentarily tearing her eyes away from Nathalie. Carmen chuckled, nudging her again to suggest they take off. Faith and Nathalie didn't need any more convincing.

"Have I missed something?" Rita asked.

"It seems Nathalie and Faith met a few days ago on a bus."

"That's who Nathalie was talking about. Wow, okay."

"Nathalie mentioned Faith?"

"She most certainly did. Nat didn't give me a name, but she wouldn't stop yammering about this cute girl she met."

Carmen smiled warmly. A sense of nostalgia washed over her as she watched Faith and Nathalie chat by the pool. Their feet dipped in the water.

Carmen was twenty before she had any hands-on experience with a woman. Sure, she'd known for years she was gay, but with all the upheaval, and the work both she and Mateo had to do to get themselves in a good place, women came second. That was until she met Hattie Belmont during her third year of college.

Hattie was the heart and soul of any room she walked into. Carmen noticed her on the first day of college, but was far too focused on her studies to think too much about the buxom blonde.

Then, one Friday night, Mateo convinced Carmen to attend a LGBTQIA2s+ fundraiser. Lo and behold, Hattie Belmont was the student president in charge of the event. After a couple of shots of bourbon, Carmen accessed a pool of confidence she didn't know she had. After a few minutes of chatting, Carmen had charmed the pants off of Hattie—literally.

And there began Carmen's journey into the sapphic world. The rest of her college experience involved a few more nights with Hattie before she moved on.

Carmen liked the idea of a girlfriend, but not the feelings. Caring for anyone else but Mateo was too daunting, and she didn't trust anyone enough to let herself try.

For years, Mateo behaved similarly, but over time, he put their therapist's help to good use. Mateo wanted a boyfriend; someone to build a life with. That was when his opinion on Carmen's less than permanent arrangements with women bugged him, and in turn, he bugged Carmen.

Now, watching Faith and Nathalie muddle their way through their *second* first interaction was hitting Carmen in the feels. What would it be like to really let someone get to know her? Could she allow herself to be vulnerable and give another person the trust needed to build a relationship?

Carmen's mind wandered to Molly Parsons, which was odd. She had no idea who the woman was, or what she was like.

"Earth to Carmen." Rita's voice pulled Carmen out of her head. A Pride party wasn't the time or place to be pondering life-altering things.

"Sorry, just watching those two," she replied, nodding in Faith and Nathalie's direction.

"Cute, aren't they?"

"Very. It's nice to see Faith coming out of her shell. The difference today, from just a few days ago, is astonishing."

"Mateo gave me a rundown of the situation. She'll be okay, especially with you two on her side. Plus, kids are resilient."

If that were true, why hadn't Carmen bounced back so easily? She was in her mid-thirties and still dealing with crap from her childhood. Hopefully, Faith wouldn't be like her.

"You know," Rita began, "you could do that." Rita pointed at the girls.

"Do what?"

"Talk to a woman. Get to know them. Start something that lasts longer than an evening."

Aside from Mateo, Rita was Carmen's closest friend. At ten years her senior, Rita offered both Mateo and Carmen an older sister slash mom support. Rita worked at the shelter where Mateo and Carmen had stayed for several months after they'd bolted from the system. They became friends and Rita helped Carmen get her first job.

"Mateo has been harping on at me to open up more," Carmen sighed.

"Is he wrong?"

Carmen shrugged. "Over the years, I was happy having fun. I was more worried about Mateo than myself."

"And now?"

Another shrug. "I don't know."

"I think you do, considering the fact that we are even having this conversation is a massive step. You will always worry about Mateo—he's your family—but he's okay. In fact, he's better than okay, and that's because of you. Maybe it's time to circle back to yourself. Work on what's going on up there." Rita pointed to Carmen's head. "Mateo is ready to settle down. He wants the same for you. So do I."

Carmen wondered if Mateo and Rita had been discussing the subject at length. It wasn't unusual for Mateo to seek Rita's advice, especially if he was frustrated with Carmen.

"Has he said something?"

It was Rita's turn to sigh. "He's just worried about you. He told me you've been spending more and more time in the house. Apparently, you hardly visit the offices anymore."

Carmen ducked her head. "I've not become a hermit intentionally. I'm just comfortable in my house. What's wrong with that?"

"See, when you adopt that petulant kid tone with me, I know you think you're getting bullied. But Carmen, that's not the case and you know it."

"I just... I don't know," Carmen mumbled, slamming her drink back. So much for enjoying the party. No wonder Mateo had slinked off as soon as he could. The little asshole probably knew Rita was going to call her out on her bullshit.

"Don't go on the defensive. Look, if all you want is casual, then fine, have at it if that's what you truly want. But, if the only reason you prefer casual is because of past trauma, then you know it's time to figure your shit out. Maybe give Christine a call?"

Carmen had been discharged from Dr. Christine Stark's care for nearly two years. They still checked in now and then, but Carmen wasn't a patient. Did she really need to go back to therapy?

If this were Mateo, Carmen wouldn't hesitate to advise him to return to the good doctor.

Rubbing her forehead, Carmen tried to soothe her irritation. She wasn't irritated at Rita or Mateo, but at herself. Huffing out a breath, Carmen knew what she had to do.

"Thanks, Rita. I'll give Christine a call. Even if it's just for a refresher."

"Nothing wrong with that. Actually, it's probably sensible for you *and* Mateo to check in now you have Faith in your lives. She needs support, and you guys need to be in the right headspace to give it to her."

Carmen nodded in agreement. Faith appearing in their lives had shaken something loose. The contentment she once felt by hiding away in her house failed to provide the same comfort of late.

Watching Faith discover the world was a privilege. How many people got to reinvent themselves like that? Not too many, Carmen would wager. And here she was, wasting her life, cowering from the world and hiding in her house.

"Alright, Ms. Dark and Gloomy, I can see you getting pissed off with yourself from here. Whatever you're thinking—stop. At least for now. Enjoy the party and then tomorrow, call Christine."

Carmen laughed at Rita's observation. Nothing got past that woman.

"You're right. Come on, let's get a drink."

Carmen clutched her head. "Oh dear God."

The pain radiating through her skull was enough to make her eyes water.

"Shhh," Mateo's voice hissed.

"Ow, ow, ow," Carmen chanted as she sat up.

"*Hermana*, I'm going to beat you to death with my butt plug if you don't shut the fuck up."

Mateo's room swam into focus. Carmen had no memory of getting home from Rita's house. In fact, she had no memories after Mateo made her drink... Oh Christ, those bright pink cocktails with candies at the bottom of the glass. What the hell kind of concoction had she drunk?

Gently rubbing her stomach, Carmen willed herself not to vomit. Counting to five, she exhaled slowly. A deep inhale and she was feeling bett—

"Oh crap," she moaned, running to the bathroom as fast as her still-drunk ass could carry her.

"Feel better?" Mateo mumbled from his pillow when Carmen returned.

"I just got very intimate with the porcelain throne."

"Gross."

Carmen closed her eyes and rested her head against the headboard. "What the hell happened yesterday?"

"We got smashed," Mateo groaned.

"You both got completely wasted," Faith giggled from the bedroom door. Carmen's eyes shot open. Fuck, they'd taken Faith to a party, told her to be safe, and then got totally annihilated.

"Faith, oh crap, are you okay?"

Faith laughed again. "I'm fine. Rita helped me get you both home."

"We are *so* sorry." Carmen went to stand, but her body revolted.

"Stay in bed. You both look bad. I'll grab you some water and Tylenol."

Carmen waited for Faith to disappear before turning to Mateo. Jabbing him hard in the ribs, Carmen got a face full of pillow.

"Mateo, get up. We have to make this right."

"She's fine. *We,* are not."

"*We* cannot let that girl look after us. We're supposed to be the responsible adults."

"Caarmmeeennn," Mateo whined.

"You know I'm right. Jesus, *hermano*, that was her first Pride party."

Rolling over, Mateo pushed himself up the bed. "I hate you."

"Tough shit, we need to get up. I'll make the coffee and order breakfast."

Together, they stumbled out of bed, still dressed in their party outfits.

"I'm going to shower," Mateo croaked. Carmen made it to the kitchen. Faith was sitting at the table, messaging someone with her phone.

Faith looked up from her device and blushed. "Sorry, I got distracted."

Faith went to get up, but Carmen stopped her. "No, you carry on doing whatever you're doing. I'm going to order breakfast."

Just the mention of food was making Carmen feel unwell.

"Then we can talk about tomorrow."

"Are you sure? No offense Carmen, but you look almost green."

"I'm sure. I just need some caffeine."

By the time Mateo made it out of the bathroom, Carmen was in a much better state. The fact she still couldn't remember a thing, weighed on her mind, but maybe she didn't want to know. God knows she and Mateo had done some questionable things before when drunk. Hopefully, yesterday wasn't one of those times.

"Okay kid, give it to me straight," Mateo sighed dramatically. "How much of an ass did I make of myself?"

"No more than anyone else," Faith giggled. "There was a lot of singing. You were particularly into Cher," Faith laughed.

"Well, that's not too bad," Mateo smiled. "If singing Cher badly is the worst of it, I think we can relax."

"I didn't say that was the worst of it," Faith grinned.

Carmen let her head hit the table.

Faith laughed. "I'm not sure I want to repeat some of the things I saw last night."

Carmen groaned out loud. "Faith, please believe me when I say that is not how I usually behave. What the hell was in those drinks, Mateo?"

"How should I know?"

"You handed them out!"

"I just passed them along. Rita made them."

"You let us drink Rita's cocktails? Are you insane?"

For the next ten minutes, Carmen laid into Mateo. Rita was a legend for her strong drinks. Both Carmen and

Mateo had sworn never to touch her mixtures ever again after a very unfortunate incident with a police officer and a pineapple.

"Are you finished?" Mateo deadpanned.

Carmen rested her head back on the table and nodded.

"Good. Now, forget about our sorry state and tell us, Faith..." Mateo grinned wickedly. "How was *your* night with Nathalie?"

Carmen laughed at the way Faith ducked her head. Every inch of skin was red.

Carmen couldn't help but join in the gentle teasing. "Yeah, Faith, how was Nathalie?"

"So, tomorrow," Faith interjected, ignoring them both. "Are you sure you want to drive? We could look into taking a train."

"I prefer driving. At least that way we're in charge of the travel time."

Faith was twisting her fingers together. A sign, Carmen knew, which meant the young woman was feeling uncomfortable.

"I'm sorry we can't fly," Faith mumbled.

"Hey, we get a road trip out of it. And, as soon as you get your driver's license, you'll be good to fly."

"I call dibs on the music," Mateo sang.

"That will be shared equally. I'm not having three days of Cher or Kylie. I mean, I love them both, but not forty-five hours' worth."

"Can we get snacks?" Faith asked, her body relaxed again.

"Oh honey, we are going to have a stash of snacks. That's like a road trip rule *numero uno*."

"What time are we heading out?" Mateo asked over the top of his coffee cup.

"Nice and early. Be ready by seven."

"A.M.?" Mateo screeched.

"Yes, a.m. Obviously. And don't get all diva on me now, *hermano*, it's not like you will be driving first. So, be ready at seven and sleep in the car."

"When do you think we will get to Vermont?" Faith asked.

"Hopefully, by Wednesday."

"You know, there must be a way of finding out if Molly is at that address before we haul our asses to the other side of the country," Mateo remarked. Carmen had thought about that too.

"True. But say we look up the address and it doesn't have Molly listed as the tenant. That doesn't mean she isn't still in Vermont. We would need to ask the neighbors and the current tenant if they have an idea where she might have moved too. Plus, I really want a road trip."

"Alright. In that case, we need to get packed. Plus, it's Sunday, and we all know what happens on a Sunday," Mateo said expectantly.

"Facials and Manicures," Carmen and Faith chanted back.

"Correct. Let's get to it ladies!"

The day had started out horrifically, but by the time early evening rolled around, Carmen felt human again. The bucketful of coffee and three breakfast sandwiches had helped.

With the car packed, Carmen was ready to go. The worst part about a road trip was the wait before going. She felt almost giddy, which wasn't an emotion Carmen associated with herself very often.

At 9:45 p.m. the doorbell rang, causing each of them to scream individually.

"Who the hell is that?" Mateo demanded, rubbing his chest. "I almost poked my eye out with my tweezers."

Carmen headed to the front door, equally irritated there was someone at the house. Ripping open the door, Carmen was more than surprised to see Enid on her front porch.

"Evening dear," Enid chirped. "I just came to drop off my bag."

Carmen—who towered over the old lady—stared down at Enid's perfectly permed hair and bright green tracksuit. Next to her feet was a carry-on case adorned with palm trees.

"Um..." What was happening?

"Be a dear and toss it in the car. I'll be over before half past seven." Enid reached up and squeezed Carmen's cheeks before retreating to her house. Carmen stood frozen for a few more moments, not sure how to process the interaction.

"Um..."

"*Chica*, who is it?" Mateo called.

"Um..."

"Carmen, are you alright?" Faith stood by her side, regarding the small suitcase. "Did Enid stop by?"

"Yeah, I...I think she believes she's coming with us tomorrow." Carmen frowned. "How the hell does she know we're going tomorrow?"

"Oh, I told her yesterday evening. Enid saw Rita and I carrying you in the house. She came around to make sure I was okay. Um...she may have taken a few photos of you two." Faith waved her hand between Carmen and Mateo.

Carmen's eyes stared back in horror. "What photos?"

"Oh, um, just you guys asleep while she drew things on your face. I washed them off when she left though."

"I..." Carmen was lost for words again.

"She said it served you right," Faith laughed. "Anyway, we got talking, and I told her about our plans. She asked if she could tag along. I think she's lonely, and honestly, I think she misses Molly."

"She's traveling with us?"

"Yeah, um...is that okay?"

"I mean sure, I suppose."

"What is happening out here? Why are you having a powwow by the front door?" Mateo's hand-on-hip stance made Carmen roll her eyes.

"It was Enid at the door. Seems we have another travel companion."

"Enid, the lady who said I'm as smooth as a Ken doll?"

"Yup, the very one."

"Well, this is gonna be interesting," he laughed.

Carmen scratched her head, still clueless about how the last five minutes had unfolded.

"Are you positive you're okay with it?" Faith asked again. Carmen's face was obviously giving off uncomfortable vibes.

"Of course. The more the merrier."

Following Faith and Mateo back to the living room, Carmen tried to mentally prepare herself for the next few days. Not only was she going to have to put up with Mateo and his Cher obsession, she was also going to share space with Enid, a woman who, frankly, scared her a little bit.

But, as she contemplated her reality, another thing struck her. Faith *wanted* Enid to come along. She must have felt a connection to the old dear. And after all, this was Faith's journey. Her life had already changed so much, and if what she needed now was to be surrounded by people she trusted and made her feel safe, then that's what she would get.

Carmen just hoped she was still sane enough to support Faith after what was going to be a testing trip.

9

Faith

Faith was brimming with feelings. Not only was she about to embark on a journey across the country to find Molly, but less than thirty-six hours ago, she'd reunited with Nathalie. Nathalie!

The Pride party had been eye-opening in the best way possible. Faith could count on one hand the number of fantastic days she'd had in her life, and by a wide margin, the party claimed the number one spot.

When Faith first laid eyes on Nathalie, all the clichéd things happened: she was left breathless, the world around her disappeared...the usual sappy stuff. But Faith didn't care. All she'd ever wanted was to experience those emotions, and with Nathalie, she'd felt them in spades.

Their talk by the pool had been shy to begin with. Faith's mind kept traveling back to the dream she'd had on the bus, and if she were honest, several other dreams she'd had since. None of them were family friendly.

It wasn't easy trying to get through an awkward conversation when certain parts of the body were waking up and causing mayhem. Faith was certain her face flushed more times than was humanly possible. If Nathalie noticed, she didn't say anything.

Nathalie had commented on Faith's new look. Faith didn't dare comment on how Nathalie had looked in that bikini she'd had on. It'd taken all her strength not to lower her eyes to Nathalie's ample chest.

Once the initial shock and awe had dissipated, they'd talked for hours. Faith had given Nathalie the CliffsNotes version of her reason for being in Seattle. The last thing she'd wanted was to bring the party down by talking about her family issues.

When it became clear Mateo and Carmen were far from sober, Faith had stuck close to them. As much as she wanted alone time with Nathalie, Faith also needed to make sure the Ruizes were okay. Thankfully, Nathalie found their antics completely entertaining.

By the end of the party, Faith had gotten Nathalie's phone number and a promise they would meet up again when she got back from Vermont. They'd started messaging the moment Faith sat in the passenger seat of Rita's car. Carmen and Mateo had passed out on each other's shoulders. Rita had made polite conversation, but she could see Faith was preoccupied.

Maybe the funniest part of the night had been sending pictures of Carmen and Mateo, with crude drawings on their faces, courtesy of Enid. Faith had never seen a woman cackle so hard as when Enid drew pieces of anatomy on each of their cheeks.

Today, however, the party was over and Faith had to bring herself back to reality. The reason she'd traveled thousands of miles and would travel thousands more: Finding Molly, and where she belonged in the world.

"Everyone ready?" Carmen called from the driver's seat.

Faith was in the back with Enid. The group decided they would rotate seats after each rest stop. Enid brought out a book with a half-naked man on the cover. Faith gave her a little side eye and a smirk.

Letting her head fall back on the headrest, Faith donned her headphones and selected the playlist Nathalie had shared with her.

As the hours flew by, Faith's mind wandered. In such a short space of time, she'd slipped into a completely new life. How would that life look after she found her aunt?

The prospect of possibly never again seeing Carmen and Mateo was like a punch to the chest. And what about her budding relationship—could she call it that—with Nathalie?

What if Molly didn't want to be responsible for Faith? How would she deal with that potential outcome? As usual, there were so many questions she simply didn't have the answers to.

The first rest stop was entertaining. Carmen wanted to stop for lunch, as did Faith, if she were honest, but Mateo—of course—had so many rules and regulations regarding "roadside food," it took them an extra hour to find somewhere suitable. Carmen had looked ready to murder Mateo. Enid sat, heckling them both when they argued with a few well-timed jabs of "Oh damn, she's going there!" and "You just got burned, Ken doll."

Faith urgently needed the bathroom by the time they stopped.

The next leg of the journey saw Faith up front with Carmen. The Ruizes definitely needed a cooling-off period. Faith found it bizarre they lived together successfully, yet the road trip was already causing such friction. When Faith noted Mateo had fallen into a food-induced coma, she broached the subject.

"You guys live so well together. What's with all the stress now?"

Carmen huffed out an irritated breath. "We get along because we both have our own space. Plus, Mateo is out of the house nearly all day. When we're cooped up like this, our immature sides emerge. I know it's stupid, but he just gets on my last nerve. Especially when he whines and gets all demanding."

"Ah, the dark side to having a sibling," Faith grinned.

"It's not all facials and glitter," Carmen laughed. "You know…" Carmen trailed off, her eyes darting from the road to Faith. "You're a part of that now—our odd little family. I just… I wanted you to know, that no matter what happens with your aunt or your parents, you have a place with us."

Faith's throat tightened and tears stung the corners of her eyes.

"Thank you," she croaked.

"Carmen, why is Faith crying again?" Mateo barked. Carmen rolled her eyes and pumped the brakes a little hard, causing Mateo to jerk forward, his head hitting Carmen's seat. "Fuck, what did you do that for?"

"Because you keep insinuating that I make Faith cry, on purpose. Stop butting in."

"I'm fine, Mateo."

"That was a nice move, Carmen. I'll remember it the next time Mildrid yaps on about how precious her dog is, even though it shits on my lawn. Maybe a good knock to the head will shut her up," Enid laughed. Mateo scowled at everyone.

"Mateo, what time did you go to bed last night?" Carmen asked, her eyes boring into him through the rear-view mirror.

"You're not my mother, Carmen."

"No, I'm not. But you only get this bitchy when you run out of cucumber face mask or you've had less than six hours of sleep. I know for a fact, you have at least three tubes of cucumber goo."

"Ugh, fine. I was a little late going to sleep."

"Why? We all turned in early."

Faith turned in her seat to look at Mateo, who had uncharacteristically blushed. His gaze darted everywhere but at Carmen or her.

"Mateo, were you talking to a boy?" Faith teased. Being silly and teasing came as second nature to Faith now. She called it the 'Ruiz Effect'.

"Mateo, *were* you talking to a boy?" Carmen parroted.

Mateo huffed dramatically, but it was all for show. He couldn't suppress the smile on his face. "Daniel gave me his number and we may have been chatting."

"About time," Enid clapped. "That boy is as smooth as you!"

"How the hell would you know that?" Mateo laughed.

"I Insta-stalked him."

Three sets of eyes whipped around to look at Enid.

"What? You think because I'm old I don't know how to find shit out? Hmm...that's the problem with young people now—they assume we're not as capable of using technology, even though we invented that shit!"

"What else did you find out?" Mateo asked nonchalantly.

"He's got the goods to fill out a Speedo."

Faith burst out laughing, as did Carmen. Mateo looked thoroughly delighted.

"Well, maybe I should invite him to Rita's. We can have a pool party."

Many, *many* hours later, Mateo finally stopped grilling Enid for information on Daniel. They'd stopped again for a pee break and began looking for a place to crash for the night.

The motel was alright. Faith couldn't really complain. It wasn't like she was the one paying for any of it. Somehow, she needed to work out a payment plan with Carmen. Although she was sure both Mateo and Carmen would decline any money, Faith was determined to pay them back for everything.

Everyone seemed in better shape after a good night's sleep. Carmen shared a room with Faith, and Mateo with Enid. Allowing Carmen and Mateo to get some space away from each other had done them both a world of good.

The miles flew by with laughter and intrigue. Enid had lived a full and interesting life. Her stories helped keep Faith's anxiety at bay. However, after a second night in a motel and a few more hours on the road, Faith saw a road sign for Vermont. In less than an hour, she would stand on

Molly's front porch. As they drew closer, everyone in the car grew quieter.

"How are you feeling, *chica*?" Mateo asked softly from the back seat.

Faith drew in a breath. "Nervous. It feels like a lifetime ago I found out I had an aunt. So much has happened, and now...now, I'm hopefully going to meet her."

"She's going to be thrilled to see you, kid." Carmen winked.

"But what if she's not there?" Faith had to vocalize her primary worry. All of this could have been for nothing.

"If she's not there, we go home, regroup, and continue looking."

A buzz from the center console alerted Faith she had a message. A quick look down at the screen made her smile like an idiot. Just seeing Nathalie's name on her phone turned her into a silly, love-struck teenager.

Nathalie 2:30

Are you there yet?

Faith 2:30 p.m.

Not too far away.

Faith bit her lip in anticipation.

Nathalie missed her. An excited squeak made Carmen jump. Faith couldn't stop the giggle, even if she wanted to.

"Nathalie, by any chance?" Carmen laughed.

"She said she misses me."

"Oh shit, this is too cute," Mateo chimed.

"Dental dams," Enid barked. "Always have dental dams. That's a thing, right? I'm sure I heard a lesbian say it once."

"Was that back in the day? 'Cuz ain't no one using those anymore," Mateo replied.

Faith scrunched her face. Should she know what a dental dam is? It felt like one of those things a good lesbian *should* know. Dammit, one more thing to add to her *lesducation* list.

"Can we stop saying dental dam, please?" Carmen shouted, her face a little red.

Faith summoned whatever courage she could to ask, "Um...what is a dental dam?"

The car fell silent. Faith looked back at Mateo and Enid, who were both staring expectantly at Carmen.

"Um..." Carmen began, clearing her throat several times. "It's...um...it's something that is used for oral sex."

"Oral sex," Faith parroted.

"Yup. Um..."

"Oh my God, Carmen, you are the worst fairy queer mother I have ever met," Mateo announced dramatically. "Faith, a dental dam is a piece of latex that is placed over a woman's vagina or anus. It creates a barrier for safe sex."

"For cunnilingus, dear," Enid tacked on.

"That doesn't sound very romantic," Faith answered, shaking her head. She didn't like the sound of it at all.

"They're good if you plan to sleep with different people. I suppose most U-Haul lesbians don't see the need for them, right Carmen?"

"I've never U-Hauled," she shot back, clearly uncomfortable.

"Have you used them?" Faith asked, then immediately regretted it. Carmen's eyes were wide and hyper-focused on the road. "Sorry, you don't have to answer that."

"No, it's fine. Um...yes, I have used them before. At the request of the woman I was with. I rarely use them, though. I prefer no barriers. That is, as long as both parties are consenting, of course."

"Faith, honey, don't worry about it. That's something to discuss with your partner when the time comes," Mateo reassured.

"I haven't even kissed a girl yet, so I think it will be a while before I need to worry about safe sex," Faith tittered nervously.

As she'd got to know Nathalie more, her dreams had increased to the point where, for the first time in her life, Faith considered touching herself. Masturbation was a sin, according to her parents, after all.

Faith remembered that discussion vividly. It was part of her mother's "sex education" speech. Acting on desire didn't come easily, no pun intended, but Faith was determined to push herself. Wanting a full, rich life wasn't a sin.

"Everything happens in its own time, *chica*."

"Is that something you want to do with Nathalie? Kiss her, I mean?" Carmen inquired, clearing her throat.

Faith nodded her head with certainty. "Nathalie is wonderful. She's so pretty, and she makes me feel comfortable. We've been talking a lot. I filled her in a little about my parents, etcetera. Not once did she make me feel like a loser—"

"You're not a loser, Faith. Never think that." The severity of Carmen's voice was surprising. The intensity in her eyes was just as striking. "Don't put yourself down like that. You're amazing."

"I second," Mateo called.

"Third," Enid added from behind her book.

"I...just feel like I have so much to learn. Nathalie has seen the world. How interested is she going to be when she learns that this is the first time I've ever been away from home? Or that..."

"She already knows that, right? You said you guys talked. *Chica*, don't look for reasons it won't work before you even try." Mateo was pointing at her.

"And," Carmen interjected, "you two have been chatting non-stop since the party. If she weren't interested, she wouldn't be investing her time. Nathalie is like Rita, in that sense."

"Honestly, I'm surprised you two didn't share a kiss at the party," Mateo mused.

"Well, we might have, if I didn't have to stop you two from scaling the palm trees, while singing Cher's 'The Shoop Shoop Song.'"

"Oh shit," Carmen mumbled.

"I do love that song," Mateo remarked.

"You numbnuts stopped that young lady from getting her freak on," Enid tutted.

"I wasn't going to get my freak on," Faith gasped.

"You could have. Now you'll never know," Enid replied, head still in her book.

"Oh damn, Faith, we clam jammed you," Mateo squealed.

"Alright," Carmen barked, "As the adult lesbian in this vehicle, I am officially prohibiting any gay man or straight woman from saying things like 'clam jam' or 'dental dam.' We are going to keep it strictly PG-13 in this car. Do you all understand?"

"Ugh, you're such a buzzkill," Enid clucked.

"Fine," Mateo whined.

The car's GPS rang out.

"We're a few minutes away," Carmen announced unnecessarily.

Rubbing sweaty palms down her thighs, Faith tried to calm her thoughts.

No matter what happens, you have Carmen and Mateo.

The car finally pulled up to a cute little bungalow, not too dissimilar to Carmen's house. The wraparound porch housed two Adirondack chairs, with a small table in between. The shutters, which adorned every window, were painted a delicate blue, and stood in contrast to the brilliant white of the building.

"Are you ready?" Carmen asked, placing her hand over Faith's.

"Yeah, let's go."

Together, Carmen and Faith climbed out of the car. The four of them decided along the way, to keep the meeting to just Faith and Carmen.

Making their way up the path, Faith noticed a light shining from one window. The porch creaked as they stepped up on it.

"Okay, here goes," Faith muttered, rapping her knuckles on the door.

Could time stop? That was sure what it felt like. It was only when she heard faint footsteps, Faith knew the world was still spinning and time was indeed marching forward.

When the blue door opened, disappointment was at the forefront of Faith's mind. The person standing in front of them was not Molly.

"Hi, can I help you?" Dressed in yoga pants and a tank top, the young woman smiled brightly at them both.

"Hi, sorry to disturb you. I'm... I was hoping Molly was in?"

"Ah, Molly doesn't live here anymore. She moved to Phoenix about four months ago."

There was no stopping the visible slump of her shoulders. They'd driven all this way and Molly was gone. Carmen quickly delivered the reassurance she had tucked away in her back pocket.

"Hey, it's alright. Like I said, we'll get back, regroup, and then try again."

"I have her address. I wouldn't usually hand out information like that, but I can tell you're related. It's striking really, apart from the different shades of hair color."

"Were you together?" Faith asked.

"No, Molly was my roommate. Awesome one too, real shame she left but..." the woman shrugged. "Oh, I'm Felicity, by the way."

"I'm Faith, Molly's niece, and this is my friend, Carmen."

"And those two?" Felicity pointed over their shoulders, a smirk forming on her face. Carmen and Faith turned in sync. Mateo and Enid both had their faces pinned to the car window.

Faith chuckled. "They're our other friends."

"Is that lady...panting?"

Carmen groaned. Trust Enid to embarrass them. They watched as Mateo swatted Enid, trying to get her to stop her—rather convincing—puppy impression.

"Anyway," Carmen sighed, turning her attention back to Felicity, "thank you for the address. We'll let you get back to what you were doing."

"Can I just ask one thing?" Faith interrupted.

"Sure."

"Molly, is she...is she nice?"

"She's the best. I know about her background, so I'm guessing you had it rough, too?"

Faith nodded.

"Molly is the kind of person you always want to be around. She's warm and comfortable. We had a great time as roommates."

"Do you know why she moved?"

"Her girlfriend, Ruth, got a job in Phoenix."

"Oh, so she's got a partner?" Carmen asked.

Faith eyed Carmen. Was that a brief flicker of annoyance in her friend's eyes? Interesting.

"Yeah, well, as far as I know. We haven't spoken in a while. Hey, if you catch up to her, tell her to call me. I miss her. And tell her to stop changing numbers. How's a girl supposed to keep in touch?"

"Absolutely. Thank you, Felicity."

Mateo and Enid must have guessed the outcome as Faith trudged back to the car, feeling a little defeated.

"So, where to next?" he asked with abundant enthusiasm.

"Phoenix," Carmen answered.

"You don't have to take me to Phoenix, Carmen. I appreciate all this, really, I do, but we could be just chasing another dead end."

"Hey, less of that. And this certainly wasn't a dead end. We have an address. We will find Molly. I promise."

Faith tried her hardest to believe the words Carmen was saying, but in light of another failed search, it was becoming harder by the minute.

10

Carmen

The drive back to Seattle had been long and almost silent. No matter what Carmen said, she couldn't get Faith to perk up. It was understandable. She couldn't imagine the weight of disappointment she must be feeling. But true to her word, Carmen was determined to find Molly. Faith deserved that.

Once Enid bid them farewell, and Mateo locked himself in the bathroom for what would likely be a full body treatment, Carmen took Faith outside to talk.

"Listen, I know you feel down. I can't imagine how frustrated you are, but please, Faith, trust that I will get you to your aunt."

"It's not that I don't trust you, Carmen. Of course I do. It's just with every day that goes by, I feel further away from her. Does that make sense?"

"I think so."

"I spent so long building up the moment where I would finally meet her. And it just hasn't happened the way I thought. I wonder if anything I imagined would happen is actually going to happen, at all."

"You're still thinking Molly won't want you, right?"

Watching Faith revert to the scared child she was when she first turned up in Seattle, was difficult to stomach.

"I know there's no reason to think that, but... Ugh, I just thought I would know by now."

"I get it. Really, I do. You've had Molly in your head as your safe harbor. That's what got you through the last few months. You can't give up now. I know we will find her, even if it's not in Phoenix."

"Are you sure you want to keep helping? You have two businesses to run and Mateo has the boutique."

"Believe it or not, this last week, driving to and from Vermont, has been exactly what I needed."

"Really?"

Carmen took a second to organize her thoughts. "Mateo was right you know, about me staying in the house too much. I convinced myself it was just easier to work—less distraction—but that's a stretch. I could literally work from anywhere. I could go to the park and enjoy the outdoors, or find a quiet coffee shop. But neither of those options felt like...well, options, for me. I realized I've spent so long making sure Mateo was okay, that I neglected myself a little."

"And being stuck in a car for the better part of six days helped you look after yourself better?" Faith asked with raised eyebrows, making Carmen laugh.

"Actually, yes. Ever since you turned up on my porch, I've felt better. Faith, you are inspiring. You helped me see hiding away isn't the answer. I'm proud of you, and a little in awe, if I'm honest."

"Carmen," Faith hiccupped.

"Ah shit, don't cry. Mateo will bust a gut if he thinks I upset you again." The levity in her voice helped quash the rising emotion in them both. "Come on, let's go sort out our laundry and repack."

"When do you think we should go to Phoenix?"

"ASAP. We can rest up tomorrow and then hit the road. I'll check in with Mateo and Enid."

"They don't have to come, really, I don't want to—"

"Hey, let them decide. Come on, let's get to it."

Taking some time to unpack, wash clothes, and then repack, was a godsend. The past few days had been intense. Carmen needed a few hours away from Mateo, so she didn't end up strangling his sassy ass. God, that man could be a diva.

When everything was done, Carmen lay on her bed, staring at the ceiling, soft music playing from her JBL speaker. A calm settled over her. That was until the shrill sound of her phone interrupted her thoughts and the music.

Frowning, Carmen reached blindly for the offending item. Stabbing the answer button, she closed her eyes and spoke, "Hello?"

"Hey, Carm," Rachel answered. The noise of keyboards clattering and phones ringing, told Carmen the detective was at work.

"Hey, Rach, everything okay?"

"Yes, and no. We had a disturbance call to your address while you were out of town."

Carmen bolted up. "A disturbance?"

"Yeah, one of your neighbors reported a man shouting and hammering on your door. A squad car was dispatched. I'd asked to be notified if your address came up."

Carmen had the good sense to let Rachel know she was taking Faith to Vermont. They'd also spoken at length about Faith's parents and the worry they would turn up uninvited.

"What happened?"

"The guy screamed and shouted for a while. The officers called me."

"Was it Faith's dad?"

"A Mr. Alan Parsons. Yes, it was him."

"Shit."

"Listen, I convinced him we would haul him off to jail if he returned, but Carmen, I know men like that. He's not going to give up."

"I need to speak to Faith. She should decide what to do next."

"Okay. I take it that things didn't go to plan in Vermont?"

"Not quite, but we are traveling to Phoenix next. I'll feel better about all this business with her dad once Faith has found Molly. At least her aunt might know how to deal with him."

"Alright, keep me updated. I'll make sure nothing, and no one, messes with your house."

"Thanks, Rachel, we appreciate it."

"Take care."

The phone line went silent, unlike Carmen's racing mind. Goddamn it, she knew the son of a bitch would turn up. What she didn't know, was how protective she would feel of Faith when it happened. It was a good thing they weren't home because God only knew what she would've said or done if she'd had to face him; the mother, as well.

"Mateo?" Carmen called.

Pacing her bedroom, Carmen could feel herself getting more and more irate. Who did that fucker think he was? Turning up to do what? Drag Faith back to the prison he called home? Force her to marry some man?

"Whoa, you look like you're about to explode. What's wrong?" Mateo closed the bedroom door, his body clad in his favorite pink robe. The smell of vanilla and pears permeated the air.

"Faith's parents were here." Carmen's voice quivered with rage.

"Shit," Mateo hissed. "How do you know?"

"Rachel."

"Does she think he will come back?"

"Possibly, but not right now. I think she scared him enough he won't push it."

"Does Faith know?"

"Nope, I wanted to tell you first. I'm so fucking angry, *hermano*. That asshole was here to take her."

"I know. I understand your anger, but you need to dial it down. Faith needs us to be calm."

"That's why I called you in here first."

Mateo stood and made his way to Carmen, blocking her path. With both hands firmly on her shoulders, he ducked to look into her eyes. "Deep breaths, *hermana*. Center yourself."

"Okay, I'm okay." Carmen nodded, "I'm good, thanks Mateo."

"Let's call her in and tell her together. I'm already packed to travel to Phoenix and so is Enid."

"Is the boutique covered?"

"Of course. It's in expert hands. I just want to focus on Faith right now."

Pulling Mateo into her body, Carmen held him for a few moments. "*Te amo.*"

"*Yo también.*"

"Carmen, have you seen my... Oh, sorry," Faith said, pausing in the doorway. Neither Mateo nor Carmen had heard it open.

"Just the person we wanted to see," Mateo chimed.

"Everything okay?" Faith couldn't disguise the worry in her voice.

"It seems your parents stopped by when we were away." Carmen gripped Faith's arm when she felt the young woman falter, her legs going weak. "Sit down."

"They were here?"

"Yes, but don't panic. Rachel, my detective friend, was here to help."

"What happened?"

"Nothing overly exciting. She just made sure your father wouldn't be back."

"That won't stop him, Carmen."

Carmen drew Faith into a hug. Mateo stepped up and engulfed them both with his long arms.

"*No te preocupes, cariño,*" he whispered.

"Change of plans. We are setting off in the morning. Even if they do come back, we won't be here."

"I'll call Enid and tell her to be here at half past seven," Mateo added.

"I'm sorry," Faith sobbed.

Carmen gripped her. "Nothing to be sorry for. Let's get some rest and be ready to rock and roll tomorrow."

Feeling Faith nod against her chest, Carmen relaxed her embrace. Maybe she could plan a few stops to try and cheer Faith up? Carmen would do anything to wipe that overwhelming look of sadness from the girl's face.

The trip to Phoenix had been a lot less fraught than the Vermont escapade. Mateo had reined in his whining *and* his Cher obsession. Faith was clearly trying to stay upbeat, but couldn't fool Carmen. Enid got herself stoned on weed gummies less than half an hour into the journey. It turned out, Enid was a lot calmer when high.

Pulling onto the street where Molly's house was supposed to be located, Carmen sent up a prayer to any deity listening.

Please let Molly be here.

"Jesus, I can feel the heat already," Mateo panted, wafting his hand in front of his face. Considering they'd had the A/C cranked up since entering the sweltering state, Carmen couldn't disagree with his statement. The road looked as if it were shimmering.

"It's heaven," Enid squealed. She was aptly dressed in a Hawaiian shirt and cargo shorts.

"Alright, shall we try this again?" Carmen asked Faith when the car came to a stop. They were outside a sprawling house, the color of sand. Palm trees lined the street, as far as the eye could see.

"Yeah, fingers crossed everyone."

Carmen slid out of the car and swore under her breath. The heat was simply ridiculous. How she craved the Seattle weather—hell—even the rain.

Following slowly behind Faith, Carmen literally crossed her fingers. The bell Faith pressed, chimed loudly. Moments later, the door opened. A very attractive woman with long black hair greeted them. Not Molly, but hopefully the girlfriend.

"Hi, can I help you?"

"Yes, I'm looking for Molly Parsons." Faith's hands were as shaky as her voice. Carmen didn't miss the hurt that passed over the stranger's face.

Oh no!

"Molly doesn't live here anymore." The woman went to shut the door, but Carmen had quick reflexes and her hand stopped the motion. "Um... do you mind?"

"Sorry, but have you got a forwarding address?"

"I'm her niece," Faith interjected. "I've been searching for my aunt for months. Please, if you can help, tell me where she went."

Faith's pleas hit the mark. The woman opened the door wider. "I'm Ruth, Molly's ex."

Why did that news make Carmen feel happy?

"I'm Carmen and this is Faith."

"Do you want to come in?"

"We have two more people with us," Carmen said, gesturing over her shoulder. At least this time Enid wasn't acting like a dog. They looked a tad warm, though.

"Invite them in. I've got some lemonade in the fridge."

Carmen looked around discreetly as Ruth ushered them to a table at the back of the house. An enormous pool glimmered under the sun. The house was sparse, but Carmen guessed that was on purpose. She couldn't see herself living in a house that was so devoid of personality. Carmen needed things around her. She also needed a color that wasn't just beige.

"Um...so do you know where Molly went?"

Faith wanted answers, and Carmen couldn't begrudge her impatience.

Ruth sighed, her eyes shining with unshed tears. If Carmen was a betting person, she would wager Ruth wasn't happy with the break-up.

"Molly moved to California. A town called Woodland, in Yolo County, to be precise."

"Are...are you okay?" Carmen asked stupidly. Obviously, the woman wasn't okay. Tears had spilled over her cheeks.

"Sorry, this is embarrassing," Ruth choked.

"Don't be sorry, dear," Enid cooed.

"I'm still very much in love with your aunt," Ruth cried. "Unfortunately, we couldn't get past our differences to make it work."

"I'm sorry," Faith whispered, taking Ruth's hand.

"Molly is a free spirit. It's the thing I fell in love with first. She's also kind and generous." Ruth swiped the tears from her face. "When we moved here, it was for my job. Molly worked at a LGBTQIA2s+ shelter in the city, until she was given the chance to work with a woman in California who'd opened up her ranch to help house LGBTQIA2s+ kids that had been made homeless."

"Has she always worked for shelters?" Faith asked.

"Yes. It's her passion. I knew when she received the offer, she would want to go. Unfortunately, I'm tied to Phoenix for the foreseeable future." Ruth's shoulders slumped. "I couldn't ask her to stay, not when I could see how badly she wanted to go."

"I don't know what to say," Faith admitted. Carmen mirrored that sentiment.

"You don't need to say anything. It's sad. I should have just gone with her. Molly isn't the kind of woman you just let go. Not for a job."

"Couldn't you go after her?" Faith's question jarred Carmen.

"No. I think her leaving showed me, that no matter how much I love her, I will always come second. And that's okay. What Molly does is so important. She also moves with the wind. There would be nothing stopping her from leaving California in a few months to work somewhere else. I don't think I'm built for that kind of life."

"Would, um, would you like us to pass a message on when we see her?" Mateo asked tentatively.

"No, thank you. We said everything we needed to. I'll write down the name of the ranch. I'd give you her number but... Well, I had a bad night after she left, and the bottle of wine I drank made me do some questionable things. Deleting her contact, for one."

They fell silent when Ruth left the room. A state of contemplation descended upon them all. Carmen couldn't speak to the others' thoughts, but hers were firmly on Molly Parsons. Who was this enigmatic woman that everyone seemed to love? Why did her name stir something in Carmen's chest?

"Here you go," Ruth said, breaking the spell.

"Thank you, Ruth. I... Thank you," Faith said, smiling warmly.

The group stood to take their leave.

"Take care," Carmen said, before shaking Ruth's hand.

In the car, the atmosphere was an odd mix of hope and sadness. Ruth's pain was hard to witness, but Carmen knew in her heart Molly was still in California, and that was what she needed to focus on. It was what they *all* needed to focus on.

"How many fucking gummies has she eaten?" Mateo hissed from the back seat.

"How should I know? I'm driving, *hermano*."

"Well, I think it's time to switch out. I cannot sit here listening to her read aloud, any longer. Do you know how disconcerting it is to have a sex scene read to you by a senior citizen? Carmen, she's even making grunt noises. I'm going to be put off sex for life, at this rate."

"Oh, I have a lesbian romance she can read from if that would be better," Carmen laughed.

Enid was in a complete world of her own. Lost in her imagination, her eyes were feverishly scanning the raunchy book.

"Carmen, please, I need a break. I know what Enid's 'breathy voice' sounds like. I should *not* know that."

"No one should know that, Mateo."

"Carmen," he growled.

"Alright, keep your heels on. I'll pull over in a few miles, although, we're literally an hour from Woodland."

"I can sit in the back with her," Faith said, taking out her earbuds.

"No!" Mateo and Carmen replied together with force.

"I'll take a turn," Carmen added. No way was she going to subject Faith's innocent ears to Enid's "breathy voice."

Twentyminutes later, Carmen found herself next to a smiling Enid. The way the older woman was looking at her was a little concerning.

"I'm glad you're back here with me," Enid said smugly.

Hold on a minute. Had Enid planned this?

"Nice to be here?" Carmen replied, with more of a question than a statement.

"So, Ruth was nice."

"Yeah, it seemed so."

"Not Molly's forever person, though."

"Um, okay?"

Where was Enid going with this?

"Molly needs someone who will nurture her need to help young people, but will make her feel safe enough to stop running."

Well, this conversation was a tad on the heavy side. Carmen almost wished Enid would start reading her smutty book out loud, again.

Looking toward the front of the car for support, Carmen was out of luck. Faith had her headphones back in, typing furiously on her phone, and Mateo was obnoxiously singing a Madonna song.

"I'm sure Molly knows what or who she needs."

"I know Molly. I watched her for a long time. I've watched you, too."

"That's creepy," Carmen mumbled.

"Not creepy... Okay, maybe a little," Enid laughed. "I just think you and Molly would be good for each other."

"Enid, you know that's not going to happen, right? We're taking Faith to her, and then, well, I don't know what will happen. One thing is for sure, though. I will head home with you and Mateo and get back to work."

"If you say so, dear. Now, would you like a gummy? I think that stick in your ass could do with a break."

Carmen stared, open-mouthed. "I..."

"Okay, 'no' to the gummy. How about I read that lesbian book you were telling Mateo about? It's been ages since I've had some girl-on-girl action."

"Enid!" Carmen squeaked.

"Oh, lord. Your generation thinks you invented lesbianism, I swear it. I've had plenty of experience with the ladies."

"How did your husband feel about that?" Carmen's eyes shimmered with amusement.

"Ha! He had his fair share of men, so no big deal." Carmen's mouth fell open.

"Now, you sure you don't want that gummy?" Enid smiled, her palm open, offering Carmen a little candy.

"Mateo, we're swapping back. Pull over!"

"Oh, look, we're in California," Faith squealed excitedly. Mateo pulled the car over to the side of the road. Looming over their windshield was a large "Welcome to California" sign.

"Hey Carmen, did you know California's state flower is a sunflower?" Mateo asked, his eyes never leaving the giant sign. Carmen shoved her head through the gap in the seats.

"That's a poppy, not a sunflower," Carmen chuckled, as Mateo screwed up his face, trying to look at the picture harder, as if that were possible.

"Fun fact, though," Faith chirped, "the ranch Molly is hopefully staying at, is called Sunflower Ranch."

"Cool," Carmen mumbled. Sunflowers were her favorite.

I wonder which flower Molly likes?

11

Molly

Molly's fingertips brushed the soft sunflower petals as she walked. Soon, the flowers would be taller than her, but until then, she would continue her daily walks through the fields.

The sun beat down on her face, but it didn't matter. Molly would always look to the sky when out walking. It was a reminder that she was free and alive. Breathing in fresh air was a balm to any malady, as far as she was concerned.

Today was a day Molly needed the freedom of those sunflower fields. For most people, a birthday was to be celebrated with friends and family. For Molly, it was a time of reflection and healing. Ever since she found herself homeless as a teenager, Molly spent her birthday alone, contemplating all that had happened and all that could be.

There were a handful of people in Molly's life who knew her history; understood how tough the path had been for her to walk. But none of them could walk in her shoes. There was still a tendril of hope, that one day she would be welcomed back with open arms and acceptance. Even after all these years, that ember still burned in her heart.

The part which hurt the most, was that her brother hadn't always been so closed-minded and bigoted. Before their parents died, Alan had been a kind and caring brother. He had nurtured their relationship so tenderly. They spent all their time together, playing and learning... But then everything changed.

Once their parents were gone, Alan sought refuge in the pastor, a man who only preached hate. He taught her brother, that punishing his so-called 'wicked' sister would bring him closer to God.

The pastor's hushed words played on a continuous loop in Alan's ear, distorting his entire worldview, and turning him into someone unrecognizable; someone who saw violence as a way of cleansing his sinful family, making them pure in God's eyes, once again. But Molly knew better. The only person Alan saved was himself. His behavior only served to keep his precious reputation among the churchgoers intact.

The memories still brought tears to Molly's eyes. One man, with his poison, had dismantled a lifetime of love and support, resulting in Molly's banishment from everything she'd ever known.

But she survived. Molly would always survive. And she would always keep trying to win back her brother. It was almost guaranteed Alan threw away her letters every month, but no matter what, Molly would keep sending them. Her parents would want her to keep trying.

Fantasizing about what could have been, was possibly the hardest part of her birthday. What if Alan *had* accepted her? Would she have spent every year with Alan and Maureen? Could they have had holidays together? As couples? Presuming Molly found "The One" that is.

So many what-ifs. Today was the only day Molly allowed herself to ponder those unanswerable questions. The other three hundred and sixty-four days of the year were about the kids who needed her help. They deserved her full attention.

A voice calling in the distance made Molly pause. She could see Chelsea's red hair bobbing up and down as she jogged to catch up.

"Hey, here you are. I've been looking for you."

"The day is so beautiful, I thought I'd take a walk."

Not a lie, but not the entire truth, either. Chelsea's presence irked Molly. They'd seen each other the night before and Molly had made it clear she wanted today to herself.

In her heart, she knew Chelsea was just being a good friend. Few people understood Molly's need for isolation on her birthday. Another part of Molly knew Chelsea was trying to get close to her, emotionally. Their "friends with benefits" system had been successful throughout their friendship, but recently, Molly felt a shift in Chelsea's feelings.

"I know you wanted to be alone, but I thought we could grab a picnic or something. Just the two of us. I won't even speak if that's what you need."

Molly squeezed Chelsea's hand gently. "Thanks for the offer, but not today."

Chelsea's disappointment was visible, but not enough to make Molly change her mind. This was *her* day, and she needed it to be *just hers*.

"Can I see you tomorrow, then?"

"Sure, tomorrow." Molly smiled and then turned to leave.

They needed to talk, but not now. That conversation could wait. And, if Molly were being completely honest, she needed Chelsea for a little longer. It was selfish, she knew, but Chelsea gave Molly the outlet she needed.

Maybe one more night together, before Molly inevitably shattered the peace. Hopefully, Chelsea would still want to be friends, without the benefits.

Today wasn't the day to be making any decisions regarding anything. That's why being on her own was the best thing—for everyone. Bessie, the ranch owner and head of the shelter, knew the reason Molly wanted to be alone, and was more than happy to take over her duties for the day.

There were four kids currently living on the ranch. Four young adults, cast aside—just as Molly had been—because of who they loved. Working with four teenagers was difficult, both mentally and physically, but Molly couldn't see herself doing anything else. From the moment she was given a safe place to land—months after she was tossed out—Molly dedicated herself to helping kids like her.

So far, working with different charities and shelters meant Molly had traveled most of the country. Though she loved each city, Molly never found one that felt like home, so she kept moving, one city after the next. It was only when she met Ruth, Molly had considered stopping and settling down. But when Bessie contacted her and offered her the job on the ranch, that old tugging feeling emerged. There was so much good she could do at the ranch.

Deciding to take the job was never in question. Molly felt guilty about that daily, because she knew Ruth should have factored into her decision more. But the ugly truth was, she hadn't. Molly loved Ruth, and really had wanted to settle down.

Maybe it just wasn't in her future? There would always be LGBTQIA2s+ kids in need, and as long as Molly could help, that's what she would do. Always.

How could she expect a partner to understand that internal drive, let alone allow her the freedom to do what she needed to do without the promise of more?

As she thought about it, Molly wasn't sure if she would ever settle in one city. In her heart, she knew if she found a place that made her feel at home, she would stop. Not the charity work; the roaming.

Maybe that would be when Molly could safely give her heart to someone—when she finally felt at home.

Her wandering thoughts brought her full circle to Alan. If he'd only loved her more, she would have still had her home.

A gentle breeze shifted the straw hat sitting delicately on Molly's head. Placing her hand on top to stop it from taking off, Molly inhaled deeply, letting the summer air fill her entirely.

All she had to do was get through the rest of today and she would be fine. All she had to do was write Alan another letter, and keep her fingers crossed *this one* would be the letter that made him contact her.

The dawn had barely broken, but Molly was up, showered, dressed, and ready to start the day. As usual, it took her a few minutes to stuff the previous day in a box and secure it in the depths of her mind. Molly'd had her allotted time. Now, it was back to business helping her kids.

Every young person Molly helped felt like hers. They became a part of her family. The proof was on her bedroom wall. Hundreds of pictures of Molly and the people she'd helped were pinned up, as well as the beautiful people she had worked with professionally.

Standing for a minute to soak up all the love and joy that poured from the Polaroids, helped Molly dispel the melancholy her birthday brought. The ranch was silent as she made her way to the kitchen.

To help the kids feel at home, Molly and Bessie had a routine. Breakfast was at eight, in the large kitchen. It wasn't mandatory for everyone to sit together. Sometimes, one or more of the residents weren't at the stage where they could socialize. But Molly encouraged the shared time, anyway.

As well as feeling like the ranch was home, Molly and Bessie wanted to foster the feeling of family. The residents ranged from sixteen to eighteen. And Molly knew having friends to lean on was imperative for the healing process.

There had been plenty of times when Molly dealt with a kid who fought the idea of getting close to other people their age. The idea of rejection was often far too potent to allow their barriers down, however, Molly also knew those kids were the ones that benefited the most from having supportive peers.

It was the reason Molly and Bessie tried to encourage the teenagers to bond, lean on each other, and become support pillars.

Micah, Liam, Courtney, and Lisa had, so far, bonded well. Micah was the oldest. They had just turned eighteen. Courtney and Liam were seventeen-year-old twins, and Lisa was a few weeks away from turning seventeen.

So far, the four of them were getting along well. Lisa was the newest addition. Her background left Molly wanting to commit murder. When Lisa was caught with a girl, her mother—if she could even be called that—beat her. If that weren't bad enough, her mother's boyfriend raped Lisa, believing it would set the girl straight.

Molly had years of experience, and unfortunately, Lisa's story wasn't unique, and yet, it still took Molly's breath away when she heard the heinous acts committed against these young and vulnerable people.

Lisa adapted well to the ranch. It took her a little time to open up to Molly and Bessie, and even longer to open up to the other kids. But Molly could proudly say Lisa was doing *so* well now. Her therapy sessions were really paying off, and Lisa had become an integral part of the ranch.

Thinking of the youngsters asleep upstairs, boosted Molly's resolve. This was where she belonged. Well, right now, she belonged in front of the stove, because teenagers were savages if they didn't get fed. First things first, though, Molly needed caffeine.

Bessie would be down shortly and they would spend a little time discussing the ranch and any jobs that needed taking care of. They'd also go over each teenager's case, filling each other in on any incidents or worries. Thankfully, none of them currently gave Molly cause for concern.

Creaking wood signaled Bessie's arrival. The four foot five firecracker bounced into the room. Molly had known Bessie for nearly a decade. Their paths crossed several times over the years and they'd formed a friendship.

When they first met, Bessie worked for a nonprofit, while her wife tended to the ranch. Three years ago, Carol, Bessie's wife, passed away. Bessie opened up the huge ranch house to homeless LGBTQIA2s+ kids, so she could still tend to the farm.

Now, Bessie was getting older and needed support. As soon as Molly got the offer to move to California and help Bessie, she'd taken it. They were a formidable team, and with the aid of different charities, they'd helped dozens of teens find their places in the world.

"Coffee's up," Molly called over her shoulder. Both women drank a bucket of coffee first thing in the morning.

"Oh, you're my favorite. Do you know that, Molly Parsons?"

"And so I should be," Molly chuckled. "What's on the agenda today?"

"I'm taking Lisa to therapy at eleven. Micah has that job interview at two-thirty, but they insist on going alone."

"They just want to feel in charge of themselves—can't fault that."

"That, and the guy who runs the coffee cart next to the building where the interview is being held is 'hot', according to Liam."

"Ah, okay, they don't want us senior citizens cramping their style," Molly laughed, rolling her eyes playfully.

"Courtney wants to help in the fields today, which is fine by me." Bessie sat down at the kitchen table, her feet dangling an inch above the ground.

"I'll work with Courtney today. It's been a minute since we've had some time to talk."

"Is there something in particular you want to talk with her about?"

"No, I just want to check in. Liam has been spending more and more time with Micah, and I just want to make sure Courtney is okay. They've only had each other for so long. I don't want Courtney to feel pushed out now that Liam is exploring outside of their little support bubble."

"Good idea. Is Chelsea coming over later?" Bessie's eyes twinkled.

Molly rolled her eyes again. Bessie had tried to set Molly up several times. When those attempts didn't work, she went all in on Molly and Chelsea's relationship.

No matter how many times Molly explained she wasn't interested in more than they had, Bessie continued to push.

"She is coming over later, but you need to simmer down. We are friends and that's it. I told you I don't want more than that, so listen, you stubborn old goat."

"Hey, less of the old." Bessie scowled.

"But you agree with the stubborn part of that sentence?" Molly grinned.

"I just don't want you closing yourself off, Molly. We both know how hard this line of work is. Everyone needs someone to go home to."

"Not everyone, Bessie. And besides, I didn't say I never wanted that, I just haven't found *The One* yet. Pushing me towards Chelsea isn't going to magically resolve that."

"So, it's just not there for you? Between you and Chelsea, I mean?"

"That's what I'm saying. Chelsea is a great friend and yes, great in bed, but she doesn't feel—"

"Like home?" Bessie finished.

"Exactly. For now, I just want to concentrate on this place. I promise I'm not shutting myself away."

"Well, alright then. I'll stop harassing you about Chelsea, but I can't promise I won't interfere if someone comes along who could be yours forever."

Molly rounded the table, so she was standing behind Bessie. Bending down, Molly wrapped her arms around Bessie's shoulders and squeezed.

"Shall we get breakfast started?"

The rest of the morning went by without Bessie bringing up Molly's love life again. Micah, Courtney, Liam, and Lisa demolished their food before scurrying back to their rooms. Molly caught up on a few chores before Courtney came back down, ready to start work outside.

"How is it going, Court?" Molly asked as they walked through the fields, inspecting the sunflowers.

Courtney shrugged. "I'm fine."

The lack of enthusiasm worried Molly.

"Hey, come on now, you know better than that. Talk to me."

Courtney stopped and sighed heavily. "I'm totally crushing on Lisa."

That wasn't where Molly thought Courtney was going to go.

"Okay, and so why do you look like someone just ate the last double-stuffed Oreo? Having a crush is supposed to be a good thing, Court."

"Yeah, if the object of that crush felt the same way," Courtney mumbled.

"Lisa doesn't feel the same way?"

"I don't think so."

"You haven't talked to her?"

"Are you nuts? I'm not going to tell her, just for her to say she doesn't like me back."

Molly knew Courtney found rejection hard, just like most people, but for these kids, the act of rejection was deeper than most. Understandably, they shielded themselves from further hurt, but that often led them to reject others first.

"You've written her off before even giving her a choice," Molly began softly. "I understand your worry. You know I do."

Molly was always upfront with people about her past. When kids came to the ranch, they needed to know the people helping them understood what they were going through.

"I know," Courtney whispered.

"She might not feel the same way, and yeah, that would suck, but on the flip side, she could be interested. Court, sweetheart, if you never take the risk, you could end up losing out on something wonderful. That's the same with everything in life, honey."

"Yeah, maybe."

Molly knew the conversation was over and Courtney needed the space to process.

"Come on, let's go grab a lemonade. It's hot as hell out here."

They ambled back to the ranch slowly. Courtney dropped onto the porch bench while Molly fetched them a pitcher of ice-cold lemonade.

Sometimes, sitting in silence, looking out over the sunflower fields, was all the therapy needed. Courtney did better when given the room to work through her thoughts, but she also needed to feel she had support close by. Sitting on the porch, watching the world go by, was the perfect compromise.

"Hey, who's that?" Courtney asked a few minutes later. Molly had been in her own world and hadn't noticed the car which wound its way up towards the house.

"No idea. Maybe someone is lost?" Molly commented.

They weren't due to have another house guest, and it wasn't Bessie's car. Micah had only just left, so it wasn't him, either.

Standing from the bench, Molly made her way down the steps. The car came to a stop a few yards away. Molly's eyes locked with a young woman sitting in the front passenger seat—eyes which were so similar to her own.

The shock caused Molly to stumble back. The passenger door opened slowly, and the girl stepped out. Molly froze. With long honey-colored hair, blue eyes, and the same dimples as her, Molly knew she was looking at Alan's daughter.

"Hi," the girl breathed, "I'm Faith. Um...I'm your niece."

12

Faith

Faith felt sick the entire drive to Yolo County. After another disappointing trip, she didn't know what she would do if Molly wasn't in California anymore.

Carmen, Mateo, and Enid had done their level best to keep the atmosphere positive, but Faith knew, until she laid eyes on her aunt, nothing would make her feel better.

As they traveled dirt roads, sunflower fields flanking either side, a feeling wound itself around Faith's heart; a sixth sense, which told Faith she was finally going to find Molly Parsons.

When the large ranch house came into view, Faith's gaze met that of a woman Faith knew instantly. Yes, her hair was slightly darker than Faith's, but her face...her face was like staring into a mirror.

When the car came to a stop, Faith slid out of the passenger side in a trance. The only thing on her mind was meeting Molly. If Molly's shocked features were anything to go by, Faith would guess Molly knew they were related.

"Hi, I'm Faith, Um...I'm your niece."

"Niece?" Molly gasped. Tears pooling in her eyes.

Faith hadn't known what to expect. How could she? It's not like she went around meeting long-lost family members every weekend. At the sight of Molly's tears, Faith's eyes misted over. For months on end, Faith's only goal was to find this woman and hope she would keep Faith safe.

The journey hadn't been that simple, and Faith had met some wonderful and unexpected characters—that she now deemed family—along the way. But even now, after having Carmen, Mateo, and Enid looking out for her, Faith's instinct was to rush to Molly, a woman she didn't even know, yet pulled her like a magnet. The last vestige of home running through Molly's bloodstream.

"I...I've been searching for you." Faith's brain struggled to form full sentences.

There was so much to say and discuss, but the sight of her aunt rendered Faith almost speechless.

Staring at each other, Faith wondered what to do. Should she carry on talking, or fall silent, allowing Molly to process what was happening?

"Faith," Molly sobbed, lunging forward, scooping Faith into her arms.

Nothing could have prepared Faith for the tsunami of emotion that overtook her body. Tears flowed freely between the two women. Faith gripped Molly hard, scared that if she left any amount of space between them, Molly would slip away.

"I didn't know," Molly cried. "I didn't know you existed. I'm so sorry."

Faith shook her head against Molly's shoulder. "It's not your fault."

Minutes passed with neither woman willing to let go. Only when a hand landed on Faith's back did the hug break apart. Carmen stood, her eyes watering and a soft smile on her face.

"Sorry, Carmen," Faith chuckled. She'd completely forgotten there were other people standing around.

"Don't apologize. Maybe you and Molly should sit and talk properly. I need to get Mateo a bathroom before he disgraces our family name by peeing himself, and Enid could do with some water."

Faith laughed. "Molly, this is Carmen Ruiz, her brother Mateo, and you know Enid."

"It's a pleasure," Molly replied. "It's wonderful to see you again, Enid. You look fantastic."

"Of course I do, dear. We'll catch up later."

"Carmen and Mateo took me in when I arrived in Seattle."

"Seattle?" Molly asked. "You thought I was in Seattle?"

"It's the last address I could find. My dad..." Faith cut herself off before another sob tore from her throat.

"Alan? He kept my letters?" Molly gasped, a hand coming to her mouth.

"He did."

"How is he?"

Faith hated the look of hope in Molly's eyes. How could she tell her aunt that her father was a brutal monster? Did Molly really not know who her brother was, or what he was capable of?

"I... We need to talk, catch up," Faith offered. A few minutes to unscramble her thoughts were needed.

"Well, hello there," a kind older woman said. Nobody had noticed the other car pull up next to Carmen's vehicle.

"Bessie, this is Faith, my niece."

Faith surmised Bessie was the owner of the ranch, and the one who had offered Molly a job. Standing alongside

Bessie was a girl, probably around Faith's age. Her long brown hair hung over her shoulders in waves. Faith liked her ripped jeans and tank top.

"Niece?" Bessie asked, raising her eyebrow.

"Long-lost niece," Faith answered.

Bessie took in the group of people. "Okay, then. How about we all head inside for a drink and snacks? Maybe you and Faith could sit out here and have a chat?"

Faith looked from Bessie—who gave Molly a little wink—to Molly, who nodded in agreement, squeezing Faith's hand.

Mateo almost sprinted into the house, which made Carmen roll her eyes and Faith laugh. Molly seemed to be amused by Faith's companions, which was nice. If she and Molly were to get along, Molly had to like Carmen and Mateo. At least Enid was a sure thing. The old woman might be nuttier than squirrel poop, but she'd become like a grandma to Faith.

Molly led Faith to the bench on the front porch. Both had grown quiet, each happy to spend a little time looking the other one over in awe. Faith really felt like she was looking at herself twenty years in the future.

"I don't know what to say," Molly laughed.

"Weird, right?" Faith smiled.

"So, your parents..." Molly trailed off, giving Faith the space to take over the conversation.

Puffing out her cheeks, Faith tried to find a place to start.

"When I mentioned my dad," she began, "I saw this look in your eye, like you were hoping he wanted to talk. Because he kept your letters." Faith had to just rip the band aid off. "That's not the case."

Molly stiffened slightly but remained silent.

"It's difficult for me to talk about. Living with him—with them—hasn't been easy."

"Tell me," Molly said, her face full of concern.

Faith drew every bit of confidence Carmen and Mateo had instilled in her and let her mouth do the talking. Nothing was skipped or watered down. Faith knew Molly had to hear it all. Maybe then her aunt could forget the idea of a joyful family reunion.

It felt cruel of Faith to be this honest, especially when she could see the light in Molly's eyes dim. Faith had to remember her experience and Molly's were different. The way Alan Parsons behaved now was the only way Faith had ever known him. But that didn't mean Molly's life with him had been the same.

"Faith, I...I really...I just don't know what to say."

"It's a lot, I know."

"Alan, your dad, wasn't always like that. Maybe that's why I kept sending him letters. I hoped one day he would snap out of it and go back to being the brother I grew up with."

"Would you mind telling me about him, about you, and what happened?" Faith couldn't imagine a world where her parents were anything but what they were now.

"I suppose I should start before it all went to shit," Molly chuckled mirthlessly. "Our parents—your grandparents—were the best people I ever knew. God, they loved us so much. Your grandad was a mechanic and your grandma worked in the library. We had little, but what we lacked in money, they made up for in love."

Faith wanted to wipe away the tears falling down Molly's face.

"Your dad was the best brother, too. He didn't mind having his baby sister following him around, even when he was with his friends."

"It's just so hard to believe," Faith replied, the earth shifting beneath her feet.

Molly nodded. "When our parents died, that's when things changed. I honestly believe if they'd still been around, your father wouldn't have cared about my sexual orientation."

"Really?"

"Really. I think he was just so angry, that when he turned for guidance to the church—to the pastor—he couldn't see the poison being spewed into him. He started changing. He was always angry and short-tempered, despite being able to usually keep that part of him in check."

"That's the man I know," Faith muttered.

"When he caught me with my best friend, in my room, I thought he would get angry but then calm down. I didn't think he would..."

"Would what? What did he do to you?"

"It's not something I like to talk about," Molly admitted.

"He hit me and mom," Faith confessed. If she wanted Molly to be vulnerable and trust her, she needed to open up.

Molly shook her head and drew Faith into another hug. "God, I wish I'd known you were alive. I would have done something."

"It's not your fault."

"How...how did you find out about me?"

Faith explained about her mother's slip-up and the conversation she'd had with Mrs. Baker in the library.

"I thought that if I could find you... I don't know, I just needed someone..."

"You needed someone to understand."

"Yes, and make me feel a part of a family."

"Your grandparents would have adored you, Faith. I promise you that. It's cruel you never got to have that with them."

"Can we take a walk?" Faith asked. Her emotions were running wild and the urge to move became insurmountable.

"Sure, let's go."

Walking through the sunflower fields offered Faith the peace she needed to continue with the deep dive into a shared family history. She'd learned more in an hour talking to her aunt than the entire sum of her existence with her parents.

Her brain was finding it impossible to reconcile the father and mother she knew to the ones Molly described.

As well as her father being completely different, Molly said her mother, Maureen, used to be an outgoing, free-spirited young woman. Apparently, Faith's parents dreamed of traveling the world.

"They're looking for me," Faith sighed as they strolled lazily. The sun caused sweat to drop down Faith's back, but she didn't care. Moving and breathing in the fresh air helped.

"How do you feel about that?"

"Scared."

"You're safe here, Faith. I won't let anything happen to you."

"You sound like Carmen." Faith smiled.

"Ah, yes, Carmen and Mateo. Tell me about them."

Faith's smile brightened when she thought of them. Mateo was her fairy godmother—his words—and Carmen was Faith's anchor.

"They live at the address I had for you in Seattle. When I turned up, Carmen could see I needed help. They took me in and... It's hard to explain what they've done for me."

"I'm glad you had them."

Faith's phone buzzed from her back pocket. Nathalie's name scrolled across the screen. As usual, Faith lost the ability to school her features. Her face heated when she saw Molly giving her a sly smile and side eye.

"I just..." Faith pointed to the phone.

"Go ahead. I'll mosey on over there," Molly chuckled, causing Faith to blush harder.

"Hey," she sighed into the phone. Nathalie's voice had a way of calming and exciting Faith in the same breath.

"Did you make it to California?"

"Oh crap, I'm sorry. I said I would message you. I totally spaced."

"Is she there?" Nathalie asked eagerly.

Faith smiled and looked over at her aunt, who had her face in a sunflower.

"Yeah, I found her, Nat. We've been talking for the past hour. It's been intense."

Nathalie let out a long breath. "Oh, thank God. I was so worried you'd be disappointed again. Faith, I'm so happy for you."

"Gosh, me too. I don't think I could've coped with another road trip, especially with that motley crew," Faith laughed. "Enid spent the entire trip...tripping." Faith grinned. "Mateo made all our ears bleed with his renditions of every Cher song ever released, and Carmen, well, I think she was as nervous as me."

"Those crazy cats," Nathalie laughed. "I miss you."

The change in Nathalie's tone made Faith's breath hitch. Their messages had grown more intimate over recent days. There hadn't been a particular catalyst to the change, just their ever-growing closeness.

One particular conversation stuck out. Faith was recounting the book she'd just finished. They were laughing because the book was one of Carmen's and they were still teenagers, embarrassed to talk about sex. But then, Nathalie asked Faith if there was anything in particular in the book she'd enjoyed.

There were one of two ways for Faith to interpret the question. First, Nathalie could have been asking about the plot. Faith was an avid reader and enjoyed storylines with complex characters. Second—and secretly what Faith hoped Nathalie was asking—was if any of the sex scenes appealed to her.

Risking embarrassment, Faith answered honestly. She said she enjoyed the scene in the shower, and that she thought it would be something she would enjoy.

Faith had come a long way in her *lesducation*. The idea of kissing a girl didn't send her into a panic attack. Nathalie was so open and caring, Faith had no problem talking about her lack of experience. To Faith's surprise,

Nathalie confessed to only ever having one girlfriend, and they'd never got as far as the bedroom.

So, if she and Nathalie wanted to take it there, they would be each other's first. Still, Faith would like them to have a first kiss before even considering taking their relationship to the next level.

Unfortunately, the timing was always off. Faith traveling around the country didn't help, and when they did have time alone, they were never *really* alone. Messaging and video calls were all they had at the moment, which was becoming increasingly frustrating.

"How's your day?" Faith asked. It felt dangerous to tell Nathalie just how much she missed her.

"Good, but it would be better if you were here."

Okay, so Nathalie wasn't going to make it easy for Faith.

To hell with it. "I miss you too, Nat. I..."

I want to kiss you so badly, feel your body close to mine.

"I want to kiss you, Faith. I can't believe I haven't been able to do that yet."

Oh boy. Faith peeked over her shoulder to check where Molly was. No way she wanted her estranged aunt listening in on this conversation.

Plucking up the courage, Faith dropped her voice, hoping it sounded sexy.

Ha, as if you know what sexy sounds like.

Faith rolled her eyes at herself. "There are a lot of things I can't believe I haven't gotten to do with you yet."

The tiny gasp from Nathalie was a victory worth savoring. Faith had to bite her lip to stop herself from laughing when Nathalie stuttered and cleared her throat.

"Faith, you...you can't say things like that, not when you're so far away."

"Why not?" Faith asked innocently.

"Because...because...I can't do anything about it."

"Would you...do something about it?"

"Would you want me to?"

Alright, so they still had a way to go in the communication department. Faith hoped they'd get to a point where neither of them felt so self-conscious and nervous.

"Yes, I would." Faith wanted Nathalie. She'd wanted the girl since spying her at the back of the bus.

"Well, hurry home then."

A bucket of ice would've served as less of a shock than Nathalie's words. Home. Where was that now? Faith had spent so long focused on finding Molly, she hadn't given a lot of thought to the 'after' part.

Several months ago, Faith would have said her home would be with Molly, but now? Carmen, Mateo, Nathalie, and Enid's faces swam in front of her eyes. They were a mishmash of people, but they were Faith's people. But what about Molly? They'd literally had an hour together, but Faith needed far more than that.

"Hey, where'd you go?" Nathalie's voice echoed over the line.

"I'm here," Faith replied weakly.

"Did I say something wrong?"

"Not at all, I suppose it just hit me I have some decisions to make."

Nathalie must have understood what Faith was thinking, because she went silent. Faith's decision affected Nathalie, too.

"Whatever you decide, I support you, Faith. You deserve to be happy."

Faith closed her eyes and willed herself not to cry. "I miss you so much."

"I miss you, too. Will you call me later?"

"Of course."

They said their goodbyes and Faith's heart cracked ever so slightly. The last thing she wanted to do was hurt anyone.

The ping of her phone drew Faith out of her head. Alice had sent a message asking if she was okay. Faith tried to keep Alice updated, but everything had been such a whirlwind she'd forgotten to let her best friend know where she was.

Firing off a quick reply, Faith shoved the phone back in her pocket. There was plenty of time for her to decide. Right now, Faith needed to take advantage of having Molly to herself for a little longer. They had so much to catch up on.

"Hey, sorry about that," Faith called, jogging over to Molly, who was sitting on the ground, her face raised to the sun.

"No worries. Someone special?" Molly grinned.

Faith scratched the back of her neck and scuffed her shoe across the ground. "Yeah, she's special."

"Girlfriend?"

"I'm not sure we're official," Faith laughed. "We met on a bus when I was traveling to Seattle. I think we spoke for like five minutes."

"Wow."

"Yeah, and then we met up again, completely by accident, at a Pride party. Nathalie is Rita's niece, and Rita is Carmen and Mateo's friend."

Molly laughed. "Jeez, small world, right?"

"Yeah." Faith smiled. "We just hit it off. She's so sweet."

"And cute, I'm guessing, by your blush."

"She's gorgeous."

Molly laughed. "Ah, to be young and in love."

"We can't be in love. We haven't even had a first kiss."

"Hey, the heart wants what the heart wants."

"I'm not sure it's my heart that's doing the talking," Faith muttered under her breath.

13

Carmen

oly hell in a handbasket. Molly Parsons was Hot with a capital H.

Yes, she looked like Faith, but there were subtle differences. Her figure was fuller, and her skin a golden brown from days spent under the sun. Her hair was a darker shade of blonde. Actually, it was more brown, and her eyes were closer to gray than blue.

It had taken all of Carmen's strength not to drool when they pulled up to the ranch. Molly was a sexy vision in her short denim cut-offs and yellow tank top. Thankfully, Faith was too preoccupied to notice Carmen's ogling of her aunt. Mateo, not so much. He'd noticed alright. Carmen was going to get ribbed as soon as they were out of earshot.

Until then, though, Carmen had to navigate standing in the ranch's kitchen surrounded by people she didn't know. Mateo had charged blindly inside to look for a bathroom. Enid had automatically started chatting with

Bessie, which left Carmen alone with two young women she didn't know the names of.

"Hey, I'm Carmen."

"Hi, I'm Lisa and this is Courtney."

Carmen caught the subtle heart-shaped eyes Courtney was throwing Lisa. Young love made Carmen's heart sing.

"Pretty nice place you have here."

"Oh, it's the best. Bessie and Molly are awesome," Courtney chimed.

"So, who else can we expect?" Carmen asked, hoping Mateo would come and save her soon. He was the social butterfly.

"There's Micah, who is at a job interview right now, and my brother Liam," Courtney answered, her eyes never straying too far from Lisa.

"That's better," Mateo sang as he strutted into the room.

Who knew you could strut in flip-flops?

"I was about to burst. Remind me not to take the extra shot next time, *hermana*."

"I told you not to this time."

"Hmm, anyway. Who are these two fabulous ladies?"

"Courtney and Lisa," Carmen replied, pointing to each girl, respectively.

"Mateo Ruiz, Esquire," Mateo announced.

"There is no esquire in your name," Carmen huffed playfully.

"Well, there should be."

"Are you two siblings?" Lisa asked, her face full of amusement.

"In every way that's important," Mateo answered as usual.

"And you know Faith?" Courtney asked.

"We do. It's a long story. I'm sure Faith would be happy to share once she's chatted with Molly."

"I can't believe Molly has a niece," Courtney mused, "and one that looks just like her."

"I take it you ladies know Molly well, then?" Mateo asked, dropping into the nearest chair, flinging one leg over the other, resting his hands on the top knee.

"Oh yeah, Molly is like... She's like family. Everyone who comes here loves her," Lisa replied.

"It's true. We love Molly and Bessie. I don't know what any of us would do without them."

"You'd be fine," Bessie answered, carrying a tray of lemonade over to the table. Enid stood beside her, cradling a cup of coffee. "You just needed a helping hand, but you're all survivors. We're proud of each one of you."

A lump formed in Carmen's throat. What she would have given to have had that kind of influence and support in her life, even if it had just been someone to chat with other than Mateo.

Her mind wandered to Camila Ruiz. What would have happened if she hadn't died? Would she have taken Mateo and Carmen in permanently? They'd gotten a brief glimpse of what a mother could be, only to have it cruelly ripped away.

"Ah shucks, Bessie, you're gonna make me cry," Courtney laughed.

"Wiseass," Bessie laughed. "Everyone, grab a drink. I'll make some sandwiches too."

"Please don't go to any trouble," Carmen interjected.

"No, please, go to trouble. I'm famished," Mateo added.

"That's because you loaded up on candy instead of actual food, *hermano*."

"Sorry, I forgot you were the candy police," Mateo scowled, then stuck his tongue out.

"You two are like children," Enid chimed.

"She started it," Mateo chuckled, causing Carmen to grin and flick his nose.

"You two are hella funny," Courtney giggled.

"So everyone says." Mateo grinned.

Bessie settled in the chair next to Mateo. "Enid, here, tells me you live in Molly's old house."

Carmen got the gist they might be here for some time, so she took a seat.

"Yeah, we didn't know that until Faith turned up. It's been an interesting few weeks."

"Hey, what's going on?"

Carmen looked up to identify where the deep voice came from. Standing in the entry doorway was a young man who resembled Courtney, but with a beard. No, not a beard. That was way too generous.

"Li, this is Carmen, Mateo, Enid, and outside with Molly, is Faith."

"Is Faith joining the house?" Liam asked.

"No, Faith is Molly's niece," Lisa added.

"Cool." That was as far as Liam's interest stretched by all accounts. "I'm gonna go play on the Xbox. Call when you want a hand with the laundry."

"Your twin, I gather," Carmen asked Courtney.

"Yeah, real bag of laughs, that one," she replied, shaking her head. "It's like puberty hit and turned him into a hungry hippo with a side of attitude."

Carmen laughed at the comparison. Mateo would never admit it, but that's what happened to him. Carmen couldn't keep food in the fridge longer than a couple of hours when he went through that stage. God knows how Bessie and Molly coped with four teenagers in the house.

"Everyone goes through puberty differently," Bessie softly chastised.

"Well, if he ever wants to get laid, he needs to chill the fuck out," Courtney stated.

"Dear Lord," Bessie sighed. Everyone else laughed.

When the coast was clear, Carmen leaned over to Mateo. "Do you think Faith is okay?"

"I'm sure she's fine, Carm. Don't worry. They need a bit of time to adjust and talk. Faith's come a long way."

"Oh, I think my gummies are finally wearing off," Enid interrupted. "Those green little shits are potent."

"You have gummies?" Bessie asked.

"Oh yes, want one?"

"I'll take you up on that later. As soon as the gang clears out."

"Excellent, I'll join you."

"Um, Enid, we need to find a place to stay for the night. You need to stay reasonably sober."

"Nonsense, you're staying right here," Bessie exclaimed, as if Carmen had just said the stupidest thing possible. "We have two extra rooms and the couch pulls out."

Carmen was grateful for the warm welcome, but she was also aware things with Molly might not go how Faith planned, and if that happened, staying in the same house wouldn't be appropriate.

"Stop worrying," Mateo whispered. "It will be fine. Please, *hermana*, relax."

The sound of tires on the gravel pulled everyone's attention. In strolled a very dapper young man. His hair was pitch black and swept stylishly back.

"Hello everyone. I didn't know we were having guests, Bess."

"Micah, how did the interview go?"

"Nailed it." He grinned. "I start next week."

Rapturous applause broke out, as Lisa, Courtney, and Bessie swarmed Micah. Carmen and Mateo exchanged a smile.

"That's it. We need to celebrate Micah's new job and Molly meeting her niece," Bessie sang.

"Molly has a niece?" Micah asked.

"Yeah, long story." Carmen smiled. "Hi, I'm Carmen and this is my brother Mateo."

"Hey, nice to meet you."

"What am I? Chopped liver?" Enid barked. "I'm Enid Butcher. Pleasure to make your acquaintance, young man."

"You too," Micah laughed. "I'm Micah, they/them."

"Alright, how does pizza sound this evening?" Bessie asked. A deafening round of agreement echoed through the kitchen. "Lovely. Now you all get your chores done. Let us old folks have a quiet five minutes."

The three teens smiled, kissed Bessie on the cheek, and waved goodbye.

"They seem like great kids," Mateo remarked.

"They are. All of them have done so well. You wouldn't have recognized Micah if you'd met them when they first turned up."

"Are the kids referred?"

"Yes, we work with a couple of shelters in the city. We do what we can, but there is always more demand than we can accommodate. That's the part of this job I hate." Bessie rapped her knuckles on the table. "But we do what we can, and for kids like those four, it's worth the heartache."

"You're doing a fantastic job. If we hadn't been there to take Faith in, I hope she would have been able to find a place like this," Carmen said sincerely.

Carmen hated the thought of Faith being anywhere but with them. That led her thoughts to Molly and the time she must have spent in shelters after her brother disowned her. Reaching out instinctively, Carmen took Mateo's hand. It was times like this she was so grateful to have him by her side.

"Thanks, sweetheart. It's nice to hear sometimes."

"How are those sandwiches coming along?" Mateo asked, earning a slap upside the head from Enid.

The sandwiches were eaten, and the kitchen tidied. Carmen and Mateo accepted a tour around the house from Micah, who kept looking at Mateo's ass every five seconds.

Keep dreaming, Micah.

With the sun setting, Carmen got antsy again. Molly and Faith were still outside talking. Carmen spotted them walking through one of the fields earlier. They seemed to be doing okay. Faith's body language was relaxed. If only Carmen could feel the same.

As the pizza delivery guy dropped off eight large pizzas, Faith and Molly finally came inside. Both faces showed signs of crying. Carmen swiftly made her way to Faith.

"Hey, you okay?"

Faith pulled Carmen into a fierce hug. "I'm great. Thank you, Carmen, for keeping your promise."

"You're welcome, kid." Carmen smiled, her chin resting on Faith's head. Molly stood a few feet away, smiling, and Carmen felt her belly tingle.

"Alright guys, let's get some food in our stomachs," Bessie shouted over the din.

Chairs scraped and plates clanged as they all dug into the food. Carmen sat next to Faith. Maybe she should have let Molly sit next to her, but selfishly, Carmen needed to be close to Faith, just in case.

If Molly was put out, she didn't show it. In fact, the woman made a beeline for Enid. They embraced each other tightly and began chatting.

Conversation flowed between the mix of people. Faith quickly got into a discussion about music with Lisa. Carmen had to stuff down the chuckle she felt when she caught Courtney scowling at the two girls talking without her.

Oh dear, there's some lesbian drama on the horizon.

As soon as the last piece of pizza was claimed, Enid stood from her seat.

"I'm taking Bessie out to the porch. Us seniors need a break." Enid winked, kissing Molly on the cheek.

"Hey, do you want to come and chill for a bit?" Lisa asked Faith.

"Sure," she replied, looking at Carmen for reassurance.

"Go for it. I'll help clear up. You go relax."

"You're the best, Carm."

"I'm going to take a shower and then hit the hay," Mateo whispered into Carmen's ear. His eyes darted between her and Molly, which was weird. Well, Carmen thought so anyway.

Once the masses cleared out, she suddenly felt nervous. Molly was clearing the table, and Carmen couldn't help but watch just for a minute. The gentle sway of Molly's hips was almost hypnotizing.

What is wrong with me?

Leering after a woman wasn't Carmen's style, so why was she finding it so hard to tear her eyes away from Molly, a woman she didn't know?

"Want a beer?"

Molly's sudden proximity to Carmen's ear made her jump.

"Shit," Carmen exhaled, her heart rocketing inside her chest.

"Sorry," Molly giggled, "I didn't mean to scare you."

"No, it's all good. I spaced out and didn't hear you approach."

Didn't hear you approach? What is she, a fucking wild animal? Christ, Carmen, get your shit together.

Molly wiggled the cold beer bottle she was holding. "So...drink?"

"Sure, that would be great, thanks."

"Want to sit out back? I'll leave Bessie and Enid to the front porch. I don't want to know what kind of trouble those pair are going to get into."

Carmen chuckled. "Yeah, I'm not sure it's a good idea we let them become friendly."

Molly tipped her head towards the kitchen door that led to the backyard. "This way."

Carmen followed a few paces behind because she couldn't stop being a creep and Molly's ass in those shorts was criminal.

I need to call Rachel when I get home!

Molly settled down on the grass and looked up at the darkening sky. Carmen mirrored her actions. They fell silent for a few minutes.

"Thank you," Molly began, "for being there, for Faith."

Carmen glanced over at Molly. "It's no problem. She's a great kid."

"She is..." Molly trailed off. "I can't believe I never knew about her."

"Would you have done things differently if you had known?"

"I want to say yes, but honestly, I don't know. There's no way I could have ever moved back, not without Alan accepting me. But..."

"But?"

"I would have made sure I was there for her. She must have felt so alone all those years."

"Faith is a strong girl. Well, young woman. What she went through was pretty terrible, but she coped and she did the right thing by staying as long as she did. Trust me,

I wanted to find your brother and rip him a new asshole when I heard how he behaved."

"I... He was so different. I honestly thought he would come around at some point."

"The important thing is Faith. She's safe now, but Molly, you have to be prepared for Alan to come looking for her."

"Yeah, Faith told me he'd already turned up in Seattle. He doesn't know this place, though. I hadn't gotten around to writing to him and giving him this address."

"Can I ask—"

"Why do I keep writing to him?"

Carmen nodded. It made little sense to her. Not when she'd done her level best to keep people at bay, even the nice ones. Why would Molly willingly invite that kind of person into her life?

"After our parents died, he was all I had. I think I clung to the guy he was before my life turned to shit. By holding onto that version of him, I kept my parents close. I know they wouldn't want me to give up on him, but now? Now I've heard the things he's done to Faith, and to Maureen, and I think I finally have to let that version of my brother go."

The overwhelming desire to pull Molly into a hug almost became too much. Just like Faith, Carmen wanted to keep her safe.

"I won't offer unsolicited advice about any of that. It's up to you to decide. Just know you have someone to talk to if you want. Faith means a lot to me and Mateo. We're happy to be there for you, too."

Molly's gaze finally dropped from the sky and Carmen felt those gunmetal eyes bore into her.

"You're a good woman, Carmen Ruiz."

Oh mama! Molly saying Carmen's full name, all quiet and whispery, was not helping Carmen resolve to stop being a pervy perv about Faith's aunt.

"Thanks, but I like to think most people would have done what we did."

"I would like to think that too, but we both know the world isn't like that."

"Can I ask how you coped?"

"Not sure I did," Molly laughed. "I was a mess for a while. There were some hairy moments. A young girl on her own, with no money or place to stay."

Carmen shook her head. That same anger she felt when Faith explained her situation when they first met, began boiling to the surface again.

"Asshole," she hissed, conjuring a mental image of Faith's father.

"Thankfully, I met a group of kids on the street who helped me out. I got into a shelter. After that, I moved from city to city when I could. I found under-the-table cash jobs to fund my way. I knew I wanted to work in the shelters. They gave me my life back by keeping me safe."

"Yeah, um...Ruth said you were passionate about your work."

Why was she bringing up Molly's ex?

"Oh, of course, I didn't think about the fact that you would've met Ruth. Do you think I'm a monster?"

"For what? Following your heart?"

"Ruth wanted to be the one that had my heart," Molly sighed. "I loved her, but she..."

"Wasn't the one," Carmen answered.

"I've always said I would know the right woman for me because I'd feel safe and at home. I didn't have that with Ruth, even though she did everything possible to make me feel that way. I don't know, something was missing."

"I get it. Really, I do."

They fell silent again. Carmen hadn't meant for the conversation to wade into such deep waters.

"I'm sorry," Carmen said after a few more silent minutes. "You don't know me and here I am getting all up in your business."

Molly chuckled. "It's fine. It's been a while since I've had someone to talk to, apart from Bessie. And I know we've only just met, but we have Faith in common. I think we're going to become friends."

Carmen's belly clenched at the thought of growing closer to Molly. Her heart also ached at the thought of losing Faith. They were a unit now. She needed to talk to Mateo.

"I think I'm going to head in," she whispered, not wanting to disturb the peacefulness of the night.

"Good night, Carmen," Molly replied with a sweet smile.

"Good night, Molly Parsons. I'm glad we finally found you."

14

Molly

To quote Dinah Washington: What a difference a day makes!

Yesterday, Molly spent the day by herself, pondering life and all the things that had happened and what could have been. Now, she was processing the fact she had a niece—a gay niece—who'd suffered at the hands of the brother she'd hoped and prayed would change his ways. Nope, that wasn't going to happen and Molly needed to rearrange her way of thinking.

After hours of talking to Faith, Molly was sure of one thing: If Alan and Maureen found them, Molly wouldn't be looking for a reunion. She'd done her part. There was no way their parents would've put up with Alan's actions towards his daughter and wife.

Standing, Molly shook out her arms and legs. There was a reason she only let herself mull over all her personal baggage on her birthday. Molly was inherently an upbeat, positive person, and that was due to limiting her personal pondering. If she allowed her brain to continue chewing over everything like this, she'd become a depressed husk of a person.

She'd done enough ruminating and questioning. There was plenty of time for that on her next birthday.

The sound of laughter drew Molly back to the present. Bessie and Enid were still on the front porch, obviously having a great time. Seeing her old neighbor again was right up there with finding out she had a niece.

Enid Butcher was one of the best people she knew. She was also one of the most interesting. Molly met Enid the first day she'd moved into the Seattle rental. It was a fortuitous meeting and one that Molly treasured to this day.

Enid acted as her surrogate grandmother and Molly returned the sentiment, looking out for the woman as she would have with her own grandparents.

"... And there he was, in his birthday suit with a pool noodle and an Alpaca," Enid roared, her entire body shaking. Bessie was doubled over, tears streaming down her face. Molly wondered what the hell she'd just walked in on. Maybe she should turn around and find something else to occupy her—

"Hey, Mol, come and grab a seat," Bessie wheezed. "You have to hear this story."

Smiling, Molly sank into the bean bag nestled next to the porch bench. "I don't think I want to know," she chuckled.

"Want a gummy?"

Enid and her friggin' gummies.

"No thanks, I'm good."

"You're *looking* good, dear. It seems California is suiting you."

"You've already said that," Molly laughed. "We had an entire conversation over pizza."

"Well, I wasn't three gummies deep at that point."

"Hey, how's that neighbor? You know, the one who likes to get kinky with her husband."

Molly and Enid had taken part in several hours of covert surveillance once Enid spied her neighbor's affinity for dressing her husband up in her clothes.

"Well, she's still at it, but now she makes the poor man wear her stilettos. You remember the size of him, right?"

Molly burst out laughing. "Oh God, he's going to injure himself," she cackled.

"I sure hope they have good medical insurance."

"I think I want to live with you," Bessie giggled, pointing at Enid. "You seem to have all the fun."

"Oh, it was much better when this one lived next door," Enid commented, throwing her thumb to one side, pointing at Molly.

"What about Carmen and Mateo?" Bessie asked, thus saving Molly from attempting to subtly inquire about Carmen.

"I only met them when Faith turned up. Oh, don't get me wrong, I'd been spying on them for months," Enid grinned, "But they kept themselves, to themselves."

"Not very neighborly," Bessie remarked.

"I don't think it was that. I think they've been through some god-awful shit and are careful about who they hang around," Enid said matter-of-factly. "Mateo is a sweet man. Gayer than a unicorn on steroids, mind you, and hopelessly in love with the pizza delivery man. I've gotten to know him well on this little adventure. It's my guess he will eventually ask Daniel out on an actual date and that will be that. Mateo is looking for his forever love."

"And Carmen?" Molly inquired.

"Now, she's a different matter. It's not really my place to tell you about their background. I'm sure I only know the basics, but from what I gather, Carmen is super careful around everyone. She's guarded and very protective of Mateo. I think I've seen her with one or two women, but none of them stick around, or she doesn't let them."

"You got all that from looking out your window?" Bessie laughed.

"It's amazing the shit you pick up just by watching," Enid answered, side-eying Molly, which was strange. "I told Carmen I thought you and her would hit it off."

"I'm sorry, what?" Molly spluttered. Surely she'd misheard.

"You would. I think you two would balance each other out wonderfully. She's all deep and guarded. You're light and outgoing. Yes, definitely a good match, and can you imagine the babies you would make?"

"Enid!" Molly chastised, completely shocked at where the conversation had ended up.

Okay, so Molly may have a *slight* curiosity towards Carmen. From the moment Molly laid eyes on the woman, she was intrigued. First, because Carmen had so selflessly offered Faith help. Actually, Carmen and Mateo had gone above and beyond for Molly's niece. Second, because Carmen had caught her eye, in the physical sense. To put it bluntly, Carmen was hot. She was tall, athletically built, and her hair was thick and luscious. Molly also couldn't forget those big brown eyes.

Whoa, mama.

"I can see that," Bessie casually added after a beat of silence.

"Bessie!"

"Oh, calm your tits, Mol," Enid tutted. "I know a good match when I see one."

"Sure, we would look striking together."

Yes, we would!

"But we literally just met a few hours ago. Oh, and I live in California and she lives in Seattle. And you have no idea if she is seeing someone, or for that matter, if I'm seeing someone."

"Are you?"

"Well, not seriously," Molly mumbled.

"Chelsea doesn't count as dating," Bessie huffed.

"Who's Chelsea?" Enid asked.

"A friend," Molly answered.

"They bang now and then," Bessie supplied.

"Jesus, Bessie."

"What? You do. But let's be honest, you're not into her like that."

"How do *you* know?" Molly asked indignantly.

"For starters, you've told me enough times, and because you, my dear, will settle down with 'the one' and no one else."

"Ah, yes, I see that," Enid chimed in.

"I'm not settling down. Ruth wanted that, not me. I like my freedom."

Molly was so full of shit, but for some reason she continued to argue her point.

"Horseshit," Enid barked, then laughed. "You need a woman who makes you feel like you've come home. When that person comes along, you'll settle."

"Oh, because you guys know me so well. We've known each other for what...a few years? That doesn't mean you're experts."

"We know you well enough to understand that when you get defensive like this, it's because you don't want to admit the truth yet...which is fine."

Molly sat, stunned, her eyes shooting from Bessie to Enid. Both women had a satisfied smile on their faces.

"Whatever," Molly grumbled, snatching a gummy from Enid's open palm.

"Are you at the high school tomorrow?" Bessie asked, breaking the awkward silence.

"Yes. I thought about taking Faith with me."

"What's happening at the high school?" Enid asked.

"I've been asked to give a talk about being young and queer."

"Are you still classed as 'young' in your thirties?" Bessie grinned.

"No," Molly laughed. "But I'm the only one willing to do it. That's why I want Faith with me. Maybe she'll earn me some street cred."

"Maybe stop saying *street cred,* first of all. That's uncool now, Molly," Enid said rolling her eyes at Molly's obvious faux pas.

"Maybe I should take *you*?" Molly quipped.

"They ain't ready for me, kid," Enid stated seriously.

Molly wholeheartedly agreed. Most fully formed *adults* weren't ready for Enid Butcher.

"I think Faith would love to go," Bessie added. "I've not had much of a chance to talk to her, but she's clearly interested in this place, and getting to know you."

"She sure has gone through a lot to find you," Enid stated.

"Yeah, she has," Molly began. "But now I want to help her move past the bullshit in Kentucky and look forward to her future."

"Carmen and Mateo have set her on the right track. You should have seen the poor girl when she first turned up. I thought I'd taken too many gummies and was tripping."

"What do you mean?" Bessie chuckled.

"Think *Little House on the Prairie* or *The Waltons*, and that's what Faith looked like. I half expected her to start milking a cow in the front yard."

"She was a disaster," Mateo said from the doorway. All three women turned. Molly grinned at Mateo's nearly six-foot frame wrapped in a silk robe. His hair was still perfectly coiffed.

"Thought you went to bed?" Enid asked.

"I couldn't sleep, and Carmen is like a goddamn elephant when she gets into bed."

"Is she still up there?" Enid inquired.

"She jumped in the shower after I beat the crap out of her for waking me up. She knows I need my beauty sleep."

"You need a gummy," Enid said, holding out her palm.

"Are you, like, the oldest drug dealer?" Bessie laughed.

"It's legal. And let's be honest...kids these days need to chill out."

"You're chill enough for all of us," Mateo commented, but took the offered gummy and sat himself down next to Enid, crossing his legs. "So, Molly, how are you feeling after today?"

"It's been...unreal, to be honest. I'm beyond happy she sought me out."

"And your brother?"

"That's going to take some time to filter through the ol' noggin," Molly laughed. "It's more important that I get to know my niece and support her."

"Carmen's taken a real shine to her," Mateo said, a hint of protectiveness in his voice.

"So have you," Enid added.

"Yeah, that's fair."

"I can't thank you both enough, really. You've been a godsend. I won't presume to know what Faith wants to do next. From what she was telling me, you and Carmen have helped her set up a life for herself in Seattle."

"She needed a little guidance, is all. As soon as we did a makeover, that girl took off. Her confidence soared." Mateo smiled wistfully.

"Well, from what I know, you provided her with everything she needed, so thank you."

"We're in her life now. No matter what she wants to do or where she wants to live, she's a Ruiz."

Molly smiled widely. Faith really had found the best people possible to help her out. The affection in Mateo's eyes was palpable, which led Molly to question if she would be seeing a lot more of Carmen and Mateo in the future.

"You guys are so noisy," Carmen yawned.

Molly looked over her shoulder and nearly choked on her tongue. Carmen's hair was piled up on top of her head, showing off an undercut.

Holy hell!

The hair, along with Carmen in boxer briefs and a tank top, was a vision of pure eroticism. Molly squirmed in her seat and forced herself to look away. The smirk on Enid's face pissed her off because she knew she'd been caught drooling.

"*We're* noisy?" Mateo laughed sardonically. "Carmen, you woke me up through earplugs when you stomped your way into the room."

"You're so dramatic, *hermano*," Carmen tutted. "You weren't asleep, because you didn't sound like a jackhammer."

"I do not snore!" Mateo shrieked.

"Mateo, seriously, we're having this argument again?"

"Are they always like this?" Molly whispered to Enid.

"Yup, it's very entertaining. Especially high."

"I have sinus issues," Mateo argued.

"I thought you didn't snore?" Carmen asked pointedly.

"And I thought we had agreed you wouldn't be seen out in public looking like *that*?" Mateo shot.

"Mateo, not all of us feel the need to dress like a French hooker to go to bed."

"That is *so* insulting! I'm a French *Madam*—there *is* a difference, you know."

Mateo and Carmen both stared at each other before falling into laughter. Molly couldn't help but join in. Bessie shuffled inside and brought out a tray of beer.

"Might as well have a drink. It's only us adults," she said, passing out the bottles.

Carmen settled next to Molly, which was awkward because Molly's eyes kept involuntarily traveling to Carmen's long caramel legs.

They look so soft.

"What is it that you do?" Molly asked Carmen. Enid and Bessie were busy discussing French whores.

"I'm in graphic design."

"Cool."

Oh Molly, come on, you can do better than that.

"So who do you work for, or are you freelance?"

"I own two companies, but I prefer the design side of things rather than managerial."

"Wow, okay, that's impressive. You're like what? Thirty?"

"Yes, I am definitely thirty. Let's stick to that," Carmen laughed.

"Oh, come on, you can't be much older, right?"

"Thirty-seven. But I like your guess better."

There is no way Molly would have put Carmen close to forty.

Jesus, what the hell kind of skin care routine does she have?

"I can see what you're thinking and yes, it is due to a skin care routine. One that is forced upon me by that butthole over there," Carmen said, pointing with her bottle to Mateo, who was currently in the middle of doing a Cher impression.

Qué sorpresa.

"He forces you to look after your skin," Molly laughed.

"Yes, since we were kids. I'm happy to wash with soap and maybe stick a bit of moisturizer on once a day, but

Queer Eye throws a hissy fit if he doesn't get to perform weekly facials. We would be millionaires if he stopped buying skin and hair products."

"I have to say, looking at you, I think I have to agree with him. Your skin looks amazing."

Molly saw a slight blush creep over Carmen's face, and for some odd reason, she felt proud.

"Don't let him know you think that. I'll never hear the last of it," Carmen smiled, bumping Molly's shoulder.

"Your secrets are safe with me... If—"

"If?"

"You tell me what brands he uses."

"Shit, um, one is white with a blue logo," Carmen began. Molly threw her head back, laughing. Every pair of eyes on the porch turned in her direction.

"You can't be serious," Molly cackled, ignoring Enid and Bessie's not-so-subtle interest.

"If I learn what the brands are, it encourages him more," Carmen laughed.

"What's going on over there?" Enid called.

"Nothing, keep your beak out of it," Molly shot back playfully, knowing her refusal to answer would drive Enid and Bessie nuts.

"Charming," Enid huffed.

A chime from Molly's phone interrupted their conversation. Molly saw Carmen turn her head away, but she was sure she'd seen Chelsea's name on the message. It was definitely not PG-rated. Shit.

"Excuse me," Molly mumbled to Carmen, eager to get out of viewing range. Standing alone, leaning against the porch railings, Molly typed a reply to Chelsea. The gist of Chelsea's message was that she desired a booty call. Molly did not.

Bessie's voice echoed in her ears. Chelsea was just a friend, and they weren't dating, and Molly wanted nothing else from their arrangement. Actually, she wasn't sure the "friends with benefits" agreement suited her needs anymore.

After the brief conversation Molly had with Carmen earlier, the one where she pretty much told a complete stranger she wanted to find a woman who made her feel at home, the thought of casually hooking up with Chelsea—well, anyone—turned her stomach sour.

Molly'd lied when she'd told Bessie and Enid it was just Ruth who wanted to settle down. Molly had those dreams, but she wasn't prepared to fulfill those dreams with anyone less than her soulmate. Was that too much to ask?

Was she being unrealistic? Possibly, but it didn't stop her from wanting it.

A difficult conversation with Chelsea loomed on Molly's horizon. She'd been foolish to get involved with Chelsea so soon after Ruth. Now, Molly was certain she was about to lose a friend. Chelsea wanted a girlfriend. That was plain to see.

Sagging her shoulders in defeat, Molly typed out a quick reply, asking Chelsea for a rain check. But it wouldn't be a booty call; it would be Molly putting a stop to their bedroom antics.

As soon as the screen read *sent*, Molly peered over her shoulder. Carmen quickly dropped her gaze from Molly's ass. A lightness bloomed in Molly's chest. Were Enid and Bessie right? Would she and Carmen make a good couple?

You have literally just sent a message asking your current fuck buddy to talk. How about you sort out that shitstorm first, before trying to mix up another one?

"I'm heading up. The day has suddenly caught up with me," Molly announced to the group, unable to look Carmen in the eye.

"Alright, dear, see you in the morning," Bessie called, blowing her a kiss goodnight.

Mateo, Enid and Carmen all said good night in chorus. Making her way up the stairs, Molly paused outside the kids' rooms. Opening their doors, she took a second just to look at them, making sure they were safe and sound.

Tiptoeing over to the room where Faith was sleeping, Molly cracked the door and peered in. It was astonishing how alike she and Faith were. They both had the habit of sleeping on their backs with one foot hanging out of the covers, by the looks of it. The sight of Faith sleeping warmed Molly's entire body.

I need to stop thinking about relationships and focus on what's important. Faith. She deserves all my attention.

Resolved to put women to the back of her mind, Molly closed the door and headed to bed. Tomorrow was a new day. The sun would rise and the birds would sing. And Molly would have the chance to build a family with Faith.

15

Faith

Waking up to the sun shining through the windows was a pleasant break from Seattle's gray skies. It must have been around 3 a.m. before Faith could finally sleep. The sound of adrenaline-infused, raucous laughter coming from Bessie and Enid made sleeping before then impossible.

Faith rolled over and stared out of the window. As much as she wanted to process meeting her aunt, there was something else on her mind: Nathalie.

After their brief conversation yesterday, the pair had continued to message throughout the day and night. Even when Faith was being entertained by Courtney and Lisa, her mind, and often her gaze, wandered at the thought of her girlfriend.

That's what they were now—girlfriends. They'd labeled the relationship last night.

Out of their many messages, one of them kept Faith up, thinking. Discussing the book Faith read seemed to have propelled them to another level in the relationship.

So far, Faith didn't know when they would get to see each other again, so calls and messages were all they had. Something new and exciting was stirring in Faith, and after last night's string of texts, she wanted to do something about it.

It wasn't that easy. Well, not for her. A lifetime of being taught a woman's pleasure was sinful, tended to make a lasting impression. But Faith couldn't ignore her body any longer.

Every time she closed her eyes, she saw Nathalie. Her dreams were becoming more and more vivid. This morning, Faith had woken with a start. Her skin was flushed and she was panting. If she'd just stayed sleeping for a second longer, she would have surely experienced her first orgasm.

Wiggling her butt, Faith felt the evidence of her arousal between her thighs. Her mind was warring with her body and with the voice she always heard, repeating how wrong it was to want to touch herself.

Grabbing her phone, Faith opened the last message Nathalie had sent. It was a picture of Nathalie's torso. A sliver of Nathalie's pink lace bra was visible at the top of the picture. Faith hadn't felt confident enough to send one back, but that was okay. Nathalie said she didn't have to do anything. She'd said she wanted to show Faith what was waiting for her when she got back to Seattle.

Faith's breathing hitched at the sight of Nathalie's tanned abs. Looking from the picture to the bedroom door, Faith made a decision. Scurrying over to the door, she flipped the lock. The bed was warm when she got back in, pulling the sheet up and over her head.

"It's natural," she whispered to herself as she slid her panties down. "You're not a sin," she said, a little stronger.

Faith had come such a long way. She was damned if she was going to listen to that godforsaken voice in her head for a second longer.

Propping her phone against her leg, Faith let her hand wander. Closing her eyes, she took a couple of steadying breaths. Before her fingers could move past her belly button, her phone rang.

"Crap," she hissed.

"Hi, hello," she answered.

"Hey, sorry, did I wake you?" Nathalie asked.

"No, nope, I'm awake."

"Are you alright? You sound flustered."

Faith *was* flustered. She was about to do something to herself for the first time, while thinking about Nathalie, and Nathalie had called. How else was she supposed to feel?

"I'm fine."

"Shit, did I freak you out with that picture?"

Faith smiled. She should have known Nathalie would worry about that. A burst of confidence washed over her. If Nathalie could put herself out there again, so could Faith.

"I was...I was just thinking about that picture," she whispered.

"Oh, um, were they good thoughts?"

"Very, I...I was about to..."

Oh damn, this was difficult. Faith desperately wanted to be sexy and alluring, but she felt far from it. What in the world did Nathalie see in her?

"About to what, Faith? What were you going to do?" Nathalie's voice was low and gravelly.

"I was going to touch myself," Faith stuttered.

"Oh fuck," Nathalie growled. "Are you still in bed?"

"Yes."

"Hold on, give me two seconds."

Faith listened. It sounded as if Nathalie was running, her breaths coming faster. Faith heard a door close and then there was a lot of rustling.

"I want to do it with you," Nathalie panted.

Faith closed her eyes and bit her lip. Yes, this was much better.

"Okay," she gasped, her excitement already building. Was that normal?

The sound of Nathalie popping a button and sliding a zipper down made Faith's heart pound.

"I...I've never done this before."

"That's okay, I'll guide you."

"Yes, I'd like that."

"I think you would also like it if you close your eyes and imagine that I'm there with you."

"Yes," Faith sighed.

"My hand is your hand, okay? Every time you touch yourself, it's my hand," Nathalie purred.

"What about you?" Faith asked.

"I can feel you here with me, Faith. Your hand is running over my nipple."

Faith groaned. "Yes, I want to feel you."

Lost in their imaginary world, Faith let herself drift into pleasure, Nathalie's voice guiding her. The first time her fingers dipped into her folds, Faith almost cried in sheer relief. The soft tones of Nathalie's voice and moans urged her on.

Nathalie told her what to do, and yet Faith didn't feel instructed. Instead of being in her own head, worrying about the act she was performing, Faith basked in the knowledge that Nathalie was there, doing this very intimate thing with her. And, by the sounds emanating from Nathalie, she was enjoying it as much as Faith.

"I want you to rub a little harder, Faith," Nathalie panted. Faith, happy to oblige, picked up the pace.

"Oh, oh..." Faith mumbled. There was a storm gathering in her abdomen. Electricity surged through her clit as she continued her ministrations. "Nat," she gasped.

"Yes, that's it, Faith, feel me touching you."

"I'm... Oh, wow. Oh..." Faith's back arched, her head slamming into the pillow as an all-consuming force of pure pleasure unleashed itself upon every part of her body. The distant cries of Nathalie's orgasm added wonderful background music as Faith rode her climax.

Minutes must have passed before Faith fell back to earth. Everything felt different.

"Faith?" Nathalie whispered, her voice sounding awestruck.

"I'm here," Faith replied, panting.

"Are you okay?"

"I'm wonderful," she sighed. "Thank you, Nat."

"It was literally my pleasure," Nat chuckled, causing Faith to giggle.

"I can't believe we did that," Faith mused.

"Do you regret it?"

"No, it was perfect."

"Perfect will be when we can do it together, in the same bed."

"I can't wait."

Was the sun brighter? The air clearer? The birds were definitely singing louder, right?

Faith was floating on an orgasm-shaped cloud as she descended the stairs to join Carmen and the gang in the kitchen for breakfast.

"Morning all," she singsonged, earning confused looks from Carmen, Mateo, and Enid. Molly offered her a sweet smile.

"Sleep well?" Molly asked.

"Like a log. Where did you sleep, Enid?"

"On the porch with Bessie. Got a little hammered and couldn't crawl into the house. Was a great night. I can't remember the last time I saw so many stars. Plus, I was high enough to see other stuff too, so that was cool."

Faith stood for a second and let that conversation sink in. "Well...um, that's awesome."

"Hey, are you coming to the high school with us today?" Micah asked, their mouth full of bacon.

"Micah, seriously, keep your trap shut when you're eating," Courtney grimaced.

"What's going on at the high school?" Faith asked, helping herself to a glass of OJ.

"Molly's doing a talk," Lisa answered.

"Oh cool, yeah, I'd love to go along if that's okay?" Faith directed her question at Molly, who beamed back.

"Absolutely. You're all welcome to tag along."

"Carmen?" Bessie chirped, "Are you up for it?"

"Oh, um...yeah, sure."

Faith narrowed her eyes. Something was off with Carmen. They may not have known each other for long, but Faith was pretty attuned to Carmen's body language.

Why were Carmen's eyes flicking from the table to Molly?

Hm, Interesting.

Faith regarded Molly, who was hellbent on avoiding looking at Carmen.

Now, Faith was a sexual novice of the lowest order, but even she could recognize sexual tension, and if she wasn't mistaken, that tension was bouncing all around Molly and Carmen.

"I'm going to stay here and prepare for this evening," Mateo announced, pulling Faith's attention back to the room.

"What's happening tonight?"

Faith had clearly missed everything while she'd been upstairs... Faith shook her head, willing her cheeks to remain pale. Sitting at the kitchen table with a bunch of people was not the time to be reminiscing over her first foray into masturbation.

"Makeovers for everyone," he squealed. Carmen rolled her eyes. Courtney, Lisa, and Micah cheered. Liam looked horrified. Molly laughed, along with Bessie and Enid.

"Awesome," Faith cheered.

"Can you be ready in half an hour?" Molly asked.

"Sure, no worries."

Cramming breakfast down her throat, Faith ran upstairs, showered, and dressed. Her fingers itched to message Nathalie, but now that she knew where those messages could lead, she restrained herself, vowing to call her girlfriend as soon as they got back from the high school.

Sitting in the passenger seat of Carmen's car, Faith smiled as they traveled. It really was a wonderful day.

"You look happy, kid," Carmen remarked, her eyes flitting from the road to Faith.

"I am."

"So, meeting Molly is everything you hoped it would be?"

Molly, right, of course. That's why Carmen would think Faith was as happy as a kid in a candy store.

"Yeah, Molly seems great," she spluttered, feeling guilty. Carmen, Mateo, and Enid had all given up their time to help Faith find and connect with her aunt, and here she was thinking of her girlfriend and all the things she wanted to try with Nathalie.

Selfish! You're selfish, Faith!

"Hey, what's that look about?" Carmen's eyes crinkled with concern.

"Nothing, I'm fine."

"Faith?"

"I was feeling guilty because as much as my happiness today, *is* over finding Molly, it isn't completely about that."

"Okay, why would that make you feel guilty?"

"Because you guys took time away from work to help get me here and I'm in my head thinking about…"

"Ah, thinking about a cute girl, right?" Carmen laughed.

"Yeah," Faith chuckled.

"Sweetie, you don't have to feel guilty for being happy, no matter what the cause of that happiness is. I think you know as well as I do, in this life, you gotta take what you can get where happiness is concerned."

Faith mulled over Carmen's words, wanting to question her friend's ability to take her own advice, but she didn't.

"Things with Nat…um…progressed," Faith stuttered.

Surely average teenagers wouldn't be caught dead trying to have this conversation with an adult, but Faith needed it. There had never been someone she could open up to and ask the awkward questions.

Carmen felt steady. She was a person Faith knew she could talk to about anything. Molly was the same, although their relationship still needed a little more time to develop before she felt able to go *there* with her aunt. Thank God Faith and Carmen were following behind Molly in a separate car.

"Progressed as in…"

"Um, well…we did some stuff over the phone."

"Stuff? Are you saying you had phone sex?" Carmen's voice squeaked a little, but Faith could see the woman was trying her hardest to remain cool and collected.

"I suppose so, yeah."

"And…um…how do you feel about it? You weren't pressured, were you?"

"God, no, I started it."

Carmen laughed. "Well, alright then."

"We've been getting closer recently. Um, our chats have become more intimate, and I started having dreams."

"It might have been back in the Stone Age, but I remember those times," Carmen winked.

"Did you find it embarrassing?"

"Well, I was living with Mateo. What do you think?" she laughed. "I think we all feel that level of embarrassment when we begin to feel sexual. It's a weird transition."

"Before I did that with Nathalie, I hadn't even…um, masturbated before."

"Not everyone feels comfortable doing that, Faith. It's nothing to be ashamed of."

"That's not what was making me feel ashamed." Faith's teeth worried her bottom lip. "I was told it was a sin to do that."

"Ah," Carmen sighed. "So, how is it sitting with you after the fact?"

"Better than I thought. Before Nathalie called me, I was thinking about it and I had this voice in my head telling me I was wrong to have those urges. But...then I talked to her, and we did it together. Nothing felt wrong to me."

"That's because it wasn't, Faith. I know how experiences in your past can leave scars. It still takes me a little time to move past certain things. Maybe I will never fully leave it all behind, but I will keep trying. That's all you can do. Your parents did a number on you. There's no denying it, but you aren't them. You're not their beliefs. I'm proud of you and I think I'm gonna be saying that a lot in the future. You're a kind and loving young woman. Keep moving forward and keep talking. Whether that's to me, Mateo, or Molly. You have people now, and we'll do our best to guide you."

"Does it make you uncomfortable talking about...sex stuff with me?"

"A little, but that's okay. You're being vulnerable with me, so the least I can do is return the favor. I had Mateo to talk to, which wasn't always the easiest. I would've loved to have had a queer woman who understood what I was going through back then. I mean, I had Rita, but we didn't have a close friendship until later on. If I can be that for you—that support—I'm happy to put any minor discomfort aside to talk these things through with you."

"Thank you, Carmen."

"Anytime."

They fell silent for the rest of the trip into town. Carmen had given her what she needed. Only a few minutes passed before they pulled into a parking space next to Molly.

"Okay, gang, are we ready to go talk about all things queer?" Molly smiled.

"Always," Courtney sang, skipping off in front.

Faith smiled and slowly walked alongside the group, who were chatting animatedly, apart from Carmen, who was happy to meander silently, a step behind Faith.

Stepping through the doors to an actual high school felt surreal. How many times had Faith wished to attend a school with other kids? And not just any school, but one that made her feel welcome. How different her life may have been if she'd had friends and learned more than the Lord's Word.

"So, we're going to go into the main hall. I'll do my thing and then we can grab ice cream after," Molly announced. "You guys just take a seat near the back."

The group filtered through a set of double doors. The hall was packed with adolescents chattering away among themselves. A pang of envy ricocheted through Faith's body.

Stop, focus on what you have now.

Settling down next to Carmen and Lisa, Faith watched in awe as Molly spoke. Her aunt had everyone's attention as she skillfully answered questions and spoke of her own experiences. Faith understood why Courtney, Lisa, Liam, and Micah loved Molly so much. She was warm and open. The passion she had for helping queer youths was evident in every syllable she uttered.

"How was that?" Molly asked after they gathered in the parking lot.

"Wonderful," Faith answered. "They loved you."

"They're just happy to have someone to talk to." Molly shrugged.

"No," Carmen began, her voice commanding, "they love you because you understand them and connect with them. Don't sell yourself short, Molly."

Lisa nodded. "Yeah, what she said."

"Can we get ice cream now?" Liam mumbled, already opening the car door. Faith laughed. She'd never met someone as grumpy as Liam before.

"Sure, let's go."

Thankfully, the ice cream parlor was only a few minutes away. The day was hot and Faith hadn't hydrated herself enough. Sitting in a booth, Faith finally gave in and checked her phone. Nothing could stop the smile that bloomed on her face when she saw several messages from Nathalie. Each one was sweeter than the last.

Is this what love feels like?

"Is that Nathalie?" Courtney asked from across the booth.

"Yeah," Faith sighed. She was such a sap and she knew it, but equally, she didn't care. She had something good for once in her life, and she wasn't about to feel bad about it.

"I'm a little jealous," Courtney chuckled, but Faith knew it was a mirthless laugh. Courtney was pining after Lisa, hard.

"Tell her, Courtney. You'll never know if you don't."

It was nice when Courtney had confided in Faith last night.

"I can't," Courtney sighed. "I'd be crushed if she rejected me."

"You're not giving her a chance to do anything," Faith argued.

"I won't get hurt that way. None of us know how long we will be at the ranch. She could be gone tomorrow if she decided she wanted something else."

"All the more reason to give her something to stick around for."

Smiling gently at a forlorn Courtney, Faith let her eyes wander around the parlor. Her mind was buzzing. When had Faith become the bearer of advice? And why hadn't she noticed Carmen checking out her aunt's ass?

16

Carmen

Carmen's mind seemed to be hyperfocused on all things Molly Parsons at the moment. From overhearing Molly speaking with Enid and Bessie—because their voices traveled from the front porch—to attending the high school to watch Molly talk to a group of young adults, Carmen couldn't focus on anything else.

Well, maybe the fact Faith had told her she'd masturbated with her girlfriend for the first time didn't help, either.

Is this what being a parent feels like?

Carmen felt honored Faith felt comfortable enough to have that conversation with her, but it would have been nice to receive a little warning. Maybe she could have prepared her answer better. Molly would have known what to say. She wouldn't have felt embarrassed.

Ah, there she went again, allowing her mind to settle on Molly Parsons. It was plain to see why Molly worked with young adults. The talk she'd given at the school was informative and confident. Molly naturally oozed calm, allowing the kids to feel instantly at ease with her.

A pool of envy filled Carmen's stomach. She loved being a graphic designer, but was it something she was passionate about? The businesses she'd started served a purpose. Now that she and Mateo were financially stable, Carmen had retreated to the safety of her home and laptop.

Watching Molly work as hard as she did to help those around her, made Carmen a little ashamed. Not everyone could do what Molly did, but Carmen could definitely do more; be more. These kids struggled and fought, but they never gave up, even when they wanted to. Could Carmen say the same?

The fight to survive and the fight to live were very different things. Carmen and Mateo spent a lifetime fighting to survive. Mateo was making the transition to living his life. It was a transition he wanted Carmen to embrace as well. It seemed everyone around her had fought their demons and were moving on to better things. Why couldn't she?

"You look full of thought," Molly's sweet voice whispered close to Carmen's ear. Once again, Carmen squealed in shock at the unexpected presence.

"Holy crap," she gasped.

"I don't think I've ever met someone so jumpy," Molly laughed, settling down on the grass next to Carmen.

After they'd returned from the high school, Carmen had taken it upon herself to wander around the property.

The Sunflower Ranch was huge. It must take an awful lot of work to maintain. Looking out onto the fields must make the slog worth it, though. The view was spectacular. Before long, Carmen stopped walking and had taken a seat on the ground, quite content sitting in silence, contemplating.

"It's Mateo's fault. He always liked to sneak up on me as a kid. Little asshole."

"You two are incorrigible," Molly chuckled. Carmen smiled.

"It really was a pleasure to watch you with the kids today, Molly."

"Nothing makes me happier."

"I can see. Do you think you will stay here?"

The question had been on Carmen's mind. Molly liked to go where she was needed. Whether that was because she liked to spread the love or because she needed to keep moving, Carmen wasn't sure. What worried Carmen now, was Faith.

It was already going to be heart-wrenching to say goodbye to her if she stayed with Molly. But what if Molly took her on the road? Carmen might not get the chance to see either of them again for a very long time, and that didn't feel good.

"Bessie needs me. The farm and kids are too much for her to handle, and to be honest, this place feels close to a home."

"I can see why."

"Do you think Faith likes it here?"

"Sure, although her head is in the clouds at the minute." Carmen grinned.

"Ah, yes, Nathalie."

"They're good together. I've known Nat nearly her entire life. She's one of the good ones and she seems completely enamored with Faith."

"I'd say the feeling is mutual, if Faith's goofy face is anything to go by," Molly laughed.

"She's changed so much, Molly. I'm in awe of her confidence."

"I think she's had wonderful role models."

"Are you going to ask her to stay?"

"I want to give her the option."

Carmen nodded, her gaze shifting back to the golden fields.

"Faith will love the idea, I'm sure of it. All she's wanted is a family member who understands and loves her for who she is."

"I'd say she's had that family for a few weeks now."

A lump formed in Carmen's throat. "Thanks," she whispered.

Surprise etched itself across her face when she felt Molly's hand slip into hers. They sat silently for a few minutes, peacefully enveloped in the calm California air.

"Hey, I took a look at the ranch's website. I hope you don't mind."

"Not at all. So, what do you think?"

"Honestly?"

"No, lie to me please." Molly grinned.

"It needs work."

"Yeah, I guessed as much. To be honest, I'm not very techy and Bessie, well, she's still using a rotary phone so..."

"I can help, if you'd like?"

Carmen spent a few minutes in bed this morning browsing the ranch website. It was there as a landing page for the work Bessie and Molly did with the kids they housed, but also for the local shelters and charities they coordinated with. The website was missing some key ingredients, and the design was outdated. Carmen might not actively save young lives like Molly and Bessie did, but she could certainly put her skills to good use and help them out.

"I can't ask you to do that," Molly balked.

"Good thing you didn't ask then, isn't it?" Carmen quipped. "I really would be happy to help. I have my laptop with me, and it wouldn't take long for me to come up with a few design ideas."

"Are you being serious right now?"

Carmen couldn't quite place the mix of emotions zipping across Molly's face. She did *not* expect to be tackled by the woman and given a hug that rid her lungs of air.

"Molly," she wheezed, unable to breathe.

"Oh shit, sorry, I'm…I'm just so thankful. Places like this need all the help they can get. I'll see what we have set aside moneywise. I can't say it will be a lot."

Carmen furrowed her eyebrows. "You're not paying me a cent. That's not why I want to help, Molly. Actually, I feel a little insulted."

"Whoa, please don't be upset."

"Then don't offer me money again." Carmen's tone was firm. Molly offering her money felt gross.

Was she being irrational? Probably, but Carmen needed Molly to understand she cared and just wanted to contribute, because she cared.

"Noted, and I swear I will never offer you a single dime, ever again. Scout's honor."

"You're not a Scout."

"I could be."

"Really?"

"No, alright, I couldn't. But the promise is still the same."

Carmen let herself relax again. "Alright, good. So, do you want to go over the website now?"

"Yes, let me grab Bessie and we can get to work."

Carmen watched Molly scuttle off toward the ranch. Dressed in a fresh set of jean shorts and tank top, the woman screamed sexy.

You're letting Enid get in your head. You don't know Molly, for God's sake.

That's all it was. This crush Carmen was feeling was all make-believe, brought on by Enid and Bessie's meddling.

Shaking away her intrusive thoughts, Carmen headed inside to fetch her laptop. The kitchen was buzzing with laughter. Faith, Courtney, Lisa, and Micah were sitting at the kitchen table, playing cards. Faith flashed her a bright smile as she passed through the room. It hurt to think about, but Carmen knew Faith would be happy here with Molly.

Having kids her own age to hang around with had to beat spending nights staying in with Carmen and Mateo. Although, she knew Faith would miss them, as they would her.

A blanket of acceptance settled on her shoulders. This was where Faith belonged and as long as she was happy, Carmen would be, too.

The work session didn't happen. Carmen was setting up her laptop when Molly rushed in.

"I'm sorry, Carmen, I need to leave. The shelter just called. They're down two workers and they need help, otherwise they won't be able to open tonight, and that isn't acceptable."

"Hey, that's fine. Do you need another body?"

"Really?"

Carmen laughed. "Yes, really. I mean what I say, Molly."

Molly flashed a smile and gave two thumbs up. "Great, grab...whatever it is you need and let's haul ass."

"Where are you two going?" Faith called from the kitchen.

"To help out at one of the shelters," Carmen shouted back without stopping. Molly was already sliding in the car and Carmen didn't want to keep her waiting. She was also secretly happy they were going to have a little more time alone.

The shelter housed a dozen beds, a small kitchen, and a communal bathroom. Carmen wasn't sure what to expect. The tsunami of emotions shouldn't have come as a shock, but the sheer weight of them took her by surprise.

Memories of holding Mateo's hand as they stood in line, hoping to get a bed, filtered through her mind. It felt like a lifetime ago, and yet, the memories unearthed feelings so strong it could have happened yesterday.

"Hey, you okay?" Molly asked as they made their way through the room.

"Yeah, it's just been a while," Carmen answered vaguely. Only Mateo and Carmen's therapist knew the full extent of her trauma and experiences. Honestly, though, the times she spent with Mateo in the shelter where Rita found them were some of the happiest memories she had. Everything before then had been bullshit and painful, but Rita's shelter was the start of their lives.

There were several kids already lined up outside, waiting to see if they had a bed for the night. Carmen knew they would have to turn some of them away, and she hated it.

"Everything is set up. We just need to get them settled and fed," Molly called from the kitchen.

"Tell me what you want me to do."

"You can get the food sorted while I let them in."

Carmen was thankful Molly was going to take over allocating beds. A little space, to acclimatize to once-familiar surroundings, was what she needed.

Busying herself with sandwiches and drinks, Carmen settled in. The room outside was alive with quiet chatter. It was clear some of the kids knew each other from either the shelter, or the streets.

Making her way around the room, Carmen handed out food and drink, chatting with each person as she went. Considering what these people were going through, Carmen found them to be open books, happy to talk about their backgrounds.

Lights out happened at 11:30 p.m. Molly took her turn patrolling the bed area, making sure no one had brought anything in which they shouldn't have.

"They're all settled," Molly whispered. Carmen was sitting at one end of an old couch, tucked away in one corner of the room.

"It breaks my heart," Carmen replied. The crack in her voice gave away how affected she was by being there.

"It's hard, but all we can do is to be here for them. They're tough kids."

"They shouldn't have to be. None of them deserve to be here. What the fuck is wrong with people?"

Carmen's distress was quickly turning to anger. Parents abandoning their kids was unforgivable.

"They don't deserve it. I wish I could make everything better, for every kid that passes through here." Molly's eyes swam with unshed tears.

"I know you do," Carmen assured. "You do a fantastic job, Molly."

In the dim light, Carmen could just make out Molly's features. Even in sadness, Molly Parsons was a captivating sight to behold. How easy would it be to lean over and press those soft lips against her own? Carmen felt herself leaning in. Would Molly reciprocate?

She never got to find out. A deafening crash outside the building entryway made both women jump.

Molly was on her feet in a second, with Carmen hot on her trail. The scene Carmen came across outside left her breathless. Slumped in the doorway was a young man, maybe eighteen. Blood poured down his face from a cut above his eye. He had a swollen and split lip.

"Can you hear me?" Molly questioned gently, laying her hands on him. The boy nodded and winced. Carmen swooped down and began checking his vital signs.

"We need to get him inside and cleaned up," she said after determining nothing major was broken. The first aid course she'd taken finally came in handy.

Together, Molly and Carmen scooped the boy up and helped him to the couch. The disturbance had alerted the other kids. Curious and frightened faces greeted them as they laid him down.

Molly didn't waste time comforting the scared youths. Carmen set about cleaning the blood from the boy's face.

"What's your name, honey?" she asked softly.

"Darren," he gasped.

"Can you tell me where it hurts?"

"My side. I think I have some broken ribs."

"Can I look?"

Darren nodded before shifting slowly to allow Carmen a look at his left side of his torso. Deep bruises marred his skin. Faint yellow bruises were also visible. This wasn't the first time he'd been beaten.

"Can you tell me what happened?"

"My dad caught me with my boyfriend," he sobbed.

Carmen gritted her teeth and willed the tears she felt forming, to stay where they were. Darren needed her to be strong. Looking at him closer, the resemblance to a young Mateo almost bowled her over.

"You're safe now, okay? I think we might need to take you to the emergency room—"

"No," he shot, fear lacing his voice. "They'll call him. If he finds me, I'm dead."

Carmen believed it. Looking at the damage done, she could well imagine the boy wouldn't survive another round.

"Okay. No hospital. I need to monitor you, though."

"Okay."

Carmen spent several more minutes cleaning Darren up. She got him settled on his side and draped a blanket over his shivering body.

"I'm going to make you a drink to help with the shock. Try to relax, okay?" Darren simply nodded, a single tear running down his cheek.

Molly was waiting for her in the kitchen, her face ashen. "How is he?"

"Hurting and scared. He won't go to a hospital."

"And his injuries?"

"It's a safe bet he has a couple of broken ribs. The cuts above his eye and lip have already stopped bleeding. I don't think they need stitches. He needs to be watched tonight, and woken regularly to make sure he doesn't have a concussion."

"Did he say how it happened?"

Carmen balled her hands into fists, anger coursing through her veins as she thought of the scumbag who'd hurt Darren.

"His father. Caught Darren with his boyfriend."

"Fucking bastard," Molly hissed.

"My thoughts entirely."

"He'll need time to recover. The shelter isn't the right place. I need to call Bessie." Molly was talking to herself rather than Carmen, which was fine. Carmen began making a cup of sweet tea for Darren as Molly continued to mutter to herself. "I'll be back in a minute," Molly announced.

Carmen carried the tea to Darren, who was fast asleep. Hating herself a little, she nudged him awake. She wished she could let him sleep and forget for a little while, but the risk he had bumped his head took precedence.

"You need to drink this. Can you tell me what day it is?"

Darren mumbled his answer, but Carmen didn't mind. As long as he wasn't confused, mumbling was okay.

"I'm Carmen, by the way. I realized I didn't introduce myself."

"Thank you," Darren said, looking into Carmen's eyes.

"You have nothing to thank me for. Now, drink your tea."

Carmen sat silently next to him as he sipped his drink. A few minutes later, Molly bustled in.

"Hey Darren, I'm Molly."

"Hi."

"I know this is a lot and I'm sure you just want to go to sleep, but we need to make sure you have somewhere to stay."

"I can't stay here?"

"You need a place to heal. I help run a ranch for kids who need a place to stay. Would it be okay if we took you there?"

Darren studied Molly for a second and then looked at Carmen. The silent question was obvious. Darren wanted Carmen to tell him it was okay.

"It's a great place, Darren. You'd be safe and have a place to recover."

"Thank you," he replied, this time to Molly.

"No worries, kid." Molly shifted her attention to Carmen. "I've arranged for two other volunteers to relieve us. We need to get Darren back to the ranch ASAP."

Half an hour passed before the relief volunteers showed up. After a quick hand-off, Carmen helped Molly walk Darren to her car. The ranch was lit up like a Christmas tree when they arrived. Bessie rushed out and assessed Darren. Mateo helped Carmen walk him inside and up the stairs.

"Faith is sleeping in Courtney's room," Bessie called as they scooted along the upstairs hall. It only took a few minutes to get Darren comfortable—well, as comfortable as was possible with broken ribs.

"I made tea," Enid whispered from the doorway. Molly was sitting at the kitchen table, nursing something stronger than tea. Carmen slipped in next to her, took the glass from her hand, and downed the amber liquid. Without a word, Molly pulled over another glass and refilled them both.

"An eventful night, huh?" Bessie remarked.

"You okay?" Mateo asked quietly, his hand taking Carmen's. All she could do was nod. No, she wasn't okay, not in the least, but it wasn't about her.

Looking to the side, she caught Molly's eye. Something passed between them; a new bond that needed to be explored, but not tonight.

17

Molly

Molly's head leaned lazily against the chair in the corner of what was now Darren's room. Sleep wouldn't come for her this evening. The only thing that helped, was knowing Carmen was only a few feet away.

After a subdued conversation with Bessie, Molly excused herself from the kitchen to take a shower. Her plan was to spend the night monitoring Darren. She hadn't expected to find Carmen already in Darren's room, reading, when she entered.

They sat silently, watching the young man sleep. This wasn't the first time Molly had dealt with this type of situation. Sadly, she also knew it wouldn't be the last. What made it different tonight, though, was having Carmen with her.

Now and then, Carmen would rise from her seat to nudge Darren awake. They'd have a quick conversation before Carmen allowed him to go back to sleep.

"I don't think he has a concussion," she whispered.

"At least that's something," Molly replied.

Falling silent again, Molly let her eyes fall shut. As much as she loved what she did, and couldn't even contemplate doing anything else, sometimes the emotional toll was overwhelming.

For the most part, Molly was excellent at compartmentalizing her personal feelings separate from her professional ones. Yes, she had no problem sharing some of her past with the kids she helped, but no one knew the complete picture. That was reserved for Molly alone.

It was natural, though, to feel old wounds reopen when faced with situations like Darren's. It was human. Unfortunately, adding tonight's drama to the emotions of Faith turning up, meant Molly was finding it near impossible to shut off her personal thoughts and feelings.

Looking over at Carmen, Molly wondered if she was finding it just as difficult. Carmen and Mateo had gone through the system, and from what little Molly knew about their past, she would bet they'd gone through their fair share of trauma. Was Carmen reliving it?

Molly was. Her mind catapulted back twenty years, to the day Alan had thrown her out with nothing but a few clothes in a bag. Unlike Darren, Molly had escaped physically unharmed, but not emotionally. Her brother had eviscerated her. Had he done that to Faith, too?

A wave of nausea rolled over every inch of Molly's body. Why had she deluded herself that she could get Alan to see sense one day? All those years of writing letters hoping for some sort of reconciliation... Why had she done that?

Because Molly longed for the family she'd had before her parents were killed, but that wasn't possible any longer. Alan wasn't the brother she'd known. He was a stranger.

There would be no more letters; no more hoping. Molly couldn't bear the thought of having Faith anywhere near that sort of toxicity. Molly also couldn't bear the thought of *anyone* having to live in such a hostile environment. The hardest part was going to be letting her past go, knowing she wouldn't get the closure she needed or deserved.

"You look like you are trying to solve world hunger over there." Carmen's soft voice was soothing to Molly's frayed mind.

"No, nothing so grand," Molly replied with a half-smile.

"Want to talk about it?"

"I was just making some decisions."

"About your brother?"

Molly wasn't surprised Carmen knew where her head had gone. She was a perceptive woman.

"Yeah," she sighed.

"I can't say I understand what you're going through, Mol."

Molly's heart gave an extra hard *thump* at Carmen's use of the nickname.

"Mateo is my family, and no matter what we went through, we did it together. You, for a long time, were alone. It's completely understandable you wanted, or still want, your family to support you."

"But at what cost?" Molly responded.

She knew the cost would be sacrificing her dignity and self-worth. She'd be begging a man who had cast her out at seventeen, not caring whether she wound up on the streets, or worse.

"Don't do that. Don't question yourself. It's okay to reconsider or rethink priorities. At one point, Molly, you needed to hold on to the idea that your brother would come around and embrace you. Now, things have changed—*you* have changed."

"I hate the feeling of giving up on him, but equally, I hate the person he's become. I'm sure there is more to the story than Faith has told me. Seeing Darren, and the fear in his eyes, I couldn't help but think of Faith in that position. Did she cower before him? Did he beat her and make her feel worthless? My stomach is sick at the thought. I should have been there for her, I—"

"You didn't know, Mol. And even if you'd known about Faith, that doesn't mean you would've been able to do anything. Trust me, I wish I'd known about her. I would have marched into the Parsons household, decked Alan, and walked out with Faith," Carmen laughed. "She didn't deserve to be treated that way. Hell, no one deserves that. At least you spent your time trying to help. Look at Darren. You didn't even hesitate in bringing him here. And I'll bet a million bucks you'll ensure he is well taken care of, even after he has recovered."

"How do you do that?" Molly asked, her head feeling a little light.

"Do what?"

"Make me feel better with just a few words. Make me feel..." Molly trailed off, unable to complete the sentence.

Make me feel safe and at home.

Dipping her head in embarrassment, Molly hoped Carmen wouldn't read into her rambling.

"I hope I can make you feel better," Carmen said quietly. Raising her eyes from the ground, Molly looked directly at Carmen, a shy smile gracing her beautiful face.

"Thank you."

"Anytime. Maybe we should try to get some sleep. It's been a long day."

"I'm not sure I can," Molly sighed.

"Come here." Carmen gestured for Molly to join her in the oversized armchair she'd been curled up in all evening.

Pushing up from her seat, Molly wandered the few feet separating them. It should feel weird squashing up next to a woman she hardly knew, but as her body settled snugly next to Carmen's, the only thing she felt was the tug of sleep pulling her under.

The crick in Molly's neck reminded her she was no longer in her twenties. Gone were the days of crashing on a couch. No, Molly needed her king-size memory foam mattress now.

God, what she wouldn't give for a massage. The image of Carmen's hands rubbing the sensitive area on her neck thundered like a freight train through her mind. A sudden heat rose from deep inside, touching every nerve in Molly's body. Jesus, she was on fire.

"You're red as a tomato, Mol," Bessie commented, perching a tray with Darren's breakfast at the end of the bed. Molly noted she was alone. Carmen was no longer snuggled up in the chair. Darren still slept soundly.

"What time is it?" she yawned, stretching her neck from side to side. In lieu of a massage, a few neck exercises would have to do.

"Nearly eight, sweetie. I'm glad to see you got a few hours of sleep."

"Mmm," she mumbled, still in the fog of slumber.

"Carmen slept well too."

Molly couldn't have missed the amusement in Bessie's tone, even if she tried.

"Good," Molly replied, her eyes unable to meet Bessie's.

"Mmm, she looked super comfy with your head on her boob."

Molly's eyes shot up. "What?"

"Yeah, I snuck in earlier just to check on you all, and there you were—two peas in a snuggly pod."

"It's not like that," Molly protested. "I couldn't relax last night after everything and Carmen was just comforting me."

"No need to get worked up, Mol," Bessie grinned.

"I'm not getting worked up," Molly hissed.

"Ah, told her you found her groping Carmen's breast, I see," Enid called softly from the doorway.

"Yup," Bessie replied, chuckling. Molly was most certainly the color of a tomato now.

"Oh my God. I was not groping anything."

"Not what I heard," Enid sang.

"You are the worst—both of you."

Ignoring their animated laughs, Molly peeled herself out of the chair and peeked over at Darren. His face was a mix of black, blue, and green. His eye and lip were swollen.

"He'll be alright, Molly. A few days of rest and relaxation and he'll feel as good as new."

"I hope so," Molly sighed.

"Come on, let's grab some breakfast." Enid said, not giving her much of an option.

The little old lady was stronger than she looked. Molly nearly tripped over her own feet as Enid grabbed her by the wrist and tugged her out of the room.

"Morning," a chorus of voices rang out. Molly smiled warmly in return, her eyes instantly gravitating to Carmen, who had her back to the room.

Was she cooking pancakes? Cooking pancakes in tight jeans and an even tighter T-shirt? Oh...that undercut was effective in turning Molly's thoughts R-rated.

"Hey," Molly cooed, instantly chastising herself as she stood next to Carmen, peering over at the frying pan currently cooking two fluffy pancakes.

"Hey. You look well-rested," Carmen replied, her face a picture of calm.

Clearly, she wasn't having the same thoughts as Molly. Even though she'd been asleep, Molly could feel the contours of Carmen's body, especially the swell of her breasts.

Wowzer...

"So you're saying I look less like a trash panda now?" Molly laughed.

"Definitely. Although I wouldn't rule out the trash panda look just yet. I have a feeling it's going to be a long day." Carmen grinned.

Molly squinted; her brows furrowed. "Is there something happening?"

Molly racked her brain. Apart from making sure Darren was doing well and checking off a couple of things to do on the ranch, she couldn't remember anything else scheduled. Nothing that would make her day long, anyway.

"Oh, there's something happening. Prepare yourself, Molly Parsons."

"Prepare myself for what?"

"For the greatest fashion show on earth," Mateo announced with as much flair as he could muster. Which, in his pink silk robe and fluffy slippers, was *a lot*.

"Okay, I'm lost," Molly laughed. The kids all looked giddy with excitement, and Carmen looked exasperated.

"The old queen wants to put on a fashion show in the front yard," Carmen replied, flipping the two pancakes.

"Damn right the old queen does!" Mateo shouted. "It's going to be spectacular."

"Um..." Molly wasn't sure how to respond.

"Don't try to understand it. Just go along for the ride," Carmen chuckled. "He's got all the kids involved."

"Well, I wouldn't want to stand in the way of the greatest fashion show on earth," Molly deadpanned.

That Mateo was doing something for all the kids was heartwarming. Over the past few days, he'd spent time with each of them, chatting about everything and nothing. Sometimes something as simple as giving the teens just a bit of time and focus, was more precious than gold. They'd spent too long feeling isolated, unheard, and misunderstood.

"Yeah, he's a good one, I suppose," Carmen muttered low enough so Mateo wouldn't hear her. "Come on, let's feed the horde."

How did Carmen and Mateo fit in so easily? Molly stood, watching for a second. Carmen arranged the pancakes on the table as Mateo psyched up the kids up about the upcoming fashion show. Bessie caught Molly's eye from the other end of the kitchen and gave her a wink.

With the worries and memories of last night's drama soothed and stored a little further back in her mind, Molly sat down and enjoyed a rather loud and excitable breakfast.

Mateo had apparently raided everyone's closets, including Molly's, to prepare for the show. Courtney, Lisa, and Faith were models. Liam mumbled something about music management, and Micah boasted about being Mateo's beauty apprentice.

"As fun as this is," Bessie interrupted, "we need to get cracking on the chores if we want to enjoy the show later on."

"Indeed," Molly agreed, shuffling from the table, depositing her dishes in the sink. "You guys can get this place cleaned, please."

"Yes, ma'am," Micah answered, corralling the others to move from the table.

They must be excited. I've never seen them so enthusiastic about cleaning up.

"I can help you with the ranch chores if you like," Carmen said to Molly quietly. The closeness of Carmen's body reminded Molly of last night.

Stop it.

"Um, sure, if you want. That would be great."

Suppressing the little shiver that coursed through her panties, Molly willed herself to calm the hell down. What was happening? She'd shared several conversations and a bit of cuddling. Surely that wasn't enough to elicit such reactions. The second shiver in her lower regions begged to differ.

You just need to get laid. It's nothing more than pent-up frustration.

The excitement in the front yard was palpable. Molly laughed out loud in amazement when she saw the fashion show setup. Where the hell had Mateo found a red carpet?

There were several chairs lined up on either side of the runway, an enormous set of curtains hanging off a makeshift frame, and a desk to the side that had a Bluetooth speaker on it.

"This is very…" Molly waved her hands about trying to come up with the best descriptors for what lay in front of her.

"Over the top?" Carmen laughed.

"No, it's brilliant. I can't believe Mateo pulled it off."

"Give that man enough time, he can turn anything into a runway."

"But I bet he's never made one in front of a ranch house, next to a field of sunflowers, before, huh?"

Carmen laughed. "Nope, it's a first."

Sitting down, they waited until Enid and Bessie strolled up, arm-in-arm.

"Those two are dangerous together," Molly muttered out the side of her mouth, so only Carmen could hear.

"You're telling me," she replied, laughing.

"Hello, you two. Isn't this a lovely sight?" Enid clapped enthusiastically.

Molly rolled her eyes. "If you're referring to the fashion show set up, then yes, it is a lovely sight."

Before Enid could make another comment, Liam pressed play on his phone. Music blared through the speaker.

"Welcome to the Annual Sunflower Ranch Fashion Show," he mumbled with all the enthusiasm an adolescent boy could muster. Molly chuckled, as did Carmen.

Bursting through the curtain, Mateo took center stage.

"Here we go," Carmen murmured.

"Ladies and Carmen," he shouted, "welcome to the *First* Annual Sunflower Ranch Fashion Show. In just a few short moments, our three gorgeous models will strut down this fine-ass catwalk to show you the latest trends in teenage fashion."

"*Por Dios*," Carmen mumbled. Molly laughed silently. Mateo was throwing everything into his performance.

"Do we walk now?" a garbled voice called from behind the curtain, momentarily knocking Mateo off his stride.

"When the music changes," he hissed good-naturedly. "Liam." He nodded toward the reluctant deejay. Liam rolled his eyes but pressed his phone to change to the next song.

Molly sat back and watched as Faith, Lisa, and Courtney all took turns walking down the red carpet runway. None of the clothes were designer, or for that matter, anything out of the ordinary, but those girls strutted as though they were attending Paris Fashion Week.

At the end of the show, Mateo walked out with the girls on his arms. Molly rocketed to her feet, wolf whistling and clapping. Enid whistled twice as loud and Bessie whooped in excitement.

Turning her face slightly, Molly caught the exchange between Carmen and Faith. A subtle wink and quiet round of applause, saw Faith burst with pride.

They're really close.

The celebrations came to a stuttering halt as the sound of a car driving far too fast up the lane caught everyone's attention. It was Faith's gasp that drew Molly's gaze from the approaching vehicle. Turning, Molly saw her niece's face drain of all color.

Stepping forward, Molly covered her brow with her hands, trying to keep the sun from her eyes. The moment the car door flew open, she knew who she would see.

"Alan," she gasped.

Alan screamed, "You dirty little whore, get in the car now!"

Molly was frozen. In her peripheral vision, she saw Carmen place herself in front of Faith, Mateo mirroring her movements. Both Ruizes were completely shielding Faith.

"You have thirty seconds to crawl back into the hole you came from before I put your face through that windshield," Carmen growled, her finger jabbing towards Alan.

"This has nothing to do with you. I'm here for my daughter. Faith, get in the car, now. I won't tell you again!" Alan screamed, his face puce.

The second Molly saw Carmen move, she unfroze. Stepping out in front of everyone, she came eye to eye with her brother, who, until then, hadn't noticed Molly. His eyes grew wide as recognition settled over him.

"Alan, leave now," Molly said calmly.

"Molly," he whispered. For just a second, Molly glimpsed the brother she'd known and loved.

"Faith is staying here," Molly continued.

Snapping out of his shock, Alan took a step forward. Molly held her ground.

"I should have known," he sneered. "Is this what you were planning all along, hmm? Waiting for my daughter to come of age so you could corrupt her with your unnatural choices?"

Molly regarded her brother. His hair was neatly combed. He wore slacks and a button-up shirt. All in all, he looked very respectable. A few lines graced his face, but time had been kind to his features.... Unlike his character.

"I hoped, for so long, I would get to see you again," Molly began, her voice strong. "I wrote those letters, praying that God would guide you back to me. But you are still lost, brother."

"Don't you dare speak of God to me, you filthy dyke!" Spittle flew from Alan's mouth.

"Mom and Dad would be so ashamed." She shook her head solemnly. "If they saw the man you have become, they would be so very sad."

Alan took another step forward. "I am taking my daughter home. She can still be saved," he growled, fists clenched. Molly wondered if he would actually strike her with everyone watching.

"Are you going to hit me, Alan?" Molly asked. "Isn't this a little too public for you? Don't you like to hide the abuse you dole out on your wife and child?"

It was Molly's turn to take a step forward.

"All this righteous bullshit is nothing more than a frightened and angry little boy who never dealt with his grief. You are nothing like the brother I knew; nothing like the son raised by our parents. I can't blame you fully, though. Your precious pastor picked well. Who better than an emotionally distraught child to teach and pass on his hate?"

The car door opened, and Maureen Parsons stepped out.

"Get back in the car," Alan howled. Maureen flinched but remained where she was.

"You took what you were given by God and ruined it—hurt the people you were supposed to love the most. I know it's too late now, Alan. I will never get the family back I craved for so long. But I've made a new one. Faith has made a new one. A family that treats her with love and kindness. You—" Molly pointed to Alan, her finger less than an inch from his chest, "—have thrown away your chance of happiness. You can throw all the insults you want, but you are not getting your hands on Faith."

"Faith?" Maureen's voice was soft, her eyes pleading at her daughter. Molly turned to see Faith push gently through the Ruiz body barrier.

"I'm not coming with you, Mom. I spent so long fearing you both," she said, shaking her head. "I will never go back to that. I'm sure you will cast me out, just like you did Aunt Molly," Faith said, now talking to Alan. "But that's okay, I forgive you."

"*You* forgive *me*?" he laughed mirthlessly.

"Yes, I forgive you. I will not live my life angry like you, Dad."

"Faith," Maureen sobbed.

"Mom, you need to leave him. You've taken enough beatings—enough abuse."

Pride swelled up in Molly as she watched her wonderful niece stand tall and sure.

"I believe what Aunt Molly says. Grandma and Grandpa would be devastated if they saw how we lived—how he treated us. I want more for my life. I want that for you too, Mom. But that's your choice. Dad, I hope you get the help you need, I truly do, but...if you come for me again, I will press charges. I am eighteen and a legal adult. I have enough people around me to support and love me, all of whom won't let any harm come to me."

"I'm still deciding if you should go through the windshield," Carmen growled.

Molly looked at Carmen, who was rigid, the anger pulsing off her entire body. Mateo placed his hand on her shoulder, calming her a fraction.

"Like I said, I have good people around me now. Get back in your car and go home."

Faith walked up and stood shoulder to shoulder with Molly.

"You heard her, Alan."

"You are dead to me," Alan hissed.

"You're not dead to me, Dad, or you, Mom. But I know, for now, it's goodbye."

Faith turned on her heel, walked to Carmen and linked their arms, forcing Carmen to move. Molly stood guard, waiting for Alan to leave. She could see him battling with his anger. How sad it was to see her one-and-only brother so lost.

"Go," she whispered.

Their eyes locked. Alan opened his mouth but snapped it back shut before turning and climbing back into the car. Maureen turned her eyes from a retreating Faith, to Molly.

"You have a choice," Molly spoke. "Make the right one."

18

Faith

Faith's nerves were surprisingly calm as she ushered Carmen into the ranch house. They didn't stop until Carmen's butt was planted in a kitchen chair.

"You okay?" Faith asked, filling a glass with cold water. Carmen looked beyond angry.

"Shouldn't I be asking you that?" Carmen replied, her jaw tensed.

"I'm not the one who looks like my head's about to explode," Faith chuckled.

Carmen's shoulders dropped. "Shit, sorry, Faith, this can't be easy for you. I'm fine, are you?"

"Surprisingly, yes. I thought I was going to vomit when I saw their car but then, I don't know, when he started yelling, the fear left me. I had you and Mateo in front of me. I could hear Molly, and then it hit me: I'm not alone now. Not like when I lived in their house. I think that's why he had so much power over me. I was alone, and the longer they kept me from people, the easier it was for them to keep me locked in that fear."

"But you got yourself out."

"Yes, only because I knew I had an aunt out there somewhere. For once, I had hope. Since meeting you and Mateo, and then Molly, that fear has slowly drained. I just didn't know it until I was faced with them again."

"You're an amazing young woman, Faith. Really, you should be so proud of how you dealt with that...unlike me," Carmen chuckled. "I'm sorry, I just saw red."

"Never apologize for wanting to protect me, Carmen. I...I see you as family. You and Mateo. Molly's my aunt by blood, but you guys are... How did you phrase it? My chosen family? Family in every way but blood."

Faith yelped as Carmen shot out of the chair and scooped her up into a mammoth hug.

"You have a place with us, always. Remember that you never have to be alone, ever again."

"Hey," Molly's soft voice echoed through the kitchen. "Everyone alright?"

Faith gave Carmen one last squeeze before stepping back and heading to Molly.

"Thank you, Molly."

"Nothing to thank me for. You were more than capable of handling the situation."

"Yeah, but that couldn't have been easy for you either."

Faith thought it might have actually been harder for her aunt. Molly had waited for closure for nearly twenty years. Faith knew it wasn't the end result Molly dreamed of, but she hoped her aunt could put her past to rest now.

"I'm good, really. It had to happen, and even though it's not what I expected, I wouldn't change the result. I got you out of it, didn't I?"

"You sure did!" Faith beamed, taking Molly into her arms.

"Well, that was a dramatic end to the show," Enid barked, walking in and taking Faith and Molly in her arms.

"Enid," Molly rasped.

Faith giggled. Enid was holding them both so tight it was difficult to breathe.

"Right," Enid bellowed after a few more seconds, "let's eat and drink. Erase all that bullshit and enjoy our day."

"Hear, hear," Mateo called from the doorway.

"Sounds great, but can I just steal Faith for a few minutes?" Molly asked.

"Sure, let's go." Faith followed Molly, noticing Carmen's gaze. She looked a little sad.

What's that about?

Faith walked quietly next to her aunt. The day was just as beautiful as every other day they'd had since turning up in California. The sunflowers had their colorful heads tipped to the sun. Faith mirrored them, enjoying the heat on her face.

"Are you really okay?" Molly finally asked.

"I am. Like I told Carmen. The fear I once had is no longer wedged in my chest. Having so many people around me shook it loose. I've experienced so much and learned a lot about myself. There was nothing that could make me go anywhere with my parents. I just wish Mom would open her eyes."

"Me too, Faith, me too."

"I'm sorry he spoke to you that way," Faith sighed.

"So am I, but I'm sorry for him. I can't imagine living with such hatred inside."

"No, it's poison," Faith commented.

There were times she wished and prayed her father would wake up one day and be a different man. A man who loved his wife and child, but that was a fantasy. Today showed Faith he was beyond her wishes, and her prayers.

Maybe one day he would open his eyes, but Faith wouldn't hold her breath. It was her mother who weighed on her mind. The defiance she'd shown today by simply stepping out of the car, when she'd clearly been given instructions to stay inside, was a glimmer of hope for Faith. Maybe losing her only child would be the catalyst to spark a change.

"You said my mom was outgoing once. I just can't see how she got from that to this?"

"Maureen was a sweet and adventurous girl. I can only imagine how Alan's behavior, views, and opinions have affected her—changed her. I have no clue if she truly agrees with him or if she's just so terrified of him she goes along with it. You'd know better than me, sweetie."

Faith let her mind travel back to her childhood. Had her mom ever shown signs of being different from her father? Possibly, but Faith's childhood memories were overshadowed by loneliness and sorrow, so even if her mom didn't agree with him, the woman did nothing to let Faith know she wasn't alone.

"Well, it doesn't matter now," Faith began. "I need to concentrate on me and my life. I truly hope she leaves him."

"What do you want to do now?" Molly asked, her feet scuffing the dirt road.

"What do you mean?"

"Um, well," Molly cleared her throat, "do you want to stay here with me?"

"Do you want me to?"

"I'd love you to, Faith. I've missed so much of your life. There is always a home for you here with me."

Faith stopped Molly with a hand on her wrist. "I can't tell you how long I have wanted that, Molly. The thought of finding you kept me going for so long. But can I think about it? I've got Nathalie to consider now. Plus, Carmen and Mateo."

Faith's heart was pounding. She didn't want Molly to think she was rejecting her, but Nathalie meant a lot to Faith, as did the Ruizes.

"Of course, take your time."

"Do you want to walk longer?" Faith enjoyed the quiet moments with Molly.

Even though they hadn't had a lot of quality time, just the two of them, Faith recognized they both liked silence. They both enjoyed listening to the birds, contemplating things as they wandered aimlessly. Maybe that was a Parsons trait?

"Absolutely, let's go."

They walked for another forty-five minutes. Faith smiled every time Molly stopped to plant her face in a sunflower, completely content. The buzzing of her phone interrupted their blissful peace. Alice's name flashed across the screen.

"Hey, Alice."

"Faith, oh my God, your dad, he knows where you are and it's my fault. I'm so sorry. The pastor went through my phone. I didn't know he'd done it. I left it on the church pew by mistake, after the service. When I came back to get it, it was gone. Bonnie saw him going through my messages before he called your dad and then threw the phone in the bin outside the church. I didn't know until an hour ago when Bonnie brought me my phone."

"Wow, calm down, Alice. It's okay—"

"No, it's not. You have to go. He's going to catch you."

"He already did," Faith replied calmly.

"What?" Alice screamed.

"It's okay. Molly, Carmen, and Mateo helped me deal with him."

"Shit, Faith, I'm so sorry. Can you forgive me?"

"What are you talking about? There is absolutely nothing to forgive. Alice, you have been the best friend anyone could ask for. Please stop panicking, everything is good."

Alice's heavy breathing filtered down the phone. Faith was sure she heard a little hiccup.

"O-okay. So what happened?"

Faith spent a few minutes filling Alice in on all the details. Molly wandered further down the track, leaving Faith to talk.

"Can you tell your parents what happened? And thank them again for everything they did for me."

"Of course," Alice answered, her voice wavering with emotion. "Does this mean I'll never see you again?"

"What? No, Alice, I'll visit you, I promise. And when I know where I will be, you can come and visit me. You need to meet Molly, Carmen, and Mateo."

"And your hot girlfriend, Nathalie," Alice chimed in, sounding a lot lighter.

Faith laughed. "Yes! You do have to meet my hot girlfriend."

"I love you, Faith. And I'm so proud of you."

"I love you too, Alice. I'll call you when I know what's going on."

"Where is everyone?" Faith asked Lisa, who was sitting, swinging her feet from the deck railing.

"Carmen and Mateo took Micah and Liam into the city. Courtney is in her room. Bessie and Enid... I have no idea and I don't think I want to know," she laughed.

"Molly is in the field, working. I thought I'd come back and have some lemonade, inside. It's so hot out here."

"I'll join you, if that's cool?" Lisa chirped, dropping to her feet.

Faith nodded and headed inside. The coolness of the ranch house was heavenly. How Molly was working outside was a mystery and seemed a little nuts.

Lisa sat at the kitchen table, bringing one knee up, resting on the seat with her knee tucked under her chin.

"Do you...do you think Courtney is nice?" Lisa asked. Faith stifled her grin as she poured them both a drink.

"Yeah, she's cool. Why?"

"Just wondering."

"Any reason?"

Placing Lisa's lemonade on the table, Faith sat opposite her. Lisa shuffled in her seat, biting her lip, clearly deep in thought.

"No, just... just thinking."

"Do *you* think Courtney is nice?"

Faith wanted to giggle at Lisa's doe-eyed expression. Her face turned a light shade of red.

"Um, well yeah, she's cool."

"Wow," Faith laughed.

"What?" Lisa shot.

"You have a crush on her, don't you?"

Faith needed to move them both along. Courtney was pining over Lisa and Lisa was crushing on Courtney. Left to their own devices, the pair would still be clueless this time next year.

"What? No!" Lisa shot.

"Okay," Faith singsonged, taking a sip of her lemonade.

"Anyway, it doesn't matter," Lisa mumbled.

"Why doesn't it matter?"

Faith knew what was coming. Lisa was going to say that even if she had a crush on Courtney, Courtney wouldn't feel the same way.

"Even if I had a crush—"

"I'm going to stop you right there, Lisa." Faith smiled at Lisa's shock of being interrupted. "I *heavily* suggest you talk to Courtney before you say another word."

"Has...has she said something?"

"Oh no, I'm not being the go-between. Please, just talk to her."

"Talk to who?" Courtney asked, strolling in and grabbing herself a muffin from the counter.

Faith looked between Lisa and Courtney, deliberating what she should do. She was in the process of opening her mouth to tell them she was going to make herself scarce, when Lisa blurted out, "Court, will you go on a date with me?"

Courtney blushed, but then the most beautiful smile blossomed on her face. Faith couldn't help but squeal in delight.

"Yes, I'd love to," Courtney answered rather breathlessly.

"You two are adorable," Faith laughed.

"Shut up," Lisa mumbled through her smile.

"Should I leave you two alone?" Faith asked seriously. She didn't want to be the third wheel.

"No, actually, I wanted to ask if you were doing all right. You know...after earlier events?" Courtney asked, dropping into the chair next to Lisa.

"Actually, yeah. I know everyone is worried about me, but there's no need. Honestly, I'm doing fine. It was a shock and I don't like what was said, but it needed to happen. I feel like a weight has been lifted. It's no fun having someone chase you, always wondering, looking over your shoulder. I'm more worried about the future."

"In what way?" Lisa asked, stealing half of Courtney's muffin.

"Molly has offered me a place here with her."

"That's awesome, isn't it?" Courtney questioned.

"Yes, it's everything I wanted."

"But?"

"But I have Nathalie to think of. Plus, I was thinking about asking Rita, Nat's aunt, about working with her. I know it was only a few days, but I feel like I made a home in Seattle with Carmen and Mateo."

"Have Carmen or Mateo said anything?"

"Carmen told me I would always have a home with them. I don't know what to do, guys."

Lisa tapped her finger on the table absentmindedly. "I think you should do what feels right to you. Don't feel you owe it to Molly to stay here, Faith. She wouldn't want that. If you have prospects in Seattle and you want to make a go of things with Nat, then maybe you already have your answer."

"I need to talk to Nathalie."

"Yeah, go call her." Courtney was side-eyeing Lisa. Faith rolled her eyes playfully.

"Yeah, I'll do that. Have fun, you two," she called over her shoulder. Faith was still chuckling when the call to Nathalie connected.

"What's funny?" Nathalie asked with a laugh.

"Oh, Courtney and Lisa finally figured out that they're into each other."

"Ah, sweet. It's good to hear your voice," Nathalie replied, her tone soft.

"You too. It's been a day."

Faith filled Nathalie in on the fashion show and her parents showing up. As usual, Nathalie was the perfect girlfriend and also perceptive.

"Why do I feel there is something bothering you that isn't to do with your parents crashing the fashion show?"

Faith sighed. "Molly offered me a place to stay, here with her."

"Is that what you want? No pressure, Faith. I want you to be happy. You deserve that."

"I think I want to live in Seattle."

"As much as that excites me. Please don't base your decision on me. I'm happy to do long distance, if that's what it takes."

"You'd really do that?"

"Yes, without a doubt. Faith, I like you a lot. I'm not letting you go, even if you live in a different state."

Nathalie giving her the space to decide was all Faith needed to know what she wanted: a chance to build something in Seattle with Nathalie. They might be young and their relationship new, but why should that matter? Faith had spent long enough tempering her wants and needs. Now she was free to take control and decide based on what she needed for herself.

"Thank you, Nat."

"No worries, babe. Listen, I need to run to the store for Rita before she gets all pissy. I'll call you tonight before bed. Maybe we can...you know, catch up."

"It's a date."

Okay, now the decision to go back to Seattle was made, Faith just had to tell Molly. Even though she knew it was the right decision for her, it didn't stop the sick feeling rolling around in her belly.

Molly was just walking up to the ranch house, filthy from her work, but a wide smile was etched on her face.

"Hey, honey," she called.

"Hey, Mol. Um, can we talk?"

A sudden nervousness crept over Faith's body. What if she offended Molly to the point her aunt didn't want to know her? No, that was stupid, the old insecurities raising their ugly heads.

"What's up?" Molly finally asked.

"Um, I've been thinking about what you said earlier. About living here with you."

"You want to be in Seattle, right?" Molly grinned.

"I...I just feel that's the place I'm supposed to be right now. I'm sorry."

"Hey," Molly began, taking Faith by the shoulders. "You don't have to apologize to me. I want you to be happy, and if that is in Seattle, then that's where you should be. I can visit you, if you're good with that, and we can talk on the phone."

"Yeah?" The relief Faith felt was immeasurable.

"Of course," Molly chuckled. "You're my niece, and you're pretty friggin' awesome. I want you to thrive, and I know Carmen will look out for you."

"Yeah, she will."

"That's all I want—to know you're happy and safe."

"But, I feel... I don't know, like I'm throwing your kindness back in your face."

"Well, that's dumb," Molly stated matter-of-factly. "My love and kindness aren't conditional, Faith. I can't wait to get to know you better. We don't need to live together for that."

"Do...do you think Carmen meant what she said?"

"What did she say?"

"She said I'd always have a home with her and Mateo."

"Then yes, absolutely. If I know Carmen, and okay, I don't know her well, but I think she only says what she means."

"You're really not upset?"

"Not in the slightest. Sweetie, you found me. The hard part is done. We're in each other's lives."

"You rock, Aunt Mol," Faith sobbed.

"C'mere," Molly laughed, hauling Faith into another behemoth hug. "Everything's going to be okay, Faith, I promise."

This time, Faith had no trouble accepting such a promise. Things would be okay. Faith could feel it.

19

Carmen

Alan turning up dredged up some old feelings. The last time Carmen felt such a rush of anger towards another human being was when Mateo returned to their group home, battered and bruised.

Back then, Carmen couldn't help; she couldn't protect her brother. It wasn't the case now, which was why she'd been ready to launch an attack if Alan had dared get too close to Faith.

Thankfully, there'd been no reason for her to get involved physically. Molly and Faith handled Alan, and it was over. She should be happy, but now, Carmen had to face the fact Faith would more than likely stay in California with Molly and she would go home to Seattle; back to her life, hiding in her house.

Wow, how sad was that?

Faith and Molly had gone for a walk and Carmen found herself milling about. Sitting still wasn't possible.

Her body felt as restless as her mind. Irritated with her own mood, Carmen took the stairs, two at a time, to the room she'd been sharing with Mateo. Unpacking her shorts and leisurewear tank top, Carmen stretched, readying herself for a run.

The sun beat down mercilessly as her feet pounded the dirt track. Pushing herself, Carmen ran harder. The thought of simply going back to the life she'd had before Faith turned up, sat heavy in her chest. Mateo tried for months to get her out of the house, but she'd always fought him.

The fun Carmen felt since Faith turned up and made their little family feel whole was unexpected, but welcome. Mateo seemed lighter, too. So, even if Faith stayed behind, Carmen knew she had to keep pulling herself toward something better. A flash of Molly's eyes zipped across her mind, causing her to physically shake her head as she ran.

Trying to break out of her past life was one thing; thinking about a woman, quite another.

One step at a time.

Inevitably, she would go back to therapy. The events of the past few weeks churned up too much for Carmen to push back down. Mateo wouldn't allow her to hide her feelings, anyway—it wasn't healthy.

Then there was her career to consider. Owning two businesses provided her and Mateo with a secure future, but now, witnessing the good Molly and Bessie were doing, made her crave more.

There was a deep sense of unfulfillment in her life. Rita would be a good person to speak to. Carmen could definitely help; she could give back. Rita deserved that. In fact, Carmen felt some shame she'd not helped Rita more.

That's going to change!

As she rounded the corner, the ranch house came into view. Sweat was literally dripping off her forehead, into her eyes. Running in one-hundred-degree weather wasn't the most sensible choice, but her body was satisfied and her head felt clearer.

Slowing down to a jog, Carmen saw Molly in the distance, off to the left of the house. It wasn't like she meant to stare, but holy shit, watching Molly in those tight-ass shorts and skin-tight tank was just too distracting.

Walking with her head firmly turned towards Molly, Carmen didn't see Enid standing in front of her until they both nearly hit the ground.

"Holy shit, Enid, I'm so sorry!"

"Christ on a bike, you nearly had me on my back, and I can tell you it's been a long time since that happened, but, honey, you should know I don't see you in that way," Enid cackled.

"Hilarious. Seriously, are you okay? You're no spring chicken anymore." Carmen grinned.

"Cheeky shit. Yes, dear, I'm fine. Although maybe I should ask you that. What had you so distracted?"

Carmen's eyes betrayed her by wandering back to Molly, who was none the wiser, still working hard. Her hair was piled high in a messy bun, leaving her long neck on display. Beads of sweat ran slowly down to her back.

"Hey, are you still with me, Carmen?" Enid said, snapping her fingers in front of Carmen's face.

"What? Yeah, I'm here, what's up?"

"Oh boy, I see. It's not a *something*, it's a *someone*. I called it, Bessie owes me fifty bucks."

"You can wipe that shit-eating grin off your face," Carmen huffed.

"I don't think so. You've got the hots for Molly," Enid cackled again.

"Will you keep your voice down, and no, I do not! I was in my head, thinking, and I just didn't see you. I didn't even notice Molly."

"Ha, you're ridiculous. Whatever, honey, I see you."

Not wanting to listen to any more of Enid's ludicrous ranting, Carmen politely excused herself to the house. She needed to shower and check her emails.

Once Carmen had gotten into work mode, she'd wasted a good four hours. She hadn't meant to, but it had actually provided her with the space she needed. No way did she want to run into Enid or Bessie; not after she'd made a complete jackass of herself ogling Molly and being caught doing it.

Her stomach growling eventually forced her to close down the laptop and sneak to the kitchen. It seemed everyone was out or in their rooms. Carmen could deal with that.

Halfway through eating a ham and cheese sandwich, Molly joined her, freshly showered, and her hair deliciously damp. Carmen had to drink some water to get the rest of her sandwich down her esophagus. How the hell did Molly get even hotter?

"Hey."

"Hi," Carmen half choked. "Sorry, the sandwich went down the wrong hole."

Molly laughed, swiping the rest of Carmen's sandwich off her plate.

"Mmm, wow, that's a good sandwich," she mumbled.

Carmen couldn't speak.

"Has Faith spoken to you?" Molly asked once she'd swallowed.

"Not since everything happened this morning."

Molly nodded, her eyes locked onto the last square of bread in her hand.

"How are you? Really?" Carmen asked.

Molly's shoulders dropped. "It was a lot. I'm just glad Faith is doing okay."

"And you? Are you doing okay?"

Molly suddenly teared up. "I—"

This is what Carmen had been afraid of: Molly keeping her feelings bottled up. Twenty years of waiting and hoping had ended today. That wasn't something she would move past easily.

Scooting her chair closer, Carmen wrapped Molly up in her arms. Molly's sobs were muffled as she buried her face in Carmen's neck.

"I miss my parents so much. I miss what I had," Molly finally rasped. "We were so happy, so loved, and it was shitty that it all got ripped away—for me and for Alan, but I thought I would always have him. I thought he would always be on my side. I truly believed he would come around one day. How could he not? I'm his only living family. But, after today? After seeing the hatred and anger he still holds in his heart, I know my prayers will go unanswered. And now I know I'm truly alone."

Carmen's heart broke for the young girl whose life had been ripped apart; for the adolescent who had her only brother disown her, and for the adult in front of her now.

"You are not alone," Carmen whispered into her hair. "Love surrounds you. Faith is your blood. You have a family who loves you. I know it can't wash away the pain you've suffered, but it's a new beginning, Molly."

"She's not staying," Molly hiccupped. "Faith...she doesn't want to stay."

Carmen pulled herself away from Molly, searching her face. "What do you mean? Where is she going?"

"She's leaving with you. Her life is in Seattle."

"Molly, I—"

"It's okay, honestly. She's finally building a life for herself. I want her to go where her heart takes her."

"I'll look after her, I swear."

Carmen was walking a fine line of heartache and happiness. Knowing Faith wanted to live with her and Mateo was wonderful. Seeing Molly so upset was not.

Should she talk to Faith? Urge her to reconsider? No, it wasn't her place. Faith needed to be in charge of her life. Carmen was there to support and guide—nothing more.

"We will talk on the phone and hopefully, I can visit."

"You are welcome anytime, Molly. Anytime."

"Thank you, Carmen. I feel like my words aren't enough to express the gratitude for everything you and Mateo have done for her."

"Please, no more thanks. I just want to help."

"You do," Molly whispered, her lips brushing Carmen's cheek. Carmen's eyes fluttered shut as she relished the sensation of Molly's sumptuous lips on her skin.

"Hey, there's a lady at the door for you, Molly," Mateo shouted from the hall. Molly sat back slowly, her eyes on Carmen.

"Send them in," Molly called back.

Carmen stared, unable to break the contact with Molly. The urge to take Molly by the face and kiss her soundly was so strong she had to fight to remain still.

The sound of footsteps approaching the kitchen finally snapped her out of the trance Molly had her in. Molly blinked, briefly looking down at her lap before getting up.

Carmen turned to the kitchen door where a very attractive woman stepped in, pulling Molly in by the waist and doing the one thing Carmen wished she could. Kissing Molly on the mouth. Carmen's jaw tightened so hard she was close to cracking her back teeth.

"Hey you," the mystery harlot said to Molly in a low voice.

"Chel-Chelsea, hi, um, what are you doing here?"

Molly was clearly flustered. Carmen narrowed her eyes at the intruder.

"It's been a few days since we've caught up. I have this evening off, so I thought I'd swing by. I didn't realize you'd have guests." Chelsea—*ugh, what a name*—flicked her eyes towards Carmen.

"Oh, right, um, this is Carmen," Molly stuttered, gesturing to Carmen. "And this is Mateo. They drove Faith, my niece, here from Seattle."

Chelsea smiled. "Oh, cool, staying long?"

Her gaze fell once again squarely on Carmen.

Ah, she's threatened.

"Just a couple more days. We need to get back by the start of next week," Carmen answered smoothly.

"And you are?" Mateo asked kindly.

"Chelsea, Molly's—"

"Friend," Molly interjected. Carmen didn't miss the flicker of disappointment in Chelsea's eyes.

"Yeah, friend," Chelsea repeated. "So, do you want to hang out?"

"Um, you're welcome to stay and hang out with us all. I want to spend as much time with these guys before they leave."

"The kiddos will filter in as soon as I put dinner on," Bessie said, shuffling into the kitchen. "Hey, Chelsea, good to see you, sweetie."

"Hey, Bessie."

"Who are you?" Enid shot. Her short stature meant they had missed her behind Bessie.

Carmen had to stifle a laugh at Enid. Her eyes were narrowed, and she was clearly judging Chelsea and her proximity to Molly.

"Um, Chelsea."

"She's my friend," Molly parroted.

"Oh, your fuck buddy," Enid tutted. Molly went a shade of red that Carmen didn't think existed.

"Enid, fucking hell," Carmen hissed.

"What? What did I do?"

"Go have a gummy on the porch," Mateo shot.

"I don't know why you're all getting so upset. It's the truth, isn't it? No reason to be embarrassed. I had a fuck buddy for a while once, but his hip kept locking."

"Oh my God!" Carmen hurled, mortified.

Enid cackled like a villain. "You lot are too easy," she tittered, shuffling back out of the kitchen. "Call me when there is food. I'm going to have the munchies in about twenty minutes."

"I'm so sorry," Molly whispered to Chelsea, who looked shell-shocked.

"She's a law unto herself. We can't control her," Mateo laughed.

"Hey, everyone," Faith called from the back door. Courtney and Lisa followed behind.

"Faith, hey, come and meet my friend Chelsea."

"Oh, hi, nice to meet you." Faith smiled.

"You too," Chelsea replied.

"What's for dinner? I'm starved," Liam bellowed from the stairs.

"Christ, it's busy here, isn't it?" Chelsea laughed, but Carmen picked up on the insincerity. She was pissed she had to share Molly.

"Just how it should be," Carmen replied enthusiastically. Then, for some reason, she shot a wink at Molly. A wink. What the hell was that about?

Oh, you're provoking Chelsea because you're a jealous ass!

"Hey," Mateo interjected, "How about we have a party? With us leaving soon, I think we should have a proper sendoff."

"Yes," Enid shouted from the front porch, "let's do that!"

"Um, could I talk to you both?" Faith asked, looking at Carmen and then Mateo.

Mateo rested his forearm on Carmen's shoulder. "Sure, *chica*, what's up?"

"Um, could we go somewhere private?" Faith mumbled.

Carmen nodded and led the way outside.

"You good?" she asked, even though she knew what Faith was about to say.

"Would, um...would you be okay if I came back to Seattle with you?"

Carmen didn't get the chance to answer because Mateo squealed so loud she had to cover her ears.

"Fuck, *hermano*," she growled. "You just startled every dog within a hundred-mile radius."

"Oh my God, are you serious?" he continued, ignoring Carmen. "You want to come home with us?"

Faith was laughing. "Yes, if that's okay?"

"That's such a dumb question. Obviously, it's okay. Oh my God, we are going to have so much fun."

"Carmen?" Faith asked.

"You don't need to ask. I told you earlier, you always have a home with us. But are you sure? What about Molly?"

"I've spoken to her and she knows it's for the best. It's where I feel I should be."

"Okay, say no more."

Carmen and Mateo surrounded Faith in a hug. Looking over Faith's shoulder, Carmen saw Molly watching them from the kitchen window.

"Come here," she mouthed. Molly looked like she was going to say no, but eventually she stepped outside and joined Faith and the Ruizes in an embrace. Suddenly, they were engulfed by more arms and bodies. Carmen laughed as Bessie, Lisa, and Courtney joined them.

"Hey, don't leave me out," Enid squawked as she rounded the corner from the front porch.

"Okay, let's plan a party," Mateo announced.

To Carmen's annoyance, Chelsea stuck around for the entire evening. Mateo was in full party-planning mode. Carmen reigned him in several times, reminding him the guests weren't his friends from home and he needed to keep it PG.

"So, everyone is okay for tomorrow night, right?" he asked the group. There was a general nod.

"I'll run to the store and pick up some stuff," Bessie said.

"I'll go," Carmen interjected. "Actually, I'll go now. It's still open."

Carmen ignored Mateo's pointed stare.

"Oh, I'll come too," Molly said, surprising Carmen. Chelsea looked super pissed.

"Sure, let's go. Have we got a list to follow? I don't want you throwing a fit when we get back."

"Oh, *hermana*, you know me so well," Mateo replied with a smile. "It's here. Don't forget the liquor. Once the rugrats are in bed, we're getting it on."

Carmen rolled her eyes. Enid clapped and pumped her fist in the air.

"Let's go," she whispered to Molly.

They spent the first few minutes in silence as Carmen navigated the winding roads. Why did it feel awkward between them?

Oh, maybe because you were seconds and inches away from kissing her!

"Chelsea seems nice."

Why was she bringing Chelsea into it?

"Yeah, she's cool."

"Sorry about Enid."

"It's not your fault she has zero filter," Molly laughed.

"Still, you looked really embarrassed."

Molly chewed her bottom lip. "We...we have an arrangement," Molly began.

"You don't owe me an explanation," Carmen replied quickly. She did *not* want to have this conversation, ever!

"I know. It's just, I think Chelsea wants it to be more."

"Well, yeah," Carmen laughed sarcastically. Wincing at her outburst, she side-eyed Molly. "Sorry. It's just, she made it obvious she wants it to be more."

"Yeah, I've told her it's not going to happen."

"Why not? You seem to get along well."

"She doesn't give me the fuzzies."

"The fuzzies," Carmen chuckled.

"Hey, don't laugh at me." Molly grinned, jabbing Carmen in the ribs.

"No, not laughing, I swear," Carmen chuckled.

"I... I just don't want to settle for less than love, you know? It takes something from you every time you give your heart to the wrong person, and I don't think I'm strong enough to keep doing that."

"You're strong enough for anything, Molly Parsons. But I understand."

Carmen completely understood. She'd never given anyone her heart. Well, Mateo had it, and now Faith, but that was different. The thought of making herself vulnerable with a woman scared the living shit out of her.

For a long time, she'd convinced herself she didn't need that kind of connection. Sex was good enough. But her perspective and outlook on life were changing.

"I don't think she's going to take it well," Molly whispered, looking out the side window.

"Just be honest with her. Completely. That's all you can do. You can't control how she'll react. That's on her as long as you give it to her straight."

"You're really good at this, you know?" Molly commented, turning her head to look at Carmen.

"What stuff?"

"Talking. Listening. You're easy to be around, Carmen. Easy to talk to. I feel like you really pay attention."

"Oh, um, thanks."

"I've embarrassed you?"

"No, it's just no one has ever said that. It's nice to hear."

They pulled into the parking lot of the grocery store. Molly placed a hand on Carmen's arm, stopping her from leaving the car.

"If you ever need someone to listen. I'll only be a phone call away. I know you have Mateo, but you know, if you need another ear," Molly said softly, shrugging.

The air constantly became charged when they were alone and Carmen didn't know how to deal with it. She wasn't going to let herself do something stupid. But damn, Molly Parsons was making it difficult!

20

Molly

The bell above the coffee shop door jingled as Molly pushed her way through. The smell of coffee instantly calmed her nerves. Strange, really, considering how unsettled she felt, that caffeine, of all things, should relax her.

In the far corner of the shop, Molly saw Chelsea waiting with a smile.

Ugh, this isn't going to be pleasant.

It didn't matter, though, Molly needed to break things off, even if, technically, there wasn't anything to finish, except a loose arrangement. Clearly though, after yesterday's stunt, Chelsea was pushing for more.

"Hey," Chelsea cooed, leaning in to kiss Molly once again. Molly smiled politely, shifted her face a fraction, and allowed Chelsea to kiss her cheek.

"Hi," Molly replied coolly. Chelsea saw the change in Molly's demeanor but didn't comment.

"I ordered you an Americano," she chirped.

"Thanks."

"Tonight's party should be fun."

Chelsea's upbeat attitude was irritating, and Molly hated feeling that way towards her friend.

Come on Molly, get it over with.

"Chels, we need to talk."

"Okay, what about, babe?"

Molly winced. She wasn't Chelsea's *babe,* or anything else, for that matter.

"I think it's time we stopped our arrangement and just went back to being friends full-time."

"Why?"

Chelsea's chipper mood was turning in front of Molly's eyes. Half the reason Molly continued to sleep with Chelsea was because it was easier than fighting with her. Chelsea could be stubborn and petulant. Lesbian drama was a real thing where she was concerned.

"Because I think you want more out of it than a casual arrangement." Carmen's words echoed in Molly's ears. *"Just be honest with her. Completely. That's all you can do. You can't control how she will react. That's on her as long as you give it to her straight."*

Chelsea scoffed. "No, I don't."

"Chelsea, you walked into my kitchen last night and kissed me like I was your girlfriend. I really didn't appreciate it. We were clear from the beginning what this was. You told me you wanted the same thing."

"I do! Nothing has changed!" Chelsea shot.

Molly stared at her, daring her to lie again. Chelsea had made it obvious she wanted Molly to be her girlfriend and now she needed to own up to it. The intensity of Molly's stare increased. Chelsea shuffled in her seat.

"Mol, fine, I want more. We're good together, don't you think?"

"As friends, Chelsea. I'm sorry, but I don't feel that way about you."

"So you've been using me for sex?" Chelsea growled.

"Yes, because that's what we agreed on! Openly, I might add. It was a way to de-stress."

"Well, I want more," Chelsea demanded.

"Tough shit, Chelsea. I don't! And I will not be bullied into it."

They glared at each other, neither willing to back down. How could Chelsea think acting this way would make Molly rethink their situation? It did the opposite and threw up some major red flags.

"You're still invited to the party tonight. I should go; I need to help set it up."

"So that's it? What you say goes, huh?"

"On second thought, maybe you shouldn't come. Take some space, Chels, decide if you still want us to be friends, but remember that is all we'll ever be."

Sliding her chair back, Molly stood, gave Chelsea a quick peck on the cheek, and walked away.

As awful and uncomfortable as that had been, Molly felt better. Now she could concentrate on tonight's festivities and the fact that Faith would be leaving.

Carmen's deep brown eyes swam in front of her face. It wasn't just Faith that Molly would miss.

Before Chelsea interrupted yesterday, Molly could have sworn Carmen was about to kiss her. Molly huffed out loud. She was being delusional. Carmen wouldn't kiss Molly. No, they were just getting closer because of Faith. Faith, yes, that was the reason.

And that she listens to me, comforts me, is caring and fun...oh, and for the first time in a long time, I feel safe. Shit!

Molly had no time for dwelling on silly thoughts. She had to get back and help with the party. Spending time with her niece was the only thing she needed to concentrate on today.

"This place looks amazing," Molly gasped when she stepped out of the kitchen and into the backyard.

After getting back from coffee with Chelsea, she'd thrown herself into helping Bessie and Faith in the kitchen. Although she tried to stay present, her mind often wandered to thoughts of Carmen and what she was doing.

"I know. I'm amazing," Mateo preened.

"And so humble, *hermano*," Carmen deadpanned.

"There's nothing wrong with blowing your own horn now and then," Mateo replied smugly.

"Ew, I don't want to hear about your horn, or who is blowing it," Enid announced, carrying out a tray of mini burgers.

"Ah, Enid, that's gross. Don't say things like that in front of me," Carmen whined. It was amazing how the two Ruizes became almost childlike in the presence of Enid. Molly laughed at their antics.

"At least there *is* a possibility of someone touching my horn," Mateo shot. Carmen hit him square in the head with a mini burger.

"Now, children, don't make me whoop your asses," Enid admonished, but there was no force behind it.

"She started it," Mateo whined.

"No, *she* started it," Carmen laughed, pointing at a grinning Enid.

"Are we ready for some tunes?" Liam called. This was the most animated Molly had seen him in a while.

"Yes, young Liam, crank it up," Mateo shouted.

"No one says 'crank it up'," Enid mocked. "How am I cooler than both of you?" she laughed, pointing at both Carmen and Mateo.

Deep bass pounding through the speakers, which were set on either side of the back porch, interrupted the bickering.

A long table had been dragged into the backyard. Mateo had erected a light linen canopy over it and strung up fairy lights. Bessie scurried back and forth with plates of food. Faith, Courtney, and Lisa started dancing on the makeshift dance floor.

"Grub's up. Dig in!" Bessie hollered.

Half of the crowd started piling plates with food, while the other half danced and laughed. Molly stood back, leaning against the porch, observing.

Carmen, Mateo, Enid, and Faith had injected energy into the ranch and everyone in it. Thinking of them not being there tomorrow was a hard pill to swallow.

"Drink?" Carmen asked quietly, leaning on the porch railing next to her, offering a bottle of beer.

"Thanks." Molly took a long draw, her eyes fixed on Faith, laughing loudly as Mateo spun her around.

"He's an idiot, but he loves that kid," Carmen commented, her eyes fixed on Faith and Mateo as well. "She's given us a sense of purpose, I think."

"She's happy."

"Are you?" Carmen whispered. Their bodies close. If it weren't for the fact Molly could see other people around them, she would swear they were completely alone. It was always that way when Carmen got close. Everything evaporated until it was only them.

"I will be," Molly answered honestly, her eyes drifting from the party to Carmen.

"Carmen," Enid screeched, causing them both to jump. "Get your ass over here and dance with me. Mateo has told us you have moves for days."

"Jesus," Carmen hissed. "I'm going to shave his eyebrows off tonight," she muttered, pushing off the railing and making her way to Enid.

Molly's mouth watered the second she spotted Carmen's hips sway. And then something fucking fantastic happened: the music changed as Mateo swept in, claiming Carmen. Together they danced, their bodies moving in perfect synchronicity. Was that a Salsa?

Out of the two, Molly would say Carmen was the more masculine, even if Mateo was dashing. He was effeminate, but now, as they danced, Carmen transformed, her hips swaying as Mateo led her perfectly. Everyone at the party stopped what they were doing and watched.

Molly's eyes never left Carmen's ass. Swaddled in tight black Daisy Dukes, sumptuous butt cheeks peeked out, not entirely covered by the denim. In just a few days of Californian sun, Carmen's skin had turned a rich brown.

Holy fuck!

But then it got better. In between twirls, Carmen reached up and untied her hair. A cascade of black silk tumbled over her shoulders. Molly was completely mesmerized. The dance was perfection and left Molly literally weak at the knees.

Raucous applause snapped her back to the party.

"Holy shit," Enid called. "That was fantastic. Teach me," she bellowed, grabbing Mateo. The music started again and everyone fell about in hysterics as Mateo tried to teach Enid the steps. Molly couldn't fully appreciate the hilarity because her head and her libido were still firmly on Carmen Ruiz.

"Wanna try?"

Molly sucked in a breath when she realized it was Carmen talking to her, offering her hand. Molly loved to dance, but this felt dangerous. Of course she couldn't refuse—not when she was met with chocolaty pools of goodness. Carmen's eyes were a deadly weapon.

Instead of verbally answering, she nodded and took Carmen's hand. As she moved into Carmen's body, Molly knew something had shifted. There was no denying the attraction, not when both she and Carmen were almost visibly vibrating with anticipation.

The gentle breeze was a welcome one as Molly slipped away from the party, sweating. One salsa lesson turned into hours of dancing and hours of having funny feelings towards Carmen as her body danced close to Molly's.

Taking a break was the only way Molly could stop from making a fool of herself. She didn't miss Bessie and

Enid's eagle eyes firmly trained on her and Carmen as they danced. For once, the duo was probably on the mark. Molly's thoughts had been less than child friendly.

"Where are you sneaking off to?" Enid asked from the shadows of the work shed. Molly let out a scream and almost fell over.

"Crap, Enid, what the hell?"

"I saw you heading off on your own. Just wanted to make sure you're okay, sweetie."

"I'm fine, just needed a break from dancing, and the night is so lovely I thought a walk would be good."

"Fuck, that's a long-winded ass way to say you needed to get some space between you and Carmen before you humped her on the dance floor."

Molly stood looking at Enid, dumbfounded. "Um."

Great rebuttal, Mol!

"No."

Enid tipped her head back and laughed maniacally. "I love it when I'm right."

"No," Molly repeated.

"Oh stop. The heat radiating off the two of you was scorching. Stop fighting it. Do you want my advice?"

"Not real—"

"Turn your cute butt around, grab Carmen by the hand, lead her to one of your sunflower fields, lay her down, and get busy!"

"Enid!"

"Careful of ant nests, though. You don't want those little bastards getting in the cracks and crevices."

"Enid!" Molly said, louder.

"Maybe take a blanket. Nothing romantic about mud in your ass. I did that once, ugh. I had some weird reaction and had to strap an ice pack to my puss for a week."

"Oh my God, Enid, stop!" Molly covered her face with her hands, half exasperated, half embarrassed.

"Or you know, take her somewhere else, but Molly," Enid continued, her voice softer, her mocking tone absent, "take her, because life is too damn short to not grab opportunities when they are slapping you in the face. It's one night. Enjoy each other."

Enid slinked off with the grace of a wily cat. Molly had walked away to get some space, not entertain the idea of grabbing Carmen, dragging her to a shadowy corner, and fucking her until the sun came up.

"It's a beautiful night, isn't it?" Carmen's low, smooth voice pierced the silence.

Molly closed her eyes and bit her lip. How was this happening?

"Molly?"

Turning on her heel, Molly smiled. "It's gorgeous. I was just getting some air. Got a little hot with all that dancing."

"Want some company?"

Oh, boy!

"Sure."

The music grew faint the longer they walked, neither in a rush to break the silence. The setting couldn't have been more perfect for a romantic walk. Molly rolled her eyes at the Universe. The stars shone down brightly. The moon cast a soft glow over the sunflower fields. Obviously, that brought the thought of Carmen, laid down on her back, spread wide, waiting for Molly.

Thanks, Enid!

"Are you okay? You look like you have something on your mind."

"Nope," Molly replied hastily.

"Molly," Carmen said gently, taking her by the hand and bringing them to a stop.

"Please don't," Molly whispered.

"Don't what?"

Oh, fuck it!

Molly slid her hand into Carmen's hair, drawing her in. Their lips smashed together in a heated frenzy. All the pent-up lust Molly had been trying—in vain—to push down, came roaring to the surface.

Carmen was soft and tasted of strawberries. Molly felt Carmen's hands circle around her waist, then drop to her ass.

Molly pulled Carmen in closer, unable to satisfy her need that pulsed through her entire body. A moan of pleasure ripped through the air when Carmen's tongue entered her mouth.

This was going to happen. For once, she was going to take Enid's advice and seize the day. Then Enid's earlier warning cropped up. They were making out furiously in the middle of the farmland. Mud and probably a lot of ant nests everywhere.

And then, as if ordained by the almighty herself, a ray of moonlight struck a place in the distance that was perfect: an abandoned pickup truck the kids had put a mattress in the back of. They used it to camp out sometimes. Why hadn't she thought of that sooner?

Because you weren't planning on ripping Carmen's clothes off and getting freaky under the stars!

Tearing her lips from Carmen, Molly pulled her along silently but with a speed that portrayed how desperately Molly *needed* to get to that truck.

But as they approached, doubt clouded Molly's mind. Sure, they'd been making out pretty hard, but taking Carmen to the truck which had a bed in it was a clear sign Molly planned to do a lot more than kiss. What if Carmen didn't want that? What if she stopped this?

Her out-of-control thoughts were ripped from her mind by Carmen slamming her back against the truck's passenger-side door. Molly hadn't even realized they'd reached it. Molly felt the button of her shorts snap open and the zip lowered. Carmen wanted this. And by God, Molly was going to let her have it.

Claiming Carmen's lips again, Molly was ready to take back control. Twisting her body, she took her turn, slamming Carmen into the truck. Their movements were frantic, hands unwavering in their search for each other's pleasure. This was fast, hard, and everything Molly wanted.

Another twist and Molly was once again backed up into the hard metal. Carmen fighting for domination was erotic and not something Molly usually enjoyed, but between them, it was perfection.

"Turn around," Carmen growled, taking Molly's bottom lip between her teeth.

Molly pushed Carmen's body away. Taking her time, she slowly turned. The feel of Carmen pressing back into her body caused her clit to twitch. Whatever Carmen wanted, Molly was going to do it.

"You have the most delicious ass I have ever seen," Carmen murmured in her ear.

Molly's shorts were tugged to the ground along with her panties. The sharp smack of Carmen's hand on her bare ass cheek sent electricity coursing through her pussy. Desire escaped down her thigh as she waited with anticipation for Carmen to spank her again.

The second hit was even more pleasurable than the first, especially when Carmen followed it with a rub and squeeze of her cheek.

"Spread your legs," Carmen rasped.

Molly could hear the sexual frustration in her voice. She was in sexual heaven when Carmen ran her hand from Molly's lower back up to her shoulder blades, bending her forward.

"Is this what you want?"

"Yes," Molly pleaded. Carmen's hand continued up to Molly's hair. With a gentle tug, Molly felt her head pulled back as Carmen's other hand parted her dripping folds.

"You are soaked," Carmen commented in wonder.

Molly wanted to say something, anything, but Carmen rubbed her entire palm through Molly's sex.

"I want you all over my hand," Carmen muttered.

"Oh my God," Molly whined, the pleasure of just one long stroke almost tipped her over.

"Tell me what you want, Molly."

"Inside me, please Carmen, inside."

"Hard?"

"Yes!"

Carmen entered her hard with two fingers. Molly backed herself into the motion of Carmen fucking her hard and slow. As if reading her mind, Carmen pulled gently on Molly's hair again just as she thrust forward.

"Oh fuck," Molly moaned.

The slow pace was preventing her orgasm from building to a release, instead it was stirring gently, sending raw pleasure to every corner of her body. She needed more.

"Faster," Molly panted.

"I'm not ready for you to come yet," Carmen stated simply, pulling out of Molly entirely.

"Carmen," Molly cried. A beat passed and then it happened. "Oh, yes!" Molly screamed when Carmen thrust with three fingers, fast and hard.

It was a tsunami, a tidal wave, a hurricane of unbridled pleasure that ripped through Molly, leaving her a quivering, screaming mess, only able to stay in place because Carmen released her hair, wrapping her arm around Molly's waist as she climaxed.

Molly couldn't distinguish between the stars splayed across the sky and the ones dancing in her eyes. There was no question; she'd never experienced an orgasm as powerful as that.

Molly's entire body was sated. When Carmen withdrew her hand, Molly wanted to protest, take her hand and reinsert those wonderful fingers inside her until she writhed again.

"Are you okay?" Carmen asked gently, close to Molly's ear.

She nodded, her voice escaping her. If she couldn't have Carmen's fingers buried inside, then she'd have the next best thing.

Slowly straightening, Molly pulled up her shorts and underwear before turning to face Carmen. "Climb in the back."

Carmen didn't argue. In fact, she didn't say a damn word. Molly watched her climb onto the truck's bed, her body lowering to the mattress. Standing at the foot of the truck, Molly slid her hands slowly up Carmen's smooth long legs. Flicking the button open, she pulled Carmen's tight shorts and panties down, tossing them haphazardly behind her.

Wrapping her hands under Carmen's knees, she pulled until Carmen's legs hung over the edge. Dropping to her knees, Molly used both palms to open Carmen wide. Fuck the starry sky, the Californian sun, and everything else that was supposed to be beautiful. This right here—Carmen laid bare, her pussy glistening with need—was the most beautiful thing in the world and Molly was going to claim it.

The first swipe was nectar, pure and simple. Carmen tasted as sweet as when they'd kissed. Molly didn't want to tease or torture. She wanted to feast and devour.

Sucking Carmen's clit into her mouth, Molly relished the loud moan pulled from Carmen's throat.

"Yes, oh yes," Carmen cried.

Molly worked quickly, licking, sucking, and fucking Carmen with her tongue. Gripping Carmen's thighs,

Molly held tightly as Carmen panted, moaned, and then screamed into the night.

If tonight was all they had, then Molly was going to make the most of it. Carmen Ruiz would be hers, over and over, until sunrise. Molly was going to extract every bit of pleasure from this delectable woman.

Faith

The past few days had been hard. Leaving Molly behind had almost torn Faith in two. The morning after the party had been full of hugs, kisses, and crying. It had also been rife with tension. Something had happened between Carmen and Molly. They could hardly look at each other.

Faith silently blamed herself. Even though Molly said she was okay that Faith returned to Seattle with Carmen, clearly, she wasn't. Faith wondered if Molly and Carmen had fought at the party. They'd disappeared for a while and when they returned, neither could look at the other. Yes, that must be it. Faith's decision to live with Carmen had caused a rift.

Molly had been all smiles and cheer when they'd said their goodbyes, promising to visit soon. They planned to Skype once a week. Faith watched Molly and Carmen say goodbye, and it was definitely awkward. Maybe she should talk to Carmen?

Faith brought nothing up, not when she saw Carmen's posture. The woman was rigid the entire drive from California to Seattle. Mateo and Enid were unusually quiet, too. Maybe everyone was just feeling as sad as Faith?

That was an understatement. Two days back in Seattle, and Faith was seriously questioning if she was still welcome in the Ruiz household.

Carmen had retreated into work. Faith tried to converse, but when she only received bare minimum interaction, she decided staying out of the way was a better option.

What the hell had happened between Molly and Carmen? Something that meant Carmen was now regretting having her in the house, Faith thought.

Mateo was still his lovely self, so whenever he was around, Faith hung out with him. The problem was, he was rarely around these days. As soon as they'd returned, Mateo sought Daniel and was spending most of his time outside of work with him.

To add to Faith's anxiety levels, Nat hadn't been to see her either. Rita had sent her away on a training course which wasn't due to conclude for another two days.

Huffing out a frustrated breath, Faith headed out of the house. The silence was becoming insufferable.

"Enid?" she called, opening her neighbor's door.

"Hello, dear," Enid shouted from her kitchen. "Want a cocktail?"

"Sure," Faith replied, wandering into the living room, throwing herself down on the couch.

"Well, that's a sour face," Enid stated. She was carrying two very large and sugary looking drinks. "Who's put that look on your mush?"

Faith hadn't told Enid of Carmen's mood.

"No one," she lied.

"Cut the shit, kid, what's going on? Are you regretting your decision to come back?"

"It's not me who's regretting it," Faith snapped. It was unlike her to get snippy, so Enid's raised eyebrows were warranted.

"I think this is the first time I've seen you act like a petulant teen. I like it."

Faith grinned. "Sorry, Enid, I shouldn't have snapped."

"You didn't. You're clearly upset with someone, though, so out with it."

Faith huffed. "I think Carmen wishes I'd stayed in California."

There, it was out in the open and already Faith felt better for voicing her concern.

"Bullshit," Enid laughed.

"Enid, you haven't been in the house. Carmen doesn't talk to me. Heck, she barely looks away from her laptop. She doesn't want me there."

"Oh, sweetie, it's not about you," Enid soothed.

"Like hell it isn't," Faith growled. Where was this anger coming from?

"Alright, Ms. Feisty," Enid chuckled. "Have you asked her?"

"When do you suppose I do that? In the millisecond I see her when she goes from her room to the bathroom?"

"She's really that bad?"

"Yup." Faith's shoulders dropped. "I think I'll just save us both any more issues and pack up. Molly will be cool with me going back."

"Right... wait there."

Faith didn't have time to open her mouth before Enid shuffled out of the house at surprising speed. To her horror, Enid returned less than five minutes later with a harassed-looking Carmen. The only way she could have looked more scolded would be if Enid held her by the ear like a naughty child.

"Sit," Enid barked, directing Carmen to the sofa. Faith's face paled. "Right, now repeat what you just said." This time, Enid was talking to Faith.

"Um, it's..."

"Come on, out with it."

Faith swallowed the lump that sat in her throat. "Um, I said I was going to pack up and go back to California."

"What?" Carmen whispered. Faith dragged her eyes from the carpet to Carmen's face. What she saw was raw sadness and surprise, which confused the hell out of her. "Why?" Carmen choked.

It was time to bite the bullet. "Because, Carmen, you're clearly not happy I'm here. You've barely uttered a full sentence to me, and all you do is work in your room. Look, it's okay, I get it. Having a whole other person to look out for is a big deal."

"No, Faith, it's not a big deal."

"Obviously it is," Faith snapped. Carmen reared back a little. Closing her eyes, Faith admonished herself for being so short. "Sorry," she mumbled.

"No," Carmen began, letting out an enormous sigh, "it's me that should be apologizing. You're right, I have been acting like a jerk since we left California. But Faith, I swear it has nothing to do with you being here. I'm so happy you are. Really!"

"Then what's wrong?"

"I think I've just had some stuff I need to work through."

"Did you and Molly fall out?"

"What makes you think that?"

Faith didn't miss how fidgety Carmen suddenly became.

"Because you were both weird at the party and then hardly spoke. I thought you liked each other."

Watching Carmen scratch the back of her head and then look everywhere but at Faith was interesting.

"Honestly, we haven't fallen out. I really am sorry for making you feel unwelcome."

It was clear Carmen didn't want to continue this line of conversation and Faith was going to respect that.

"Okay. But look, if at any point you need me to leave, I'd prefer you to just be honest with me."

Carmen looked genuinely hurt by Faith's curt tone. "Faith, your home is here with me, Mateo, and Enid. There will never be a time I ask you to leave. Never!"

"Well, this was all a bit fucking deep," Enid interrupted. "Anyone for a gummy?"

Faith rolled her eyes, and Carmen laughed.

"Are we okay?" Carmen asked quietly, finding Faith's gaze.

"Yeah, we're good."

"Great, let's go get ice cream. You're right, I have been spending way too much time working."

"Really?" Faith asked excitedly.

"Absolutely!" Carmen nodded.

"Shotgun," Enid shouted, shuffling at max speed toward the front door.

"Who said you were invited?" Carmen called, winking at Faith.

"Ha, screw you, I'm the glue that holds this fucked-up family together," Enid cackled.

"She kind of is," Faith muttered.

"Shh, don't let her hear you say that."

For the first time since the leaving party, Faith felt a modicum of happiness. Of course she missed Molly, and couldn't wait to talk to her later, but Faith still felt her life was in Seattle. All she needed now was for Nathalie to come home. They were overdue for some time together.

"Hey, where are you going?" Mateo called from the street.

"Ice cream," Enid sang.

"Hell, yeah, I'm getting in on that," Mateo squealed.

"What? You're actually gracing us with your time, *hermano*?" Carmen mocked.

"Yeah, yeah, I get it. I've been a little absent. Well, I'm here now and we're going out on a family ice cream trip, so hush!"

They all climbed into Carmen's car just like they had for their road trip.

"Onward, Jeeves," Enid said, snapping her fingers. Faith laughed.

Life in the Ruiz/Parsons household—as Faith now affectionately called it—was as close to normal as possible. Once again, it was something Faith was very grateful for.

Mateo was making more of an effort to spend time with her and Carmen. He admitted he'd got lost in the haze of dating and was neglecting his family. Faith couldn't get too pissy; it was nice seeing Mateo happy. Daniel was good for him.

Carmen also turned herself around. Faith was still in the dark about what had actually made Carmen act so off, but she didn't push it. If Carmen wanted to talk, she would.

The best thing about life right now was the fact that in one hour, Nathalie would be visiting. Those two days of waiting for the training course to end had crawled by. It didn't help that Nathalie was unable to message or call a lot because of her hectic schedule.

Running a comb through her hair for the tenth time, Faith inhaled deeply. Why was she so nervous? Oh yeah, because even though she and Nathalie hadn't even shared their first kiss yet, they *had* partaken in a little bit of phone sex.

Nothing had changed between them, yet Faith felt everything had. Would it be awkward between them now? Would Nathalie expect them to take the next step? Was Faith ready for that?

Her body said yes. In fact, it was almost begging Faith to do the deed. Ever since their phone date, Faith experienced nightly dreams that left her squirming the next morning. It was safe to say Faith was no longer worried about masturbation. She'd made up for the years missing out, in just a handful of days.

"*Chica*, you have a visitor," Mateo called. Faith's heart rate spiked. How had an hour gone by already?

Bolting out of her room, Faith ran full speed, into Nathalie's arms. "I missed you so much," she breathed into her girlfriend's neck.

Nathalie's arms engulfed her tightly. Faith smiled as she felt Nathalie's lips press gently against her temple. "I missed you, too."

"God, you're so cute. It's kinda gross." Mateo gagged, mocking them mercilessly. Faith didn't care, she needed to feel Nathalie close.

"Come on, let's go to my room." Glaring at Mateo as they passed, Faith pulled Nathalie into her bedroom. Now they were truly alone, the air shifted. For a time, they simply stood there grinning at each other like idiots.

"You got a tan!" Nathalie smiled, her hand coming up to stroke Faith's face. Closing her eyes, Faith leaned into the touch.

"Yeah, it's kinda hard not to get some sun at the ranch."

"Maybe when you visit, I could go with you?"

"God, yes," Faith exclaimed. "I talked so much about you. Molly would whoop my butt if I turned up without you."

"You talked about me?" Nathalie grinned.

"I couldn't stop thinking about you," Faith confessed.

"A little bit of me is really relieved to hear you say that," Nathalie sighed.

Sensing something deeper, Faith stepped forward, cupping her girlfriend's face in her hands. "Were you worried?"

Nathalie's eyes shone with emotion. "Maybe a smidge."

"Why?"

"Because I like you so much, and I got scared you wouldn't come back to me."

Caressing Nathalie's cheek with her thumb, Faith drew closer. They may have done things a little backward, but that didn't make their first kiss any less monumental. The first touch of Nathalie's lips sent shivers down Faith's spine. Their noses brushed gently. Nathalie moved her hands to Faith's hips, pulling them even closer.

As much as Faith wanted to keep her eyes open and locked onto this wonderful woman, the sensation and pleasure became too much. Closing her eyes, Faith allowed her other senses to take over. She inhaled the smell of Nathalie's skin, and felt her tongue gently brushing against Faith's lower lip.

Instinctively, she opened her lips, granting Nathalie entrance. If Faith thought the kiss was good before, she was completely floored when Nathalie's tongue danced with her own.

A groan slipped from her throat as Nathalie ran her hands over Faith's ass, squeezing gently. With her pulse thundering in her ears, Faith knew she needed to bring the kiss to a close before she took it to a level she wasn't quite ready for.

Sensing Faith's thoughts, Nathalie gently withdrew, a lazy grin plastered on her face. "Wow," she whispered against Faith's lips.

"Uh huh, totally wow," Faith replied, her eyes unfocused and her feet unsteady.

"That was some first kiss."

"That was everything," Faith gasped. Her body was thrumming and her mind was mashed potatoes.

"Are you okay?" Nathalie chuckled, her lips grazing over Faith once again, sending a visible shudder through Faith's body.

"Hmm," Faith hummed.

Nathalie laughed louder, taking a step back. "I think I should stay at least a foot or two away from you until we've both cooled down."

Faith didn't answer, she just nodded bringing her fingers to her lips, still very much lost in a post-first kiss haze. Nathalie smiled a cocky grin, perching on the edge of Faith's desk.

"So, come on, how are you feeling being back? Sorry I couldn't call more."

Finally, coming to her senses, Faith sat on the end of her bed, cross-legged. "I'm feeling much better now that you're back. It was a little intense at first. Something was going on with Carmen, but that seems to have passed now."

"Any idea what was wrong?"

"Not sure, but I think it had something to do with Molly. I hope they didn't have a falling out."

"I'm sure they're fine. If not, it's not your problem, babe."

"Yeah. Anyway, I was thinking..."

"You were thinking?"

"Would you mind if I chatted with your aunt? I think I would like to do something similar to Molly, but without all the moving."

Nathalie's smile grew. "That's an excellent idea. Rita is always looking for help, especially from younger queer people. She loves to mentor. Any idea what you want to do?"

"Um, I think, eventually, I'd like to help counsel kids. I know I need a degree to be a professional, but if there is something I can do now, I want to."

Nathalie slipped off the desk and made her way to Faith. "You would be an excellent counselor. Rita will love the idea. There's a bunch of courses she can sign you up for. I bet she would even help you look into college if that's what you want."

Nathalie's excitement was infectious.

"Really, you think I could go to college?"

College had always been a faraway dream. Eventually Faith pushed it to the back of her mind to stop herself from feeling disappointed. It was better to expect nothing, so she wouldn't feel let down.

But since Carmen and Mateo had given her a place where she could make her dreams come true, her mindset was changing. To have her girlfriend support her was the cherry on top of the metaphorical cake.

"Babe," Nathalie cooed, "you can absolutely go to college and you will kill it."

Surging forward, Faith wrapped herself around Nathalie, capturing those plump lips in a scorching kiss.

"Thank you," she gasped when they came up for air. Faith noted she was on top of Nathalie, her thigh in between her girlfriend's. All it would take would be a few well-placed hip rolls.

Calm down, not yet.

"You're welcome," Nat mumbled, her lips tracing Faith's neck. Faith closed her eyes and did the hardest thing she'd ever had to do. She pulled herself away and sat on the opposite side of the bed.

"Sorry," Faith began. She didn't want Nathalie to feel as if she were teasing her.

"No, don't apologize. You're right to pull back. I don't want us to have a quickie the first time we're together." Sitting up, Nathalie took Faith's hand in her own. "When we do that, I want us both to be ready."

"Me too. I'm...I'm almost there. I just, I don't know, I just need a little more time."

"Baby, there is no rush. I'm not entirely ready yet either. It's a big deal. I know a lot of people my age would find it stupid that I want it to be perfect. But it's how I feel."

"Me, too."

"We can still make out, though."

"Absolutely. But maybe not right now. I think I could do with a cold shower first." They both fell into giggles.

"Do you want to go out for food and then head over to my place? Rita should be there."

"Yeah, that would be awesome."

Faith watched Nathalie head out the bedroom door, her gaze firmly on her girlfriend's ass.

She has the best butt in the world.

"Come on, you can check out my ass later. I need something to take the edge off my raging hormones. I'm thinking of pizza."

"Raging hormones, huh?" Carmen laughed from the hallway. Faith saw Nathalie's face grow red. Neither of them had paid the slightest bit of attention to their surroundings.

"Hey, Carm," Nathalie grinned.

"Hey, yourself. Now what's this I heard about pizza?"

"We were going to get something to eat and then head over to Nat's."

"Mind if I tag along? I need a quick word with your aunt."

Well, Faith needed something to temper her libido, and what was better than a big sister figure playing third wheel?

"Sure," Faith chirped. Her eye caught Nathalie's, and she knew they were on the same wavelength. Shooting a wink, Faith passed Nathalie, giving her ass a quick squeeze.

"Naughty," Nathalie whispered in her ear.

"I don't know what you're talking about," Faith grinned.

"Oh, Jesus, are you going to be like this the entire time?" Carmen moaned.

"Probably," Nathalie laughed.

"All right, that calls for backup then." Carmen grabbed her wallet and car keys. Confused, Faith and Nathalie followed Carmen out the door. Both burst into laughter when Carmen walked up to Enid's house.

22

Carmen

Drumming her fingers on her work desk, Carmen let out a frustrated huff. It had been three weeks since they returned to Seattle, so why the hell was she still struggling?

Lack of focus plagued her every waking hour. Carmen's brain was only content to obsess over her catastrophic fuck-up. Sleeping with Molly was perfect, but also a colossal mistake. How could she have let one moment of weakness override her common sense?

The fact they could hardly look at each other once they'd both come was a huge indicator it should never have happened. And now it was going to be a constant source of awkwardness. It's not like Carmen would never see the woman again. If that were the case, she wouldn't still be flagellating herself. But she would see Molly. It was inevitable. Faith was already talking about inviting her aunt to Seattle.

Knowing Faith thought Carmen regretted inviting her to live in Seattle sat heavy in her stomach. After they'd left California, Carmen retreated within herself. It was the only way she knew how to deal with what she was feeling. However, her behavior had given Faith the impression she wasn't welcome, and that was an awful feeling to sit with.

As soon as Enid ripped her a new asshole, Carmen tried her hardest to act normally around Faith. Any time she was alone, however, her thoughts and mood drifted. She was stuck in a perpetual loop of regret and longing.

No matter how much her brain screamed at her for doing something so stupid, Carmen's heart and body longed for Molly's touch. Carmen knew great sex. Over the years, she'd experienced some wild things, with a multitude of women. With Molly Parsons, all those experiences amounted to nothing but vanilla encounters. It wasn't because they did anything out of the ordinary; it was the feeling that accompanied the act.

The want had been so strong. So raw. Carmen felt as though they'd claimed each other, if only for that brief time. And now she didn't know how to move on from that monumental moment.

In California, she'd decided to make a few changes in her life. Since returning, Carmen had tried to keep her word. A conversation with Rita started the ball rolling and Carmen was looking forward to challenging herself by getting out of the house more and meeting new people.

What Carmen *hadn't* banked on changing was her approach to women. Casual sex was satisfactory, and it meant Carmen didn't need to be vulnerable and open to getting hurt. For a long time that worked perfectly, but now, after the connection she felt with Molly, Carmen wasn't sure if casual sex would be enough.

The one person who Carmen relied on to talk this sort of shit through with was absent most of the time now. Mateo and Daniel had ramped up the intensity of their relationship, leveling up to lesbian standards. A U-Haul was definitely in their future. It was only a matter of time before Mateo wanted to move out. That potential destabilization was a clawing feeling Carmen didn't want to explore right now. Too many things were changing.

So here she sat, in her room again, because Mateo was out and so was Faith. She was alone and drowning in her own feelings. Great!

The ping of a text message caught her attention. Carmen almost threw the phone across the room when she read Molly's name on the screen. Why was she messaging?

"Stop being pathetic," she growled to herself. Picking up the phone, Carmen tapped the message. A picture of Darren loaded. His face had healed, and his smile was radiant. The picture showed him with an arm slung around Molly's shoulder, laughing.

Carmen's heart burst open. Darren looked so happy. A far cry from the broken boy Carmen and Molly nursed all those weeks ago.

Carmen 10:45 a.m.

Oh wow, he looks great! How's he doing?

Molly's instant reply brought a smile to her face.

Molly 10:46 a.m.

So good. His boyfriend's parents have offered him a home. Darren reported his dad. It's been a little intense, but he's coping well.

Carmen 10:47 a.m.

Oh wow, that's huge. I'm so happy he's got a place to go. Please send him my love.

Carmen began tapping her fingers on her desk again. Should she mention the party? Apologize? Or should it just be ignored?

Okay, it looked like Molly wanted to skate over the whole thing, and Carmen was good with that. Maybe she could start sleeping normally now, or you know, focus on anything else but having sex with Molly Parsons.

Later that evening, Carmen was still on her own. Faith and Nathalie were practically joined at the hip now, and ever since Rita had taken to mentoring Faith, Carmen saw less and less of her. As much as Carmen wished she could see Mateo and Faith more, she was happy they were both thriving.

The front door closed with a thud, making Carmen jump. The spoon of spaghetti sauce she was holding fell to the floor, splatting her legs.

"Jesus," she hissed. Why did everyone have to make her fucking jump?

"Hey, *hermana*," Mateo called. He glided into the kitchen, wrapping his arms around Carmen.

"Who are you, and why are you in my house?"

"Okay, I get it, I suck. I'm sorry. I told you I would be around more and have done the exact opposite."

"It's fine." She smiled, but it didn't quite meet her eyes.

"No, it's not. But I'm here now and it's high time we had an evening together."

"What's with the sudden worry?" Carmen hadn't meant for it to come out as a snarky comment, but Mateo's wince said it had.

"Enid," Mateo mumbled, his eyes dropping to the floor.

"Enid?"

"Yeah, she, um...she had a chat with me."

"Okay, about?"

"How I've dropped you for a piece of ass."

"Whoa, I don't think that. I know Daniel is important to you."

"I know, but she isn't wrong. I just got swept up in him and totally bailed on you." Mateo toed the floor. "I knew something was going on with you, but ignored it because I was enjoying being with Daniel."

Okay, that kind of stung. Carmen would drop everything for Mateo, no matter who she was with.

"It's fine." Another half-smile.

Mateo grabbed Carmen by the shoulders and looked into her eyes. "No, it's not. No man or woman, or any other person for that matter, should ever be more important than you and me. I lost sight of that for a second and I'm sorry. I'm here now, though. I've told Daniel I need to spend some time at home and he understands."

"Mateo, you didn't have to do that. I'm fine, really."

"And if I didn't know you so well, I might be inclined to believe that *mierda*! But I do know you, and you've been struggling ever since we got home."

Turning off the stove, Carmen occupied herself with serving up food for them both. Mateo set the table silently, waiting for Carmen to open up.

Halfway through their dinner, Carmen finally spoke. "I slept with Molly."

"I thought so."

"Was it obvious to everyone?" Carmen didn't like the idea of being talked about.

"I think it's safe to say Enid and Bessie knew too, but we didn't gossip. I promise."

"Sure."

"Hey, look at me," Mateo pleaded. "We didn't gossip."

"Ugh, it doesn't matter anyway. We made a mistake and made life awkward."

"Is that why you're so down lately?"

Carmen scooted her spaghetti around her plate. "It was amazing," she mumbled.

"Amazing?"

"Yeah. The sex. It was amazing."

"Okay. Why do you sound upset about that?" Mateo chuckled.

"Because it was a mistake. It would be so much easier to forget if it had been mediocre."

"Why do you need to forget it? By the sounds of it, you were both caught up in a moment. It happened, and that's it. Why are you hanging on to it?"

"Because...because she... I..." Carmen was floundering.

"Hey, come on," Mateo encouraged, rubbing Carmen's back gently.

"We connected, not just physically. I can't remember the last person who I did that with. Yeah, it was a heat of the moment thing, but *in* that moment, we were together, you know, completely in sync."

Mateo thought for several seconds. "So why does it have to be a mistake? Maybe you could explore something with Molly?"

"Nope, no way!"

"Why not?"

How could Mateo even entertain that idea? "She's Faith's aunt for one. If we started something, and it broke down, like it inevitably would, things between me and Faith would get fucked up."

"Wow, that's a bleak outlook."

"It's an accurate statement."

"No, it's not. Carm, this is much deeper than that. Ever since we were kids, you've always expected the worst in people, and I get it—you know I do—but we're not those kids anymore. You encouraged me to meet new people. To live life. And all this time, you have refused to take your own advice."

"That's not it," Carmen argued.

"That's absolutely it! I want you to set up a therapy appointment, Carmen. It's time. I've been a terrible brother, letting you continue like this. You've always done what's best for me and now I'm doing the same." Mateo handed Carmen her phone.

"You want me to call now?"

"Yes, no time like the present."

"Fine." Carmen wouldn't argue. For Mateo to be so insistent, she knew it was time to seek help. "There," she replied, setting the phone down. "I have an appointment on Wednesday."

"Okay, good. Now, tell me about your chat with Rita."

"Oh shit! Yeah, I didn't tell you, did I? I'm going to work full time for Rita. I'll take over the running of the digital content. I've already got so many ideas."

"What about your business?"

"I'm staying on as a silent partner. I've sold part of each company to the new CEOs."

"Jesus, Carmen, that's huge. Why the hell didn't you tell me?"

"Because you've been MIA!" Carmen shot.

"Fuck, yeah, I know."

"I don't want to argue or fall out, okay? I knew the day would come when you met someone who swept you off your feet, Mateo. I'm so happy for you, I swear."

"He has swept me off my feet. But I know better than to abandon my family."

"That's a bit much. You haven't abandoned anyone."

"It feels like that when I find out you've made huge life decisions and I wasn't around to help you through it."

"Alright, how about we stop beating ourselves up and just do better?"

"Deal."

Life felt closer to being on an even keel after Carmen's heart-to-heart with Mateo. He brought Daniel to their house daily, which Carmen was grateful for.

Getting to know Daniel better was a must. They might have been acquainted through pizza delivery, but that wasn't enough to scope out if the man was good enough for her brother.

Carmen quickly decided he was. She'd never seen a man treat Mateo so well. Daniel indulged Mateo's diva side, but knew how to reel him in when needed. They balanced each other out. Deep down, she knew they were going to last. Mateo had finally found his happily ever after.

As for Carmen's love life, that had shifted too. It didn't take too many therapy sessions for Carmen to understand how self-destructive she'd been over the past few months... Longer if she were being honest.

That led to a monumental decision and one that scared the crap out of her. Carmen was going to date for real. Not just a hook-up or friends with benefits. No, she was going to bite the bullet and ask a woman out.

Fumbling with her phone, Carmen cursed her ridiculous nerves. "Just message her, you moron."

Easier said than done, though. Her body was pre-wired to keep people at a distance. Changing that way of living wasn't an easy fix.

"Okay, just calm down. Send the message and go from there. No pressure."

"Did you do it yet?" Faith asked from the other side of Carmen's door.

"Not yet," she whined.

"Just hit send, Carmen," Faith replied. Carmen could hear the eye roll in her voice.

"Fuck it," she grumbled, hitting send. "Done," she called to Faith, who flung open her door excitedly.

"Really?"

"Yes, really," Carmen laughed.

"Okay, what are you going to wear for your first date?"

"Faith, she hasn't even replie—" the beep of her phone stopped Carmen mid-sentence.

"What did she say?" Faith practically screamed.

With a shaking thumb, Carmen swiped open the message. Rachel's answer was a resounding yes. Relief flooded her system.

"She said yes."

"Yeah, she did!" Faith cried loudly, whooping and hollering.

Carmen couldn't help laughing at Faith's over the top reaction.

"Shit, I've got to go on a proper date now," Carmen chuckled.

"You're going to be great. You know Rachel. Don't overthink it."

"I'll try not to."

"Where are you taking her?"

Crap, Carmen only got up to asking the detective for a date. She hadn't even thought of what would happen if she said yes.

"Um...a bar?"

"Sure, but not just a bar you would usually go to. It has to stand out."

"Okay, um...yeah, I know. There's a new place I think she'd enjoy."

"Great, now the outfit."

Carmen watched Faith scour her closet. *She's spending too much time with Mateo.*

"What's going on?" Mateo asked from the doorway, his finger pointing between Carmen sitting on the bed and Faith raiding her clothes.

"Rachel said yes," Faith shouted from the closet.

"Hell yeah, she did," Mateo cheered, entering Carmen's room. Carmen sat back on her bed and relaxed. There was zero point in her trying to have an opinion on her clothes now that Faith and Mateo were in full-tilt fashion mode.

Sure enough, half an hour and several wardrobe changes later, Carmen stood in front of her floor mirror checking out the date clothes. She had to admit; they looked good.

"And once again, I am a genius," Mateo sighed.

"Excuse you? Who is the genius?" Faith huffed.

Carmen loved this version of Faith, who had well and truly burst out of her own closet and not just with soaring confidence as a queer woman, but with sass and attitude. Faith was still the kind and gracious kid who had turned up on her doorstep, but now she believed in herself. It really was a beautiful thing to witness.

"You're right, *chica*, this one belongs to you," Mateo conceded, bowing his head slightly. Faith giggled and swatted his arm.

Another chime of Carmen's phone interrupted their antics.

"Jeez, she's eager," Mateo laughed, presuming the message was from Rachel. It wasn't. As soon as Carmen's eyes spied Molly's name, her heart gave a brief flutter.

Over the course of the past few weeks, Molly began to message daily. At first, Carmen found it difficult to engage, but Molly was good at putting her at ease. It didn't take long for them to begin daily conversations.

Most of the time, they spoke about everyday life. Molly updated Carmen on the kids. Courtney and Lisa were well and truly in the young love stage. Micah was storming their way up the ranks in their job. Even Liam was doing better. He'd joined a gaming club and was making new friends.

Carmen talked about the work she was doing for Rita. Their mutual passion for helping queer youths made their conversations easy to get lost in.

To help move past her guilt of sleeping with Faith's aunt, Carmen had been open and honest with her therapist. Since letting that night go, she and Molly had built a genuine friendship, yet they never talked about women and dating.

Carmen wasn't sure she was quite ready to hear about Molly being with someone else, which she knew was stupid because they had only had the one night together.

Despite everything, Carmen could now recognize their one night had meant something to her and she wouldn't simply dismiss it as nothing.

"Oh, it's not Rachel," Carmen commented nonchalantly.

"Is it Molly?" Faith asked innocently. Faith was still in the dark about Carmen and Molly's transgression and that's how it would stay. As far as Faith was concerned, the women were just friends.

"Yeah, it is. She's covering a night shift at the shelter."

"She's been doing that a lot lately," Faith sighed. "I think there's something going on with her, but when I ask, she dodges the question."

"I'm sure she's fine," Mateo assured.

"Has she mentioned anything to you?" Faith asked Carmen.

"No, nothing. She's probably tired and missing you, kiddo."

"Yeah, I think it's time I invited her for a visit."

The sudden thudding of Carmen's heart took her by surprise. They'd done well forming a long-distance friendship. Carmen wasn't sure she'd be so chill with Molly being close. And what if things with Rachel took off? How awkward would *that* be? Well, only awkward if Molly still thought about their night together. That was unlikely, right?

Carmen was overthinking, as usual. Laying her worries to one side, she put a hand on Faith's shoulder. "You should absolutely invite her here. Bessie, too. I bet Enid would love that."

There, she'd done the right thing. Faith skipped out of her room, presumably to call Molly.

Mateo bumped Carmen's shoulder. "Are you okay with that?" he asked quietly.

"Yeah, it will do Faith a world of good seeing her again. And I'm in a better place now. We had a night together, but that's all it was."

"Okay. If you're good, I'm good. Now let's get you looking hot as hell for your date tonight."

Yes, that's what Carmen needed to concentrate on; the person who was an option for her, not a fantasy that still haunted her dreams.

23

Molly

Stupid, stupid Molly. Of all the things she could've done—sorry—of all the people she could've done; Chelsea was the worst possible choice, and yet here she lay naked next to her ex-friend with benefits. Idiot!

"Mmm, that was good," Chelsea whispered in Molly's ear.

Covering her face with both her hands, Molly wished she could rewind the past hour of her life. "That was a mistake."

"Really? You think an orgasm is a mistake?" Chelsea answered cockily.

"In this case, yes." Molly was furious with herself. Hauling herself out of Chelsea's bed, Molly dressed, unable to meet Chelsea's eyes. "Sorry, Chelsea, I don't want to confuse you. I said we were done doing this and then..." Molly gestured between them. "It's the last time it will happen. I stand by what I said before."

"If you say so," Chelsea chuckled, causing Molly to scowl.

"Bye, Chelsea." Molly left before Chelsea stopped her or tried to convince her to stay longer.

For weeks, Molly stayed out of Chelsea's way, knowing the woman still wanted more, but then Molly found out Carmen was going on a date and that flipped everything on its head.

Instead of dealing with her feelings, Molly sought out Chelsea and did the one thing she shouldn't have: She used sex to forget her emotions, and it was an utterly ridiculous choice. Molly knew that going in, and yet she'd gone through with it anyway. But, of course, all the emotions she'd wanted to forget, came rushing back the moment the fucking had finished. And now she felt worse than before.

Breaking way too many road laws, Molly skidded to a stop at the front of the ranch house. Bessie cocked both eyebrows from her seat on the front deck. Great, now she was going to have to explain why she was driving like a maniac. And why was her shirt inside out? Fuck!

"Is the Apocalypse happening or something?" Bessie asked.

"No," Molly grumbled.

"Oh, sweetie, what the hell happened? You've got a face like someone just kicked your dog."

Dramatically flinging herself in the chair next to Bessie, Molly cradled her head in her hands. "I did something stupid."

"It can't be that bad, can it?"

"I slept with Chelsea."

"Yeah, okay, that was stupid."

Molly glared at Bessie. "Really? Is that all you have to say?"

"What? You said you did something stupid, and I agreed. Care to tell me why you slept with her?"

"Not really."

"Could it have something to do with the reason you've had a bee in your bonnet for weeks now?"

"I have not," Molly argued.

She absolutely had. Ever since the party and that sublime session with Carmen Ruiz, Molly had been a hot mess. Why, of all people, did Molly have to connect so deeply with Carmen?

A woman who lived in another state. A woman who—as of recently—didn't date seriously. A woman who had shattered Molly's idea of what good sex felt like.

No matter how hard she worked in the fields or how tired she felt after a day at the shelter, Molly's mind wouldn't quit thinking about that night. She still winced when she thought of how they acted with each other after they were both sated.

In a few moments, they went from passionate, straight to awkward. Molly remembered Carmen looked as if she wanted to jump in her car, there and then, and take off. Instead, they'd walked silently back to the party, mussed and smelling of sex.

Bessie and Enid had given them both knowing smirks, which made everything feel a hundred times worse. Thankfully, Faith didn't notice a thing. They managed a few more minutes before Carmen excused herself and went to bed.

Obviously, Molly had gotten no sleep that night. Her brain anticipated how Carmen would act the next morning. The answer had been: distant. Carmen quickly popped into the kitchen and grabbed a piece of toast before leaving again, only giving a brief wave to everyone in the room. And that was it. Molly didn't see Carmen again until they were saying goodbye.

Their hug was brief, and Molly struggled to keep her composure. If she'd known for one second how things would go down, she never would have initiated anything, no matter how much she wanted it.

Weeks passed, and Molly finally plucked up the courage to text Carmen. Believing it was best to skate over their time together, Molly acted as she did before they'd fucked. And it worked...for the most part. Their messages became frequent and their friendship bloomed. Perfect, right? Everyone was moving on.

But then Faith called, inviting her to Seattle, and mentioning Carmen was preparing to go out on a first date with some detective called Rachel. It was the same detective, Faith told Molly, who helped keep an eye out for her when Alan was still a threat. Awesome. Just fucking fantastic.

"You just went to a dark place," Bessie stated. "You're frowning so hard right now."

"It's just been a shit day, is all."

"Alright. Enough. Molly, spit it out."

Molly should've known Bessie would only hold back for so long. "I slept with Carmen."

"Tell me something I don't know." Bessie grinned.

"I slept with her and then it got weird and awkward. She left, and we've only just started talking again. Now she's going out with some woman."

"There's quite a bit there to unpack. Let's start with you sleeping with her."

"Do we have to?"

"Yes, if you want to stop feeling like this." Bessie waved her hand up and down Molly's slumped posture.

"Fine," Molly growled. "We were close. We fucked."

"Nope, try again."

"Ugh," Molly sighed. "Carmen just got me from the moment she turned up. She listened and understood what I needed. I was happy to just stay friends, but then, I don't know, I just couldn't stop myself, and I kissed her."

"Before the night of the party?"

"No, same night. Well, Carmen was more than receptive and we... You know."

"Right, so it was all passion and heat?"

"Exactly. Bessie, it was the best sex of my life. I can't imagine what a full night with her would have felt like. She might have killed me."

Bessie let out a low chuckle. "I'm glad you enjoyed yourself."

"Yeah, I did—we did. But then, as soon as we finished, it fell apart."

"Did Carmen say something?"

"No, worse. She clammed up, and we never spoke of it. Actually, apart from saying goodbye the next day, we didn't speak again."

"And how did that make you feel?"

"Like fucking garbage, if I'm being honest."

"Elaborate."

"The sex was amazing, but it wasn't just the physical act, you know. I felt safe with her, even if it was also hella hot. I never felt out of control. I thought..."

"You thought?" Bessie gently urged.

"I thought maybe we could have explored something more. But that wasn't what Carmen wanted, obviously. She couldn't get out of here fast enough."

"Or she was just as shaken up as you and didn't know how to deal with it?"

"Maybe."

"So that's why you're all bent out of shape? You thought you guys could be more, but Carmen doesn't seem to be on the same page?"

"Carmen said she didn't do relationships. And yet, Faith called and told me she's going out on a date. I've been texting with Carmen for weeks and she hasn't said anything."

"Ah, so you're jealous. I see."

"No," Molly protested.

"Yes! Hearing Carmen, the woman who broke your vagina—"

"She did not break my vagina," Molly barked.

"Okay, the woman who rocked your world and then left you high but not quite dry, who told you she wasn't into dating, suddenly starts dating. Molly, you're jealous, which is stupid."

"Thanks, Bess, you're really helping so far."

"It's stupid, because no matter who Carmen dates, if it's not you, it won't work!"

"What are you talking about?"

"Look, Enid and I might have teased you both about being a good fit, but we weren't lying. We saw how you interacted and got close. That's why you two sleeping together came as no surprise—at all. I spoke to Enid the other day, and do you know what she told me?"

"What?" Molly asked cautiously.

"That Carmen, has been as much of a hot mess as you have."

"Probably because she regrets being with me."

"Or because she has feelings and doesn't know what to do with them. Have you considered that she panicked about what Faith would think if she found out?"

"Of course I did. I worried too."

"Right, but look at it from Carmen's point of view. You know her background, you know why she's probably freaking out."

"Jesus, this is too much. It doesn't matter, anyway. Like I said, she lives in a different state."

"And you move a lot. Maybe moving north is your next stop."

"Bessie, I'm here for the foreseeable future."

"If you say so, but don't stick around here out of some sort of loyalty to me, or because you're scared to find out what it would be like to have someone in your corner."

"Bess—"

"You know I'm right, Mol. I love you, and the work you do is invaluable. You give everything you have to help, and usually at the detriment of yourself. For a long time, you have told me you were looking for *the* person who made you feel safe, like you were home. Molly, several times you've mentioned Carmen made you feel both those things. Maybe, just this once, you stop running away from things and run towards something."

"Bessie," Molly sighed.

"Sweetie, just think about it. And don't sleep with Chelsea again. Christ!"

"Molly, hey." Faith waved. Their video chats were becoming more frequent.

"Well, hey there, honey. You look great!"

"Aw, shucks," Faith chuckled. "Nat's taking me on a date tonight, so I wanted to look good. I was just trying some stuff on. I've got a shift at the shelter before we go, and won't have time to decide later."

"Oh, fancy. Where are you being swept off to?"

"I don't know, she wants it to be a surprise."

"Well, Nat has moves, huh?"

"She does." Faith winked. "So, how's it going on your end? I haven't heard from Lisa and Court in a few days."

"Ah, that's because they are having a bit of a tiff."

"Oh, no, why?"

"Lisa got into college in New York."

"Ah, and I take it Courtney is super happy, but majorly depressed at the same time."

"Yeah, something like that. They'll work it out."

"God, I hope so. They're great together."

"Speaking of cute couples, how are Mateo and Daniel?"

"Daniel is moving in here," Faith squealed happily.

"Really? Wow, you're gonna have a full house."

"It won't be too bad. Everyone works, so it's quite rare we all gather in one space. Mateo is thinking about opening up another boutique. Carmen is out and about with Rita, plus she spends a lot of time at Rachel's now."

Ugh, it still stung to hear how well Carmen and Rachel were getting along. After talking to Bessie the day she found out Carmen was going on her first date with Rachel, Molly had done her best to put her feelings to rest.

There was no point upsetting the apple cart. Molly was in California, Carmen was in Seattle, and they were friends. That had to be enough. So, for weeks, Molly plastered on a happy face and became the best damn friend Carmen could ask for.

"Wow, so they're still together, great."

"Yeah, Rachel's cool, but..."

"But?" Molly jumped all over *that* brief pause.

"I don't know. Carmen doesn't seem totally happy. I could be wrong, but I like to think I know her."

"Has she said something?"

"No, not at all. It's just a feeling."

Molly hated the idea Carmen could be unhappy, but she'd be lying if the thought also didn't stoke a tiny bit of hope that maybe she hadn't missed the boat completely. Maybe she and Carmen *could* still happen?

"Well, I'm sure she's fine. Look, I was thinking about visiting in about two weeks. How does that sound?"

Molly pushed her phone further away as Faith screamed and shouted how happy she was Molly was finally visiting Seattle.

"I'll take that as a yes, then," Molly laughed.

"Yes, yes, yes. You have to come. I can't believe you haven't visited yet."

"I know, but I wanted to make sure everything was okay here. Bessie will call in extra people to help, but you know I don't like leaving extra work for anyone."

"I know, I know. I'm just pumped you're coming here. Oh my God, there is so much I want to show you."

"I can't wait, sweetie. Have a great time tonight, say hello to everyone, and tell Nat I'll kick her ass if she hurts you."

Faith scoffed. "No, I will not, because you wouldn't."

"Ugh, can't you just pretend I'm even a little intimidating?" Molly laughed.

"Nope." Faith grinned. "I'll say hello to everyone. Shall we catch up on the weekend?"

"Sounds great. Love you."

"Love you."

Was Carmen unhappy? That was the only thing that resonated from the entire conversation with her niece. Molly had pledged to be a friend to Carmen, so calling her to make sure everything was okay seemed reasonable, right?

Checking her watch, Molly noticed it was later than she thought. Carmen and Molly's messages usually happened in the daytime, and they were yet to have a phone conversation.

Nibbling her bottom lip, Molly weighed her next move. Either she stayed out of it and continued to message Carmen daily, or she called Carmen and figured out if Faith's worries were legitimate.

"You're just being a good friend," Molly mumbled to herself, her finger already navigating to Carmen's contact info. The call connected after two rings.

"Molly?"

Oh, Lord, that voice. "He-hey, Carmen."

"Is everything okay?"

Of course, Carmen would be concerned. There was no reason for Molly to be calling this late.

"Everything is great. Um, I just wanted to double-check that you were okay with me visiting. Faith just called, and I told her I could come up in a couple of weeks."

There, that was the truth. Mainly.

"Yeah, that's more than okay. Faith's going to be buzzing until you arrive," Carmen laughed.

"I could have just messaged, huh?"

"Probably, but it's good to actually talk to you," Carmen said softly.

It was difficult for Molly not to read into anything, especially when Carmen's tone of voice gave her reason to think there was something more to that response.

"So," Molly chirped, needing to lighten the atmosphere before she said something stupid, "how's the website for Rita coming along?"

"Oh, God, yeah, it's looking great. We're going to host a fundraiser next month, so I've been incorporating that into the site. I'm so pleased I made a change. As much as I loved working for myself, I feel so much more accomplished working with Rita."

"Well, I'm proud of you, Carmen. It takes a lot for someone to change up their life like you have."

"I have you to thank, Mol."

Ah, damn her and her use of Molly's nickname.

"Nah, you would have done it, regardless of knowing me."

"No, Molly, I owe you. Watching you and seeing the difference you make, inspired me to do better. You made me better."

Silence hung on the line as Molly tried to decipher what Carmen meant.

"Carmen," Molly whispered.

She was losing the battle. Hearing Carmen, picturing her beautiful face, was destroying the meager wall of resistance Molly had built up. Scrunching her face, Molly asked the one thing she knew would snap them both back to reality.

"How's Rachel?"

The sound of Carmen's breath filtered down the phone. "She's fine, thanks."

Wow, okay, not the ringing endorsement of someone happy in a new relationship.

"Just fine? You guys have been dating for a few weeks now, right?"

"Yeah. I like her."

"Carmen, is everything okay?"

"Um, I'm not sure you're the best person to talk to about this with, to be honest, Molly," Carmen chuckled.

This was the closest they'd come to acknowledging what had happened between them.

"Why? We're friends, right?"

"You seriously want to hear about my love life?"

Nope, not one tiny little bit. But if they were to move forward and get along when Molly was in Seattle, they needed to bridge this gap in their friendship.

"Sure, why not? Come on, what's going on?"

"Molly!" Bessie yelled from downstairs. The urgent tone in her voice sent Molly scrambling for the door.

"Shit, Carmen, I need to go. I'll call soon."

Throwing the phone down on her bed, Molly raced downstairs. Bessie stood on the front porch looking out over the driveway. Molly skidded to a halt, checking Bessie over for signs of injury.

"Bess, are you okay? Are you hurt?"

"I'm fine, sweetie, but she's not," Bessie said, indicating to the woman standing in front of a beat-up car.

Whipping her head to look at the woman, Molly gasped. "Maureen?"

"Molly," Faith's mom hissed through what looked like a broken jaw and a severely bruised right eye.

Wasting no time, Molly descended the porch and approached Maureen, carefully laying a hand on her forearm. The state of the woman's body was shocking. It was amazing she could still stand.

"Come on, let's get you inside."

Bessie helped Molly gently lead Maureen to the kitchen.

"What happened, honey?" Bessie asked, sitting in the chair opposite, her eyes never leaving Maureen's.

"Alan," Maureen simply stated. It didn't take a genius to figure out Alan had done this.

"Do you want to tell us?" Molly prompted, her voice soft.

"Seeing Faith," Maureen began, "seeing her looking so happy and free." Maureen shook her head, tears falling from her battered face. "I couldn't believe the woman in front of me was my little girl. I thought, for so long, that staying with Alan was the best thing. I know I'm as much a monster as he is for allowing Faith to be hurt by him—by us. I swear to God, Molly, I never wanted this life for her, or for me."

Molly swallowed a lump. "I can't say I understand, Maureen. Faith should never have had to experience a life like that. But you're here, and I presume, looking at the state you're in, you left him?"

Maureen nodded her head. "I told him I was leaving, and he did *this*. I waited until he was asleep and left. I don't care who Faith loves. I just want my daughter back. I need her to know I love her and will do whatever it takes to make amends."

Molly looked from Maureen to Bessie. What the hell was she supposed to do? Faith was settled. Her life was just starting, but this was her mom. If Molly had the chance to have her parents back, she'd take it in a heartbeat, but that wasn't to say Faith wanted the same thing.

Taking a steadying breath, Molly faced Bessie. "I need to take care of this, Bess."

"I know, love. You need to go."

24

Faith

Faith flopped back on her bed. Today kicked her ass entirely. Working with Rita was proving to be one of the most difficult things she'd ever tried. It wasn't the day-to-day grunt work that was taxing; it was the group meetings.

Rita had wholeheartedly welcomed Faith into the fold, acting as a mentor right out of the gate. They'd discussed Faith's plans for the future and Rita felt her dreams of becoming a counselor were more than achievable. To help Faith understand what she would face, Rita asked her to take part in group sessions. All the participants had given their permission for Faith to sit and listen.

Some stories Faith heard in that room were horrifying. The trauma which had been inflicted on those people was unimaginable, but Faith did her best to sit silently. The people in that room didn't need her sympathy, they needed help to move forward.

Watching Rita navigate such rough waters was impressive. At no point did she instruct. Rita listened, asked questions and helped the person get to where they needed to be on their own.

After each session, Rita would debrief with Faith in her office. It was a good way for them to discuss how Faith was feeling and explain the methods Rita used to help the kids move forward.

Today was a particularly hard session. A young woman joined the group for the first time. Her story sent shockwaves through everyone, but as usual, Rita handled it like a pro. Bile rose in Faith's throat every time she recounted Lila's story.

Alan might have been a terrible father and husband, but he hadn't inflicted the torture Lila had suffered for years. Why were people so cruel? How could anyone do such inhumane things to another person? Was a woman loving another woman really so bad? No, of course not, the world was just a fucked-up pool of hatred.

The idea of going out tonight sat heavily on Faith's shoulders. Nathalie wanted to take her on a date, but Faith was far from being in a romantic mood. All she could do was think of Lila. The tough part of the whole thing was Faith couldn't talk to anyone about the session. It was strictly confidential, and Faith had no plans to break that rule.

"Hey, babe, are you ready to go?" Nathalie asked, entering Faith's bedroom. Faith swiped away a rogue tear that had fallen. "Whoa, what's wrong?"

"Hard day," Faith replied, sitting up. Nathalie regarded her for a few seconds before taking Faith in her arms.

"Okay, go take a shower. I'll be back in a few minutes."

And that's why Nathalie was the perfect girlfriend. She never pushed for an explanation. She simply gave Faith what she needed in the moment. Watching Nathalie scamper out of the room, Faith allowed herself a minute of reflection and thanks.

The shower helped wash the day away. Upon returning to her room, Faith couldn't help but smile widely. Nathalie had switched on the fairy lights, set up a range of naughty snacks on the bed, and opened up Netflix.

"Come on, get snuggled," Nathalie said, extending her arm to Faith.

Allowing herself to be pulled into Nathalie's body, Faith sighed in contemplation. Only after a few minutes did she realize she was still in a towel, damp from the shower.

"Let me get dressed before we start the movie." Faith noted the look of lust in Nathalie's eyes. They still hadn't taken the next step, but Faith was ready. Not tonight, but soon. Their make-out sessions became heated every time. Clothes were discarded, but they always stopped before underwear came off.

Nathalie cleared her throat, her eyes darting around the room. "I forgot hot chocolate. I'll do that while you sort yourself out."

And just like that, Nathalie shot from the room. Faith couldn't stop herself from chuckling.

Halfway through the movie, Faith was struggling to keep her eyes open. Normally, Nathalie went home after a movie night, but tonight, Faith needed her to stay close.

"Will you stay?" she mumbled through her drowsiness.

"If you want," Nat replied, holding her closer. "Let's turn this off and get some sleep. You're worn out."

Faith didn't have the energy to argue. After a day like today, falling unconscious in Nathalie's arms was the perfect balm.

Sunlight piercing through Faith's eyelids woke her early. Damn, she'd forgotten to close her blinds. For a split-second, Faith was confused by the warm body wrapped around her until she remembered Nat had stayed the night.

Turning slowly, Faith peered over her shoulder. Nathalie was holding her like a koala bear, her face buried in Faith's neck. It was a wonder she could breathe. Nathalie's entire face was smothered in Faith's hair.

The little snort and mumble Nathalie made caused Faith to laugh, which, in turn, caused Nathalie to stir. Had Faith ever seen anything more adorable than a sleepy Nat? Nope, never.

"Whatsappenin'?" Nathalie asked.

If Faith hadn't been paying attention, Nathalie's words would have been completely nonsensical.

"Hey, babe, sorry, I didn't mean to wake you," Faith cooed, turning in Nathalie's arms so they were facing each other.

"S'okay," Nat yawned, burying her head deeper in Faith's hair.

Faith chuckled again. By all accounts, Nathalie wasn't a very good morning person.

"Do you want some breakfast?"

"Nostayhere."

"What?" Faith laughed. Even *she* didn't understand that rambling. Nathalie lifted her head and gave a sleepy smile.

"I said, no, stay here."

Faith's internal thermometer was skyrocketing. Nathalie was gorgeous, her hair mussed up from sleep and her eyes a little wet from the morning light.

When Faith thought of the perfect time for them to have sex, she'd always imagined it would be after a super romantic date. There would be candles and music...all the cheesy stuff found in movies. But, here, now, looking into her girlfriend's eyes, Faith couldn't think of a more perfect time.

Nathalie had held her all night, giving Faith love and support. Waking up, tucked into Nathalie's body, was so natural and felt so right. Seeing Nathalie first thing in the morning was Faith's new favorite thing, and her body was reacting in kind.

Bringing her hand up to Nathalie's neck, Faith drew her girlfriend into a slow, deep kiss. Nathalie's hand landed on Faith's waist, her fingers scratching slightly in small circles. Who knew that was an erogenous zone?

Faith held Nathalie closer, shifting slightly to allow Nathalie to lie on top of her. The sweet kiss turned frantic. Faith couldn't seem to get close enough to Nathalie. Her body was on fire and this time she had no intention of stopping.

"Are you sure?" Nathalie whispered against Faith's mouth.

"Yes," she gasped.

The first touch of Nathalie's fingers on Faith's stomach sent tendrils of electricity through her body. Maybe because Faith knew they would go all the way this time, it felt different to all their other make-out sessions.

Gliding her hands over Nat's body, she lifted her girlfriend's top over her head. How could Faith describe seeing Nat's breasts for the first time? Awe-inspiring? Heaven-sent? Maybe life-affirming? All would be accurate. Nathalie was perfect.

Tentatively, Faith brought her hand up and gently cupped Nathalie's left breast. Their eyes met, giving Faith a little more confidence as Nathalie's eyes glazed over. Taking a chance, Faith rolled Nathalie's nipple. The gasp and moan Nathalie released was all Faith needed to proceed.

With one hand kneading Nathalie's breast, Faith took Nathalie's ass cheek in the other, pulling her body down. The friction caused by Nathalie's hips sinking into her own left Faith dizzy. There was no space for nerves; not when her body felt like it would combust at any moment.

Nathalie began slowly grinding her hips. Faith nibbled Nathalie's neck, scraping her teeth across the supple skin.

"Oh, Faith," Nathalie whispered.

"I want to see all of you," Faith replied, releasing Nathalie's body.

Wordlessly, they pulled apart, allowing the other to remove their clothing. A small wave of insecurity washed over Faith as Nathalie surveyed her body.

"You are beautiful," Nathalie choked, overwhelmed with emotion.

Laying back down, Faith pulled Nathalie back on top of her. Not missing a beat, Nathalie resumed her slow hip rolls. This time, though, her mouth found Faith's breasts.

"Oh, Lord," Faith mumbled into Nathalie's shoulder.

"Is this okay?" Nathalie asked. The nipple she was sucking on making a small popping sound when released.

Was it okay? It was fantastic! Faith was more concerned she wasn't going to last very long. Just the nipple sucking had caused an ache to build in her sex.

"It's perfect, but…"

"But? I can stop."

Shaking her head, Faith tried to articulate what she was feeling. It was proving difficult to form a coherent sentence with all the feelings she had zipping around in her body.

"I might not last very long," she finally voiced.

"That's okay. We have all day."

Hell yeah, we do!

Faith closed her eyes, completely entranced by the feeling of Nathalie's lips once again enveloping her sensitive buds.

Right then, Faith didn't think it could get any better. Well, that was until Nathalie slowly snaked her hand down Faith's torso. The hesitation in Nathalie's movements showed she was a little nervous.

When Nathalie's hand paused above Faith's mound, Faith gently slid her own hand on top of Nathalie's and guided her to where she so desperately needed to be touched.

The gasp Nathalie made when her fingers slid through Faith's folds sent a pulse of want straight to Faith's clit.

"Oh, you're so wet," Nathalie commented, almost awestruck.

Faith could only nod her head. She was struggling to keep herself in the present. All she wanted was to throw her head back and scream in pleasure because Nathalie was driving her insane.

"Is this good?" Nathalie asked, slowly circling Faith's clit.

"Mmmm, so good," Faith rasped.

"You feel amazing."

"Oh, Nat, I-I'm not sure I can hold on any longer." Faith's whole body was vibrating. The orgasm building in her body was nothing like she'd ever felt.

Faith was a little frightened it would break her. The tremors became more intense as Nathalie quickened her pace and pressed a little harder.

Gripping Nathalie, Faith bit into her shoulder as the most intense feeling of pleasure sent shockwaves racing to every nerve. It was only after the initial wave subsided that she heard herself screaming Nathalie's name.

Blinking rapidly, Faith finally came back to reality. Nathalie hovered over her, a look of... worry on her face. "Are you okay? Did I hurt you?"

"No, baby," Faith panted, her breathing still rapid, "that...that was..."

Faith couldn't find the words to give what she had just felt, the justice it deserved. Instead of trying to explain further, Faith drew Nathalie into another heated kiss.

If Faith couldn't verbally explain to Nathalie what had just happened, maybe she could show her. Pushing on Nathalie's shoulder, Faith rolled them over. A pang of nerves fluttered in Faith's stomach. It was one thing receiving immeasurable pleasure, quite another trying to give it.

But no matter how nervous she felt, knowing it was Nathalie here with her helped quash those worries. All she had to do was show Nathalie how she felt. Easy, right?

Straddling Nathalie's hips, Faith bent forward and kissed her way from Nathalie's soft, warm lips, to her neck, and down to her chest. Reflexively, Faith's hips rocked, painting Nathalie with her excitement.

The overwhelming need to taste Nathalie hit Faith like a freight train. Scooting herself lower, she continued to kiss every inch of Nathalie's skin. A smile graced her lips when Nathalie opened her legs wide. A quick flick of her eyes to Nathalie's face showed how much Nathalie wanted this.

Dipping her head, Faith brushed her nose ever so gently against Nathalie's short curls. The scent of her girlfriend caused her mouth to water. Why had they waited so long?

"Y-you don't have to," Nathalie stuttered.

"I want to," Faith replied, her eyes firmly fixed on her goal. With a delicate swipe of her tongue, Faith savored Nathalie's taste.

Oh, she is divine.

"Oh, Jesus," Nathalie panted, her hands fisting the bed sheets.

Faith reached out, took one of those fisted hands and rested it on the back of her own head.

"Show me what you want," Faith whispered.

She felt Nathalie grip her hair slightly, before pushing gently to lower Faith's mouth back to where she needed it.

Closing her eyes, Faith allowed her tongue to roam free. She explored every inch of Nathalie's folds, licking and sucking, unsure if she was doing it right, but trusting her instinct.

Nathalie's thighs tightened around her head and her moans grew louder and louder, until Nathalie fell silent, her mouth open and her body shaking.

When Faith felt a tap on her shoulder, she gave Nathalie's clit one last kiss before pulling away. Nathalie drew her in. Together they lay silently, panting, processing what they had just done together.

"That was perfect," Nathalie sighed after a few minutes. "Y-you enjoyed it too, right?"

Faith lifted her head, surprised to see genuine worry etched on Nathalie's face.

"Nat, that was everything I've ever dreamed of." Swallowing hard, Faith said the one thing that had been on her mind for weeks. "Nathalie, I love you."

A tear made its way down Nathalie's cheek. "You do?"

"Yeah, I do."

"I love you, too," she sobbed, resting her forehead against Faith's.

They lay together, gently caressing each other for what seemed like hours, basking in each other's warmth. When Nathalie's stomach gave an almighty rumble, they giggled and agreed it was time to get up.

"I'm going to jump in the shower before we go eat," Faith commented as they untangled themselves from each other. "I can't sit by Carmen and Mateo with you still on my chin," she chuckled.

"Maybe I'll join you," Nathalie grinned, wiggling her eyebrows.

Breakfast could wait!

"Hey, *chica*, no Nathalie?" Mateo asked later that day.

"No, she left about an hour ago. Are you not working today?"

"I thought I'd take the afternoon off and give myself a facial. Care to join me?"

"One thousand times, yes," Faith replied excitedly. It had been a couple of weeks since she'd had a spa day with Mateo.

"Carmen tells me Molly is visiting in a few weeks."

"Yeah, I can't wait." Chewing her lip, Faith asked the one thing she'd been wondering about since they were in California. "Did something happen between Molly and Carmen?"

Mateo froze momentarily. "Um, no, why, um, why do you think that?"

Oh, wow, Mateo was a terrible liar!

"Mateo, what happened?" Faith rounded on him, hands on hips, hoping she came across as intimidating. Well, intimidating enough for Mateo to spill.

"Maybe that's something you should talk to Carmen about, *chica*."

Narrowing her eyes, Faith regarded him a little longer until he started squirming. "So, something did happen?"

"I didn't say that," he squeaked.

"You just told me to ask Carmen. If nothing happened, there would be nothing to ask about. I knew it. Did they fall out over me moving here?"

"No, sweetie," Mateo smiled. "Nothing like that."

"Okay, but what else could they have to get upset about?"

"They weren't upset. Nothing happened."

"Hang on," Faith gasped, realization smacking her square in the face. "Did they..."

No way!

Of course, that's what had happened. Faith had caught the looks her aunt and Carmen shared.

"Ask Carmen," Mateo spluttered. "I'm going to get my face creams." And just like that, Mateo disappeared.

"Well, well, well. Carmen and Aunt Molly." Faith muttered to herself, grinning. If Mateo wouldn't give her the scoop, she knew a cantankerous pothead who would. Shouting to Mateo that she was stepping out for a bit, Faith ran over to Enid's.

Bursting through the door, Faith beelined for Enid, who was sitting in her favorite spot by the window; the one she used to spy on her neighbors.

"Carmen and Molly did it, didn't they?"

"Ha," Enid cackled. "You finally caught on."

"I can't believe it. Why didn't they tell me they liked each other?"

"Honey, they can't even admit it to themselves yet. They're not as evolved as the likes of you and me."

"That's stupid. What's the problem?" Did Carmen and Molly think Faith would take it badly or something? "Is it me?"

"No, sweetie, although I'm sure they will use you as an excuse for a while. They've both just got their heads up their asses at the minute, but I'm not worried."

"Should I talk to Carmen? Tell her I'm cool with it? I could call Molly."

"No, leave it be. Do you want a cocktail? I had a delightful Sex on the Beach earlier."

"Sure, why not! It's a day of celebration," Faith smiled, her mind transporting back to this morning.

"Oh yeah, and why's that?" Enid asked, her eyebrows cocked.

"Just is," Faith mumbled, her face flushing.

"Well, all right then. Let's celebrate."

Faith laughed as Enid did a strange Salsa dance to the kitchen. Faith sat in Enid's unoccupied seat. Even though the day was gray, nothing could dampen Faith's mood. She couldn't wait to have Nathalie back in her bed. Chuckling to herself, Faith shook her head.

"Who are you?" she asked herself playfully. She was a young, vibrant woman, with a delicious girlfriend and wonderful people supporting her. That's who she was, and boy, was that something!

Enid shuffled in with two cocktails and a tray of snacks. "Here you go, dear, get that down your gullet."

"Cheers, Enid,"

"Cheers, sweetie."

Sipping her drink, Faith smiled widely, her chest full of warmth. Yesterday was hard, but a new day brought new things, and Faith was going to hold on to them with all her might.

421

25

Carmen

You'd think after so many weeks apart and a new relationship, the thought of Molly being close wouldn't cause such a deep ache, and yet that's exactly what Carmen felt every time she closed her eyes and pictured Molly.

It wasn't fair to Rachel. Carmen was well aware of that and yet, she still didn't do the right thing and break it off. And now, Rachel was talking about their future, whereas Carmen was thinking about another woman.

She was a garbage human being!

"So, what do you think? A trip to Vermont in the fall would be so romantic." Rachel wasn't going to let the topic drop, no matter how many times Carmen tried to avoid it.

"Um, I'm not sure, Rach, it depends on what Rita needs me to do."

Bullshit excuse, but it was all Carmen had.

"Okay, sure." Rachel's eyes narrowed and Carmen felt herself shrink. "I guess I'll be the adult then," Rachel continued. "Carmen, do you want to be in this relationship?"

"What, of course!"

"Why don't I believe you? I feel like I'm the only one invested in this. It doesn't help that trying to talk to you is like pulling teeth."

Guilt. That's all Carmen felt. She should have known that Rachel, *a detective,* would pick up her growing unease.

"I think maybe we're just moving fast."

"Okay. Which part of us dating, is moving too fast?"

"All of it," Carmen sighed.

Stop being a fucking coward!

"Rachel, I just don't think I'm ready for this...for dating."

Rachel nodded her head in thought. "*You* pursued *me*. You remember that, right?"

Dropping her head to her chest, Carmen blew out a breath. "Yeah, I did, and I'm sorry I'm jerking you around. I thought this was what I wanted. I thought I was ready to try getting serious with someone."

"But I'm not the right someone, huh?"

"I—"

What could she say? Rachel wasn't wrong, but the someone Carmen kept thinking about was the one person she couldn't have. Mateo and Enid would tell her she was making stupid excuses, purposely sabotaging herself, and yes, they were probably right, but no matter how hard Carmen tried to break down her own walls, she was stuck.

"Carmen, you don't have to explain yourself to me. I just wish you would have been a little more honest with yourself before you got me involved."

"Rachel, I'm so sorry. The last thing I want to do is to hurt you. And, I know that is a bullshit, clichéd thing to say to you, but it really is the truth."

"It's disappointing. I thought we made a damn good couple, but I'll get over it. Maybe I'll call you in a few weeks, after we've both had some time."

Carmen nodded, squeezing Rachel's hand as Rachel stood to leave.

Fuck!

"I'm sorry, Rach."

"See you around, Ruiz."

Carmen scrubbed her hands up and down her face in frustration. This was not how the day was supposed to go!

Even though Rachel wasn't the one for her, a tug pulled at Carmen's heart as she watched her leave. Was this going to be her life? Alone, unable to connect or allow herself to get close?

Shaking her head, Carmen whipped out her phone and hit 'Dial'. Living this way was unacceptable.

"Hi, Doc, can you fit me in?"

For weeks now, Carmen hadn't been telling her therapist the entire truth about her feelings. They spoke about Carmen changing careers and they worked on ways Carmen could learn to trust others. Carmen was happy to talk about Rachel, Mateo, and Faith, but the one person she hadn't allowed herself to talk about in depth, was Molly.

Everyone in Carmen's life was happy. They were living for themselves. Mateo had Daniel, and Faith had Nathalie. Hell, even Enid was speed dating. And all Carmen could do was hide behind her walls, hurting people she cared for.

After a grueling session, Carmen left her therapist's office feeling raw but in a better frame of mind. Rachel was right to end things with her. Carmen was not in the right place to start a serious relationship. There was a lot of work to do on herself, and she couldn't concentrate on that with someone else in her life.

Learning to let people in was her number one goal. Getting out, meeting people, and forming connections became a priority. Since working for Rita, Carmen had been getting out of the house a hell of a lot more lately, but she was still holed up in her room most of the time.

"Okay, Ruiz, what's the first step?" she asked herself, walking towards her favorite coffee shop.

A sign in the shop window caught Carmen's eye. The owner of the café was advertising space above the shop to rent. There were three offices in total.

"Well, if this isn't a sign, literally, I don't know what is," Carmen chuckled.

Renting an office was the answer. There would be at least two other people occupying the space, which meant Carmen would have to step out of her comfort zone and socialize a little.

Pushing through the door, Carmen made her way to the counter. After ordering a large coffee, Carmen inquired about the space. The owner was a lovely lady who took Carmen upstairs to view the last available office. It was perfect.

The day may have started rocky, but things were looking up. Carmen signed the lease there and then. It was a risk and she might regret it, but drastic action was called for.

Shuffling to the bathroom, Carmen yawned while scratching her butt. After signing the lease, she'd tasked herself with organizing files and folders, getting herself ready to move to her new space. It was past midnight by the time she finished. At some point, she heard Faith arrive, and then Nathalie.

Yawning, she shuffled to the bathroom. It was relatively early in the morning, but Carmen couldn't fall back to sleep. Her foot had just reached the tile on the bathroom floor when a noise sounded from Faith's room.

Freezing, Carmen's eyes grew wide. A second groan, louder than the first, reached her ears.

"No, no, nope." Carmen did not want to be hearing what she was hearing. Actually, she wanted to bleach her ears. Turning on her heel, she clamped her hands over her ears and rushed through the house, not stopping until she made it to Enid's house.

"Why are you on my doorstep in your boxers?" Enid questioned the moment she opened her door.

"Can't I just stop by?"

"Sure you can, but you usually wear more clothes. Christ, Carmen, your tits are amazing."

Wrapping her arms around her chest, Carmen rolled her eyes. "Thanks," she chuckled.

"I remember when my boobs stayed north of the equator all on their own. Ah, the good old days."

"Your boobs look great. Now, have you got bourbon or something?"

"You know I'm not one to turn down day drinking, but it's pretty damn early to be starting on the hard booze, even for me. What's going on, sweetie?"

"I heard something I can't unhear."

"Ah, Mateo tugging one out?"

Carmen's face paled. "Oh my God, no! That's disgusting. I don't want that in my head. Gross!"

"Alright, no need to get your panties in a wad. I share a wall with you. I know you're no stranger to getting it on solo."

"Fuck my life," Carmen groaned.

"Oh, calm down. What did you hear?"

"Faith…" Carmen forced out. "…and Nathalie." There, no need to explain further.

"What about them?"

"Um, I think, I think they were…you know."

"Carmen Ruiz, you are a grown-ass woman approaching forty. You should be able to say sex without dying of embarrassment."

"I don't want to say sex and Faith in the same sentence! Ever!"

"Why? What's wrong? She's young and in love. Nathalie is wonderful. I would have thought you'd be pleased she was getting nasty with someone she loves."

"Getting nasty? No. See? Why do you have to say things like that? Faith's innocent and young and…"

"Ha, you're in full parent mode right now," Enid cackled.

"What do you mean?"

"You see Faith as yours. No parent wants to think of their kid bumping uglies with anyone."

"Yeah, okay, fine. I do feel a bit like a parental figure. That's a normal thought, right?"

"Of course. That girl definitely sees you as a parental figure. No doubt."

"So you get why I don't want to hear *that*," Carmen stated, pointing towards the wall which connected their houses.

"Kind of, but come on. You're no prude. You know how important it is to talk to kids about this sort of thing."

"I'm not qualified to do that, Enid. I barely got through the whole dental dam incident."

Not to mention the mutual masturbation conversation.

Enid let out a belly laugh. "Yeah, that was funny. But Carmen, that was a bit of fun. Talking one-on-one with Faith about her feelings and safe sex is very different."

"Maybe I should call Molly."

"Maybe you should. First thing, though, sweetie. Stop freaking out. Stay and have a cup of coffee and a bagel, then go home."

"Okay."

The house was quiet when she arrived home. Slipping on a pair of sweatpants and a fresh tank, Carmen grabbed a few boxes and headed to her new office. She'd face Faith later, after she talked to Molly.

With files littering every surface, Carmen dropped into her office chair. The phone rang several times before Molly finally picked up.

"Hey stranger."

"Hey, Mol, you okay?" The question was met with silence for a few seconds.

"Um, yeah, all good here. What's up?"

Carmen knew there was something going on, but if Molly didn't want to say, she wouldn't push.

"Okay, so a thing happened," Carmen began.

"A thing?" Molly laughed. "Okay, what thing?"

"Um, I think Faith and Nathalie are, um, you know, sexually active."

"Right, okay."

"Um, should I talk to her, or do you want to, or should we leave it?"

"Carmen," Molly laughed. "You're rambling."

"Sorry, I just feel out of my depth on this."

"Why? Faith talks to you about everything, doesn't she?"

"Yeah, but this is different, right? I mean, this is a big deal, isn't it? It was a big deal when *I* first started having sex."

"It might not be a big deal to her. Maybe wait for Faith to come to you. I'm sure she'll want someone to confide in, and my guess is that will be you."

"Shouldn't it be you, though?"

"Why? Because we're blood-related? It doesn't work like that. I'm just happy she's comfortable enough to talk to you about these things."

"Why aren't you freaking out?"

"Why are you?"

"I...I supposed it just sort of took me by surprise. I mean, I never, ever want to hear what I heard, again. But I suppose I'm happy they were somewhere safe."

"Listen, I have to go, but call me anytime, okay? And stop freaking out. Sex is natural and fun. Maybe you need reminding of that," Molly laughed.

A heat rose in Carmen's chest as she visualized Molly bent over the old truck, Carmen knuckle-deep inside.

"Ha, yeah," Carmen stuttered. "Okay, talk soon." Dropping the phone to her desk, Carmen took a few steady breaths.

"Okay, Ruiz, get yourself together. You are a successful woman. You kick ass daily. You can handle a teenager having sex."

The pep talk revved Carmen up and gave her the confidence needed until she stepped foot inside the house later that afternoon and came face to face with Faith. Instead of being a kickass woman, she melted into a nervous puddle.

"Hey, kid."

"Hey, Carmen, do you have a second?"

Oh God, she's going to talk to me about it.

"Sure, absolutely."

"Are you okay? You're flustered."

"Yes, yep, I'm fine, I'm ready!"

"Ready? What for?"

"Nothing, or anything, whatever you want to tell me."

Faith looked utterly perplexed at Carmen's behavior. "Riiight, okay. Um, so I wanted to ask you something."

"It's completely natural, and as long as you and Nathalie are both consenting, it's okay. I'm glad you were in a safe space to explore things together. I'm happy to take you to a clinic if you want to get tested, you know, just to make sure you're both safe, or I can ask Mateo, or Enid if you like," Carmen blurted.

Faith's stunned face stared back at her. Maybe Carmen could have approached it a little better.

"You...you know about...me and Nathalie?"

"Is that not what you wanted to talk to me about?"

"No, I wanted to ask if you slept with Molly."

Oh. My. God. This is not happening!

"What...what makes you ask that?" Carmen squeaked. Was it as hot in the house as Carmen thought? Pulling at the collar of her tank top, she willed herself not to sweat.

"I figured something happened between you at the party. First, I thought you argued, but then I stopped being dumb and put it together. You like each other and I think you slept with each other."

"I...um, this is a little uncomfortable if I'm being honest, Faith."

"I know, I'm sorry. I just wanted you to know that I'm okay with you guys liking each other. I don't want you to be weird because she's my aunt or whatever. That's all."

"Okay, well, thanks for that. Molly and I are just friends, though, and I doubt that will change."

Faith's face showed disappointment. "Okay, sure. It's between you guys. I just wanted you to know."

Clearing her throat, Carmen stood a little straighter. "So, do you...want to talk about..."

"Having sex with Nathalie?" Faith chuckled. "I think I'm good. We waited until both of us were ready and it was perfect. I promise I will come to you, though, if I need to."

"Excellent, right, good chat! I'm going to drink a bottle of rum and forget this morning ever happened. Cool?"

"Cool," Faith laughed.

As appealing as a bottle of rum sounded, Carmen resisted the urge to get blackout drunk. Instead, she ordered an extra-large pizza and binge-watched Netflix. After napping away the food coma she'd put herself in, Carmen worked on the task Dr. Stark assigned her in their session.

Apparently, Carmen wasn't great at voicing her feelings. Who knew! She was given the unenviable job of writing a diary; one where she tried her best to open herself up entirely. The doctor thought it would be a good way for Carmen to learn how to trust herself. According to the doc, trusting herself was the first step to Carmen trusting others.

So far, she'd doodled a flower and a cloud in the page's corner. Why was it so hard? All she had to do was note her feelings. It was hard, because for thirty years, Carmen had done her best to push her feelings to the side so she could survive.

"Christ," she grumbled to herself, before putting pen to paper and scribbling out any thought that crossed her mind.

As soon as she finished, she re-read her notes. "Jesus, am I really this cynical?" she muttered.

The page was full of Carmen's mistrust of the world. It was clear, for far too long, Carmen had regarded the world through a very jaded lens.

One sentence stood out from all others. In the middle of her ramblings, Carmen read what she had written: *If the one person you should be able to trust in the whole world abandons you, what hope is there for anyone else? Why did you leave me, Mom?*

Carmen's eyes stung as tears threatened to fall. Why had she written that? Carmen didn't think about her mom, ever! She'd never had a mother, and she'd made peace with that.

"*Hermana*?" Mateo's soft voice pulled Carmen's gaze from the paper. Words wouldn't come. Mateo sat beside her, stroking her back. His eyes fell on the mess of writing.

Pulling the paper from Carmen's grip, he read what she'd written. "Oh, honey," he sighed, pulling Carmen in tighter.

"I'm so broken," she sobbed.

"You're not broken, *chica*, you just need a little help."

"I shouldn't be like this, Mateo. Not after all this time. Why can't I just fucking get over it?"

Leaning back, Mateo cupped Carmen's face with both his hands. "Carmen, you have spent so long being strong for everyone else. There is no time limit on trauma."

"I didn't go through what you did. What the hell have I got to be traumatized about?" Carmen had never voiced her thoughts like this to Mateo.

"You went through plenty. You became an adult when you were still a child. You saw things and did things no kid should have to, and you did it while looking after me. You got me the help I needed, and I know you went to therapy as well, but I know you, Carmen. I know you didn't fully open yourself up. You think guarding your emotions and keeping everything to yourself protects you, but it only hurts you more. This paper right here shows me you are ready to work through everything—for real this time. And Carmen, I'm going to be with you every step of the way, understand?"

"Mateo," Carmen cried, shaking her head.

"No, this isn't a debate. I'm in a good place because of you. Let me be your pillar of strength now."

"I don't even know where to begin."

"Yes, you do. You're already doing it. Being open with your therapist is the biggest step you could take, and I'm so proud of you."

"I don't understand why now? Why am I breaking down now?"

Mateo paused. Carmen could see he was figuring out the best way to say what was on his mind.

"Honestly, I think it's because you found someone you could see a future with."

"Mateo," Carmen scoffed.

"It's okay. You don't have to believe me. In the end, it doesn't matter why you're struggling with this now. All that matters is you working through this shit so you can finally live a full and happy life. It will never be perfect, *chica*. I still have triggers, you know that, but I'm ninety percent there. I want that for you."

"I want that too," Carmen admitted.

"Okay, so what's the plan?"

"I think I need some time away. A lot has happened over the past few months and maybe a bit of time alone will help me see through it all. I need to clear my head."

"Alone? Are you sure?"

"I am. I'm going to listen to my doctor and spend quality time with myself. Is that okay?"

"Whatever you need, honey. I'll be right here when you need me."

Carmen had always thought she needed to keep Mateo close to keep him from harm. Control was her friend, but now, after reading her innermost thoughts on that paper, Carmen understood she'd been holding everything *too* close.

If she were ever going to get to a place of happiness, she had to leave.

26

Carmen, Molly & Faith

If Carmen wasn't so sure this was what she needed to do, she would've canceled her plans to leave after explaining to Faith why it was necessary for her to go away for a while.

It'd been a tough conversation to have, and it certainly left her feeling guilty about taking time for herself. But, after hours of discussion with Mateo and her therapist, Carmen was resolute in her decision.

Acknowledging her difficulties had never come easy, but now, for whatever reason, Carmen found it a little easier to talk about her feelings. Mateo was making a point of checking in regularly, which was nice, although it would be better if he weren't such a massive drama queen about everything. Anyone witnessing their exchanges would think she was leaving for good instead of taking an impromptu break.

The timing wasn't wonderful. After all, she had just signed a lease for the shared office, however it wouldn't go to waste. Rita was more than happy to take over for the duration of Carmen's absence. It would make a good meeting space for small groups, apparently. Carmen was more than happy with that arrangement.

Admittedly, Carmen had consciously chosen to leave in the next day or two, because she really wanted to avoid seeing Molly, who was due to arrive for her visit in three days.

If Faith's sad face had almost stopped her from going, Carmen was positive seeing Molly would completely derail her plans. She wasn't yet prepared to admit that finding Molly Parsons was the catalyst to her recent need for change, but she couldn't completely deny it either.

Molly had reached parts of Carmen—no euphemism intended—that no other woman had. If they'd shared more than a few days and one spectacular night together, Carmen might be inclined to entertain the idea that Molly was a real possibility; a woman she could really give herself to.

But that wasn't the case. Molly was Faith's aunt. She had her own baggage, and right now, Carmen couldn't allow herself to see a future with anyone; not until she felt better about herself.

Slamming her suitcase shut, Carmen realized she'd packed nearly her entire closet. Did she really need snow pants? No, not when she intended on traveling to Florida for a few weeks. Her itinerary had been decided by blindly pinning a thumbtack to a map of the U.S. Florida came up the winner.

The one benefit of Carmen working hard and never vacationing over the past twenty years, was that she had a stash of savings to fund her trip. In fact, she'd done something completely out of character and booked herself into a five-star hotel and spa—a fact she had most definitely *not* let slip to Mateo. He would jam himself into her luggage if privy to that kind of intel.

"*Chica*, did you know it's Enid's seventieth birthday next week?" Mateo called from the hallway.

"No, did she say something? Damn, we could have thrown a party if we had known sooner..."

"Faith told me. Why wouldn't Enid have said anything?"

"You'd have to ask her that. Maybe she doesn't like a fuss being made."

"No, it's because she doesn't have any family," Faith chimed in.

"Can you guys come in here or something? I hate having a discussion with everyone in different parts of the house," Carmen yelled.

"*We're* her family," Mateo protested, swishing his robe as he sank to Carmen's bed.

"Did you talk to her about it?" Carmen asked Faith, who strode in seconds later.

"Yeah. She said, and I quote, 'My dipshit husband was supposed to take me away for the big seven-o, but he went and kicked the bucket, the silly old bastard.'"

"Yeah, that sounds about right," Mateo laughed.

"That's so sad," Carmen sighed.

"Well, maybe we can do something when you get back," Mateo commented, scrolling through his phone.

"Mm," Carmen answered, her mind racing. An idea was percolating. It would change her plans slightly, but it would also bring a foul-mouthed old woman some happiness—she hoped.

"Okay, I'm packed. I'm going to pop next door and say goodbye to Enid."

"Tell her she can come around here for her birthday if she wants," Mateo called. Carmen didn't answer. If she had anything to do with it, Enid would spend her seventieth in the lap of luxury.

"Enid, you here?"

"In the kitchen. Do you want a Slippery Nipple?"

"Um...no?"

"That's a shame. I love a good Slippery Nipple."

"Are you just going to keep saying the name to make me feel uncomfortable?"

Enid cackled. "Obviously. Anyway, what brings you over here? Are you ready to take off?"

"I'm packed, but I don't plan to leave until the day after tomorrow."

A full twenty-four hours before Molly was due to arrive.

"Lovely. You're going to have a great time, dear."

"About that," Carmen started, deciding after all, a cocktail with an uncomfortable name was just what she needed. "If your 'dipshit husband' were still around, where would he have taken you for your birthday?"

"Oh, well, um, I suppose somewhere like Florida. He was too stingy to take me to Hawaii."

"And would that be something you'd still want to do?"

"It would be tough, sweetie, he's been dead for a while."

Carmen rolled her eyes. "Enid, would you like to come to Florida with me?"

"When...what?"

"Don't tell Mateo, but I'm going to be staying in a particularly fancy hotel in Florida, and I want you to come with me."

"But I thought you needed space?"

"I do, but I know you won't need me hovering around while you get pampered."

"Hell no, I don't need you clam jamming me."

"Christ," Carmen groaned. "I'm just gonna brush past that. Do you want to come? You shouldn't miss out on your birthday trip. I know how much you love the tropics." Carmen winked.

"Are you sure, Carmen? I know I make jokes and get a little silly, but in all seriousness, I wouldn't want to intrude on something you need to do to make yourself whole again, honey."

"I promise, Enid. I'll take time for myself, but I think having you close by would be a comfort."

"Well, spank my ass and call me Judy, I'm going to Florida!" Enid hollered, shaking her ass.

"Get packing, lady!" Carmen laughed.

Carmen filled in Mateo and Faith about Enid tagging along. After Mateo stopped pouting, he could see it was the right thing to do. Two days later, Carmen stood with her suitcase by her feet, ready to leave the house for their flight to Florida, looking at Enid, who was taking things *out* of her suitcase to show Mateo and Faith her new bikinis.

"Enid, we have to go. Get that shit packed!" Carmen barked.

"Yes, boss," Enid replied, saluting.

The sky was its usual gray self as the cab pulled away from the house. Goodbyes had been swift, which Carmen appreciated. She desperately wanted to look back as they drove away, a silent plea echoing within her to turn around and look one last time. Surrendering to that desire risked asking the cab driver to stop the car, an urge Carmen knew she wouldn't be able to resist.

Home wasn't the best place for her, though; not right now. Keeping her head facing forward, she muttered to herself some affirming words.

"This is the right thing to do."

Enid's wrinkled hand patted hers in support. Yes, it was the right thing to do...wasn't it?

Arriving a day early in Seattle had not been an easy decision to make, but with Maureen accompanying her, Molly didn't want to wait any longer. If there could be a chance for Faith and Maureen to heal, Molly wanted it to happen sooner rather than later.

Hopefully, Faith wouldn't be too mad Molly had kept Maureen's visit a secret. Truthfully, Molly hadn't known the best choice of what to do. She certainly didn't want Faith seeing her mother all beaten and bruised. But injuries like Maureen suffered could take months to heal and Molly couldn't put off her visit to Seattle without explaining the reason to Faith. Plus, Maureen begged her not to tell Faith, worried her daughter would reject them coming, outright.

It didn't sit well with Molly that she had gone along with it. The discomfort she felt about lying was also a major factor in fast-forwarding their plans.

The time she'd had lately with Maureen, gave Molly confidence that the woman was sincere in her pledge to make things right with Faith, although Molly genuinely didn't know how Faith would react. When Alan and Maureen had shown up in California, it was Faith who told them she would always keep the door open. Hopefully, that still rang true.

Another reason, and maybe the scariest, was the realization that Molly wanted to see Carmen. Weeks had gone by and Carmen seldom left Molly's mind. Bessie was relentless in her mission to talk about Carmen.

As soon as the kids caught on to Molly's internal dilemma regarding the very sexy Carmen Ruiz, they had joined in Bessie's crusade. The result was a night of deep conversations, hard realizations, and vodka.

Molly was into Carmen in a big way. Their night together had been hot as hell, but also deeply meaningful. Since leaving Kentucky, Molly had searched for the woman who would make her feel safe—make her feel at home. And even though Carmen Ruiz was still a mystery, she'd made Molly feel both of those things.

There was a lot to work through. Molly wasn't naïve, but that didn't mean she and Carmen couldn't explore their options.

Especially when Molly decided to stay in Seattle semi-permanently. There was too much time to make up with Faith. All Molly had ever wanted was a family again, and she'd been handed the opportunity. She didn't want to waste it.

Bessie had been the one to push Molly into making the right call. It wasn't easy breaking a bad habit, but Molly's tendency to run was just that; a bad habit, and one she had to stop repeating. Staying in one place, putting down roots with Faith—and hopefully with Carmen—felt like the right thing to do.

Molly had done her best to make sure Bessie and the kids had people around to help. They knew they could call her anytime, and she planned to visit regularly.

Maybe Carmen would go with her? If—that is—Carmen was willing to give their relationship a chance.

As the cab pulled up to the familiar Seattle address, Molly chuckled at the driver who was cursing another cab ahead of them, which seemed to have pulled out in front of their vehicle, causing him to suddenly brake.

Thanking the driver, Maureen and Molly made their way to the house. This was it; this was the day Molly actively changed her life from nomadic to settled-in-suburbia.

Giving Maureen's hand a quick squeeze, Molly knocked several times. Laughter echoed from inside, and Molly was happy to hear Faith's soft voice teasing Mateo.

"Did you forget some—"

"Hey, Faith," Molly grinned at Faith's shocked face.

"Molly!" she screamed. Molly braced herself for the full weight of her niece crashing into her.

"Hey, honey," Molly laughed.

"Mom?" Faith pulled back, looking between Molly and Maureen.

"We have some things to talk about," Molly said, holding Maureen's and Faith's hands. Faith simply nodded and ushered them inside.

"Molly, hey *chica*, it's great to see you!" Mateo gushed, dragging her in for another bone-crushing hug.

"Mateo, you look great!"

"I know, honey," he laughed. "So, what's all this?" he asked, waving his hand at Maureen. Molly couldn't fault him for being a little cold towards Faith's mother.

"*This,* is something Faith and Maureen need to discuss," Molly said plainly.

Mateo turned Faith's body so she was facing him completely. "Faith, is that what you want?"

"Yeah, I'm alright. Mom, you wanna come through to the kitchen and we'll talk?"

"I'd love that," Maureen replied, her voice cracking.

Molly and Mateo watched them walk away. Now that one of the most nerve-wracking parts of the day was done, Molly was ready to take on the next part.

"Um, will Carmen be home soon? I have something to talk to her about."

Mateo shuffled his feet nervously, his hand scratching the back of his head. "Carmen isn't here, Molly."

"Oh, yeah, I figured that. What time will she be back?"

"Molly, she's gone."

Gone? What the hell did that mean?

"Sorry, I don't follow."

"Carmen left, *chica*."

"I think we're getting good at this," Nathalie chuckled, gently stroking Faith's hair.

"Practice does make perfect," Faith grinned, turning her head to kiss Nathalie's jaw.

Nathalie pulled Faith closer. "I could stay like this all day."

Faith could absolutely stay like this all day, but they'd already started earning raised eyebrows from Mateo and Molly.

So maybe they were skipping all forms of socializing with the people they loved most to dash to the bedroom as often as possible. Was that so wrong?

Faith was just happy Carmen wasn't here to witness it. The incident where she'd heard them going at it, lead to Carmen scowling at Nathalie every chance she got.

Faith found it highly entertaining, because Nathalie would go bright red and scuttle off to Faith's room. Carmen would then smile triumphantly at her work, winking at Faith. No matter how many times Faith explained to Nathalie that Carmen was yanking her chain, Nathalie still tried to avoid Carmen as much as possible.

"How are you feeling about your mom being here?"

Well, wasn't that the million-dollar question? It had certainly been a shock to see her mom standing next to Molly on the doorstep. Sadly, it had been less of a shock to see the state of her mother's face.

The talk, which began after their arrival, had been hard. Maureen begged and pleaded for Faith's forgiveness. Of course, Faith wanted to forgive her mother, but something deep inside didn't feel right to just let everything go. Maybe her mom's link to her father was still too fresh. Faith didn't quite know. Molly seemed to be convinced Maureen meant no harm, and Faith wanted to believe that was true.

Faith asked her mom for some time to think. She was happy to keep talking and working through things, but it had to be at her own pace, and Maureen agreed.

Molly had always planned to be staying with Faith at the house. Maureen knew this and happily booked a hotel for a few nights. Depending on how things went, Maureen would travel back to California after a week's stay. Molly planned to stay longer.

After Maureen left, Faith spent some time with Molly, hearing her side of recent events. Honestly, Faith had been a little annoyed at being ambushed and would have preferred Molly warn her about her mom visiting, but she couldn't stay mad; not when she saw the toll it had taken on her aunt.

Molly looked...dejected. It took Faith a little while to realize Molly's mood was due to Carmen's absence. Instead of asking Molly about it, Faith let her be. Nathalie came over in the evening and Faith was happy to see Molly take to her girlfriend. Still, Faith could see Molly wasn't herself.

"I'm feeling okay. We'll take things day by day. I don't want to rush anything."

"That's fair. I bet you're happy to have Molly here, though, right?"

"Completely. I've been looking forward to her visiting for weeks."

"But?" Damn Nathalie and her observational superpowers.

"But she's not happy. I mean, she's happy to see me, but I think Carmen being gone has really upset her."

"Did you ask her about it?"

"No, because I didn't want to push it."

"I get that, but if you're worried, talk to her."

Faith pulled Nathalie in tighter. She loved the feeling of her girlfriend's arms around her. She really liked the feeling of Nathalie's naked body against her, too.

"I will, today. I want her to enjoy her visit."

"Good, but I think that talk can wait for a little longer," Nathalie growled in her ear, nipping Faith's lobe.

Yeah, it could definitely wait.

"Mol, want to take a walk around the neighborhood?"

"Sure thing. What time are you meeting up with your mom?"

"In a few hours."

The sun was shining as they walked. Faith thought it would be a good idea to get out in the fresh-ish air.

"So, wanna talk about why you look so down?"

Molly chuckled. "Can't get anything past you, huh?"

"Mol, it's blatantly obvious. Is it because Carmen left?"

Molly sighed. "Yeah."

"And..." Faith drew out the word, hoping Molly would jump in.

"Well, you already know we, you know..."

"Boned, yup, I'm aware."

"Brat," Molly laughed. "Ugh, I feel like a teenager talking about this."

"You like Carmen. And let me guess, you hoped to start something while you were here, but then you arrived and Carmen is gone."

"Wow, yeah, hit the nail on the head there, sweetie."

"But you know she's coming back, so what's the problem?"

"Faith, she could be gone for months. I don't really understand why she's gone. Mateo was all close-lipped about it."

"Carmen has stuff she needs to work through, Molly. She's taking time to do that."

"Okay, that's good for her, I suppose?"

"It's great for her, and for you, actually!"

"How do you figure that?"

"Because, Molly, if you want to woo Carmen Ruiz, you need to have a plan."

"Woo her? Really?"

"Yeah, really. Look, I'm having awesome sex now. I know these things!"

Molly threw her head back, letting out a deep belly laugh. "Oh, Faith, I have missed you. Go on then, pass on your wisdom."

"Carmen is away, figuring out a lifetime of stuff. She wants to change so she can get serious with someone, but until she feels better in her own head, she can't offer that. That's what she told me, anyway. But, when she's in the right headspace, you can bet your ass she will give *all* of her heart to the woman she loves. Carmen is just like that. She loves fully. If you want to be that woman, Molly, you need to be on the same page. I'm not saying you have to be ready to walk down the aisle or anything, but you will have to give her more than casual. You need to be prepared to be in it for the long run."

"Jesus, Faith."

"I know it's a lot, but I know Carmen. Actually, I think you know Carmen enough to agree with what I said."

"Okay, I see that. Carmen is fierce with the people she loves. I can see her being the same way with a woman, too."

"So, while she's away sorting her shit out, you get to be here with me preparing yourself."

"That sounds scary, to be honest."

"Of course it does. But when you think of Carmen, and the possibilities for you two, do you see yourself taking those steps? Waiting for her?"

"Yes. It's stupid, considering we barely know each other."

"It's not stupid. You guys connected. It's awesome, and you have the time to get to know each other. That's what love is, isn't it?"

"Christ, you've grown up, kid."

"I just listen to the people around me."

"So, what do you suggest I do, then?"

Faith stopped them in the middle of the street, took Molly by the shoulders and looked her in the eyes. "You figure out how you feel and then, when you're ready, you make a plan."

"And what's that plan?"

"Keeping Carmen Ruiz!"

The story continues in *Keeping Carmen Ruiz.*
Available in eBook and paperback on my website.
www.alysonroot.com

Afterword

Thank you for reading Finding Molly Parsons.
Please spare a few more minutes of your time by heading
over to Amazon and Goodreads to leave a review.

Other Titles By Alyson Root

A Dance Towards Forever

Diving Into Her

Always Emilie

Broken Parts Included

Love & Other Wild Things

Finding Molly Parsons

Keeping Carmen Ruiz

The Wisdom of Bug

Sleigh Bells Ring

Risking Immortality

Waiting for Eternity

Fighting for Infinity

www.alysonroot.com

About the author

Alyson was born and raised in the heart of England. She moved to Paris in 2015 when she met her wife. Together they moved to the west of France, where they now live with their two dogs. Alyson spends her time reading sapphic fiction books, writing and Scuba Diving.

Alyson discovered her love of writing in her mid-thirties. Her debut book, *A Dance Towards Forever,* was inspired by her wife and their very own love story. Alyson wrote *Diving Into Her* and award-winning *Always Emilie,* which added with her first book, created The French Connection series.

www.alysonroot.com

a.rootauthor@alysonroot.com

HUMAN AUTHORED™

THE Authors Guild

6524773

9 781917 785006